MW00830417

Fetching the Phonies

A Sharp Investigations Novel

Book Five

BY: E. N. CRANE

EDITED BY: A. O. NEAL & SUE SCOTT

Dedication

Thank you to my dogs: Perry and Padfoot. Their shenanigans, antics and behavior are the model for all things Winnie.

Special thanks to Crystal Calderon and Emma Wood for helping me with the two kinds of Spanish. You are way better than Google.

Chapter One: Flesh and Bone

*S**he is going to get sliced to ribbons*, I thought.

The events unfolded like a first-person shooter game. My pale hand clutched the butcher knife, the hem of a navy-blue jumpsuit just peeking into my field of view. A young woman ran upstairs, sweat and blood dripping down her face. Her torn short shorts came into sharp relief just as she fell forward on all fours, her bright red bra on full display as she arched her back to look at the approaching knife. As she rose, the white tank top tore off of one shoulder and her arms pressed the cleavage tighter and still my knife advanced slowly, a menacing swell in music and I felt the tension beside me grow.

"Rawr!" I shouted, leaping toward Mo on the couch.

My best friend leapt from her skin, screamed and upended a bowl of popcorn seeds onto her carpeted living room floor. Her arms and legs flailed violently, warding off the attacker on screen who was as real as the rubber knife that was threatening her. Her face was pale but going near her was too hazardous to provide assistance.

Sensing my inability to stop her, Winnie, also known as the retired Sgt. Winnifred Pupperson, was vacuuming up the salty kernels before the bowl settled. Despite an excellent lineage of top performing working dogs, a German Shepherd father and Belgian Malinois mother, her work ethic was sorely lacking. Not lacking was her vacuuming and gas providing skills, and the two were often related but not necessarily requested. I crumbled into a fit of giggles that shook my entire body. It had been a long time since I'd seen a slasher flick, but they were still as ridiculous as they'd always been. Just a series of poor choices and carefully chosen music.

But watching them with Mo was like taking a child to Disneyland. Half the joy of suffering through this was mocking her secondhand terror.

"Cynthia Sharp, you are the worst person…" The rest of Mo's insult was lost in my raucous laughter. My arms wrapped around my stomach and tears streamed down my face as I slid from the couch to the floor feeling every muscle bunch and release. Winnie bounded over and covered my face in doggy kisses, a mix of salty popcorn with an undercurrent of the salmon in her dog food.

"I hate movie night with you!"

Her exclamation elicited more laughter and her face went red with anger. When I'd arrived two hours ago laden down with snacks, booze, and a streaming password, we fought over what to watch for fifteen minutes until deciding we had to come to some sort of compromise. While I had wanted to watch Elf, hilarious and a reminder of when it was not summer, Mo insisted that warm summer nights begged for slasher flicks. Ultimately, she'd won the movie choice, and I won the snack consumption order of operations. In exchange, she agreed that I could mock it mercilessly if I wasn't absolutely terrified, and I promised to hold her hair back if she puked from mixing nachos and ice cream.

Frankly, she was asking for it because I'd almost been burned alive recently and none of these actors were that good. The woman being chased had clearly been ordered to pose like a Playboy model every time she stopped, and the knife man was far slower than any reasonable murderer in pursuit of bloodlust could possibly move.

Also, I'd been forced to go to therapy, so mocking the faux terror of others was necessary to keep my macho Army woman persona. It was also necessary to convince people not to ask in their calmest voice if I was "feeling OK" every ten seconds.

I was so not interested in discussing my feelings.

Unless those feelings were enjoyment at the mockery of poorly made movies and easily startled friends.

Winnie jumped from my lap toward Mo and threatened to love her to death.

"You and your dog are rotten!" She buried her head into Winnie's fur and made exaggerated kissing noises. She paused and looked up at me with a pinched face.

"Yeah, we are not as rotten as what she rolled in before we got here. You should know better than to stick your face in Winnie fur by now. Absolutely disgusting. Do you have no sense of hygiene?"

"Damn you, Cyn!" Mo threw a marshmallow at my head, missed, and crossed her arms in a pout. Not deterred in the least, I plucked the squishy treat from the floor and popped it into my mouth. Marshmallows had initially been brought out to make indoor s'mores, but Mo's crème brulee torch was out of fuel and when we asked her boyfriend Chris to bring us some, he said we were too drunk to play with fire and to eat the marshmallows raw.

Like animals or something!

Stinkin' firefighters.

"Ew! Do you even know when I last vacuumed? And you accused me of having no sense of hygiene."

"No idea, and I never said I had a sense of hygiene. I can judge you for things while still also being guilty of them," I replied, gliding back on the couch and stuffing three more marshmallows into my mouth. "But probably you've vacuumed since the swan debacle as the marshmallow wasn't coated in glitter, feathers, or rhinestones."

Mo, Mary O'Connor, was five and a half feet of freckles and red hair piled in a bun on her head. Her green plastic cat-eye glasses sat on top of a packaged face mask shaped like a panda bear. The baker and shopkeeper took the look of utter female indulgence to new heights with an oversized Sweet Pea Fire shirt and slippers shaped like dinosaurs. The slippers were a birthday gift from me, the shirt probably belonged to her volunteer fire-fighting EMT/nurse boyfriend who was notoriously curmud-geonly about treating lacerations on my butt.

A non-issue if you were anyone else, but I needed treatment somewhat frequently and his refusal was inconvenient. He made me go to the ER like every other person attacked in a freak incident with spike strips and a runaway tractor.

This after I'd been forced to dress as a swan for their com-mitment celebration and was deprived of leftover cake. There had been four feet of cake and they wouldn't let me have any leftovers for either harboring a stripper or not participating... I had stopped paying attention once the cake was off the table.

Literally and figuratively.

"I'm serious, this is why Larry foisted you off on me you gargantuan..." She pointed a finger accusingly and I clutched my chest in mock offense. Gargantuan, unfortunately, was accurate. At six feet tall and a size sixteen, I'd never blended anywhere in my life. With blonde hair and lavender eyes, I hadn't made much effort since retiring from the Army last year. Specialist Cynthia Sharp, Army MP and well documented world-renowned disas-ter, was now just Cyn Sharp. A small-town PI, animal techni-cian, and local disaster, who was dating the town's commercial veterinarian, Larry Kirby, and only occasionally causing property damage.

Weekly is a sort of occasion.

Like taco night, it was something you could count on but never get tired of.

"No! He *foisted* me off on you because you threatened to cut out his tongue if you didn't get a girl's night!" I wiggled my toes in pink rainbow paw print slippers and studied my short purple PJ shorts and camisole. My face mask was a dog and as far as I could tell it succeeded in nothing more than making my face feel damp and smell like witch hazel.

Sadly, witch hazel had zero witch related properties, so I'd probably still get a zit from the sugar.

"Which reminds me, did you pick his tongue because of this new trend to please your book nerd?" I continued, standing as Winnie circled, and I accurately guessed she needed assistance with the doorknob. She pranced to the opened front door and rushed out into Mo's yard to either do her business or barf up popcorn kernels.

My money was on the latter. Popcorn kernels were disgusting.

Mo's yard was a wild overgrowth of foliage and weeds. From the road, you received no indication that a house even sat there. Trees, bushes, and topiaries hid her front door from wayward travelers who stumbled into her veritable hedge maze.

Thankfully, Joseph made Winnie wear a jingle bell on the farm and I could hear her prancing through the garden in search of small critters who would hopefully be wise enough to run away.

"What *new trend*? You please a book nerd by giving them quiet, snacks, and an endless supply of books. If those books are spicy, you make yourself available after," she waved suggestively in the direction of her bedroom as I tuned back in. "For, you know, story recreation purposes."

"Yeah, but I guess the internet doesn't recommend waiting until after. Rather, there's a listicle recommending use of the tongue to offer satisfaction... while reading. You don't even have to put down the book, Mo!"

"Oh my god, that's so rude! How could you not put down the book? What if the scene ends? Do you just keep reading?" She bit her lower lip in thought, and I suppressed a grimace as I heard Winnie rustling through the dry grass, intent on something.

Probably Mo was right.

Putting down the book would have been the polite thing to do.

I made a mental note to have better manners moving forward... maybe. Instead of admitting my faux pas, I barreled on in ignorance.

"No idea, and I don't control the internet! Also don't get me started, Miss 'I read selkie fanfiction that includes pegging'. I read Olivia Dade's *All the Feels*. I know that whatever that is, it is absolutely filthy!"

"Selkies aren't filthy, they live in the ocean! Google it, you narrow minded prude." She chucked another marshmallow in my direction and Winnie leapt through the door to intercept the sugary treat. I beat her to it and she let out a long snort before picking up a long thin chew and carrying it to the center of Mo's living room.

"I did Google it, my computer got a virus and I still don't know what it is." Mo rolled her eyes and I pointed a finger at her chest. "Besides, Mo, you know the only sexy shifters are werewolves and unicorns. Everything else is weird and creepy. Also, if selkies live in the ocean does pegging have to do with pirates who have peg legs kicking-"

"A selkie isn't a shifter," the red head scoffed derisively, cutting off my question about pirates. I could only offer an eye roll since it was probably for the best. The woman who'd run up the stairs on television had been slaughtered on screen in a cascade of fake blood and heaving breasts that were a little too in focus for the purpose of the shot. "Ugh! Why do films do that? Like the woman was just killed, why are we ogling her dead breasts?"

"I don't think we are this movie's target audience," I conceded and noticed something strange about the bone Winnie was chewing on. That something was that I'd never seen it before and had no recollection of bringing it with us.

"It's a slasher flick! The target audience should be anyone with an aversion to a gruesome death who is also fascinated by the prospect." Mo emptied her wine glass, but I was only half listening as I studied Winnie and her new toy. "I mean seriously, this is borderline necrophilia."

To avoid mental scarring, I elected to strike that from my memory.

The woman owned dozens of slasher films and baked while listening to true crime podcasts. If a mysterious series of murders happened in this town, she would either solve it or be the one committing it.

"Did you buy Winnie toys and treats for your house?" I asked, moving closer to the dog and hearing the tell-tale pop of the chew treat losing structural integrity.

"What? No, I just give her people food when you aren't looking. Why?"

The end beneath her left paw was gnarled, a round protrusion coated in dirt. Maybe an antler or a chew modeled after a bone, but the size was wrong for what is sold in stores.

"Do you..." just as I was about to grab her chew, Winnie snatched it up and took off. "Winnie! Get back here!"

My slippers skidded when I chased her from the carpeted living room and into the kitchen. A knee buckled, hyper extended, and my legs slipped from under me. My elbow slammed into the linoleum with force, and I let loose a string of swears that would make a sailor blush.

Thank dog I was in the Army.

Sailors were such unimaginative babies.

"Dog if you don't..." I started as she trotted over, gracefully leapt my prostrate form and pranced into the living room.

Probably for the best, the room was a little wobbly and I wasn't on my threat-making A game.

"You OK, Cyn?" Mo called and I considered briefly if anything felt broken. Arm would probably be fine, butt was well padded, head hadn't hit the ground... good enough.

"Probably," I shouted back. Carefully, I hauled myself the great distance from the floor, my feet getting farther and farther away. It was like looking into a funhouse mirror that was my eyeballs. In the interest of my sanity, I looked around the kitchen until I spotted the open bottle of tequila. "Were we drinking wine or tequila?"

"Both!" She called back and I poked my head around the corner, gripping the wall tightly as the world seemed to spin on a new axis. I was definitely too old to be drinking this much on a school night... or work night.

"Both?"

"Yeah, we started with margaritas and then switched to wine when I tried to convince you to video me doing a strip-tease for TikTok-" I slammed my hands over my ears and started humming. The sound for the latest trend was going to haunt my nightmares with images of bouncing breasts and lime. Winnie, for her part, took her toy to Mo and dropped it on her lap, an invitation to play.

"Who's a good..." she started, face suddenly going pale as she picked it up with her thumb and index finger. "Where did she get this?"

"That's what I asked you," I moved closer to it, trying to identify whatever her teeth had dug into that became startlingly white without the layer of dirt and other deposits. It had long thin strings that, combined together, accounted for its shape and density.

Mo rotated the chew in her hand, analyzing it from all sides and realization dawned as she screamed in time to the newest on-screen victim.

"Oh my god, your dog killed someone and brought me the femur!"

Then she may have passed out.

About the Author

E. N. Crane is a fiction author writing humorous mysteries with plus-sized female leads and their furry friends. She is one of two authors under the Perry Dog Publishing Imprint, a one woman, two dog operation in Idaho... for now. My dogs are Perry and Padfoot, the furry beasts shown above. They are well-loved character inspiration in all things written and business.

If you are interested in joining my newsletter, please subscribe here: https://e-n-crane_perrydogpublishing.ck.page/578ed9ab37or on my website, PerryDogPublishing.com

You will receive A Bite in Afghanistan, the prequel to the Sharp Investigations Series, as a thank-you for joining. I only have one newsletter for mental health reasons, so both romance and mystery are on there! If you only want one in your inbox, follow Perry Dog Publishing on all socials to stay on top of the latest news... and pet pics.

Chapter Two:
Square Roots

"I don't understand," Larry said again, hands on hips. He was wearing his usual T-shirt and jeans, red chucks, and a hat that covered his wavy light brown hair. "How do you get drunk and find a bone?"

"You mean without going to a bar?" I joked, waggling my brows. Larry Kirby had been my quasi friend growing up and despite having grown into his ears, he still looked like a nerd. A nerd who accidentally bought a gym membership and forced himself to use it, but still definitely a nerd.

A sexy, lovable, and mostly nice-smelling nerd who always needed a haircut.

"What's sad is that if you had encountered a bone in a bar, you'd have probably let Winnie chew on that too," he ruffled the dog's ears affectionately. "Then my brother would have had to show up and take a report. Which, given your history, would probably have resulted in him having tooth marks in his ass and you being in jail."

"OK, first, it was a tree root. Not a bone," I repeated myself as I poured coffee into my mug. We were in my apartment, if one considered a four hundred square foot space with a kitchenette, couch, and a bed an apartment. "Second, Winnie would never bite your brother's ass. Give her some credit, she'd go for the hands."

Larry's brother, Daniel Kirby, was the high school hottie. Arrogant, muscled, and charmed through puberty, he'd grown up to be as procreative as a rabbit and one of the town's two police officers. The second, Barney Fife, looked like a cross between Dudley Do-Right and Paul Blart, his personality equal to his namesake despite his size. Neither officer was intelligent, hard-working, or productive, traits that meant when the Chief retired, an outsider was brought in to fill the job. It had been an ongoing source of frustration to her that the pair was all she had to work with and worse, a condition of her employment was not firing them until the end of her first year.

It had been a little over a month and a half and she was pretty certain she couldn't survive a year.

Since the chief was my sister-in-law, I had recommended psychological warfare to make them quit. She pointed out that since psychological warfare required a brain, it was wasted effort. When I suggested Winnie fart chemical warfare, she brought up the Geneva Convention and domestic terrorism.

Then we got really drunk and filled their work boots with petroleum jelly from Daniel's locker.

He had a disturbing amount of petroleum jelly and neither of us wanted to know why.

"I didn't say they'd be Winnie's tooth marks," Larry raised an empty cup from my cabinet at me.

"Ew! Not touching that. But why the heck shouldn't she play with a dead person's bone? They're dead. What do they need it for? Holding up their re-animated corpse? Who wants to be the walking dead when you can be the sleeping dead?"

Larry muscled his way in beside me and poured himself some of the magical bean water. Another reason I loved him, he knew better than to get between me and the coffee pot before I had the first probable-felony-reducing cup.

"Because it's weird and disrespectful?" He offered, doctoring his coffee with the flavored creamer I'd purchased on a whim. It was clearance Peeps creamer from Easter, and it tasted like liquid marshmallows. Arguably, since marshmallows were vanilla sugar, most creamer tasted like marshmallows. Since I like vanilla sugar, I'd buy literally any creamer that didn't have hazelnut.

Bonus, this one had a brightly colored wrapper with cute chicks to make me smile every time I opened my fridge.

"Why though? The dude is dead. He's probably not using the femur. If anything, playing fetch with his now pointless leg bone would be an excellent distraction from the boredom of being dead." I chugged the coffee in three swallows at the conclusion of my argument and poured myself another round. "I mean, have you seen Corpse Bride? Ghost dog fetch with dead body parts is a perfectly legit pastime... or aftertime? After life pastime? Past life pastime?"

"Yeah, just cuz you'd offer your skeleton to a dog and play tug doesn't make it less weird to *normal* people. And yes, Tim Burton is not normal either," he cut off my statement before I could make it. I pouted while he took a few sips of his coffee and flinched. "Why did you buy this?"

"Because the town took a vote and added keeping me in coffee to the natural disaster emergency preparedness plan and it was on sale," I said around gulps of coffee. Curious, I spun around the bag and looked at the flavor. It was a vanilla bean blend, probably one of the most boring coffees that I owned. It wasn't like I'd made him the surprise bag of Bertie Botts Every Flavor Coffee Bean I found on a website for fans of the unusual and fantastic.

Wine and internet shopping were not friends, but I enjoyed every horrifying sip of the abomination and refused to share. If one were going to go drunk shopping online, a post-therapy retail therapy if you will, coffee and novelty gifts that served no purpose were really the only way to go.

At least that's what the talking unicorn action figure on my nightstand said when she woke me up.

OK, technically she sang a song about her horn being used to stab thine enemies, but I interpreted it as "you're such an amazing shopper, people only wish they had your skills to find rare and wondrous things".

I also believed that if I didn't have a dog, woodland creatures would bring me my slippers. The Earth is flat and murder should be legal in some instances.

You know, normal stuff.

"Not the coffee, the diabetes in a container you poured into it," he made a grab for my Peeps creamer to refill his coffee and I smacked his hand. No one criticizes my brightly colored caffeination friend and gets seconds.

"How dare you insult the liquid version of Jesus's resurrection treat. I mean he came back from the dead so we can have Peeps and Peep flavored things," I made my declaration well aware that if any nearby Christians heard me, I was being condemned straight to hell. Since I'd lived in Florida for two years, I figured the dry heat wouldn't be that bad and I wouldn't have to listen to judgmental Christians. Unless passing judgment was a one-way ticket to the bad place in which case, I was back to being screwed worse than a metal pan in a house full of toddlers with ADHD and a future in percussion performance.

Larry laughed and pulled me against him for a long, tongue filled kiss.

This kind of screwed I was down for... so long as I didn't end up with any of the aforementioned toddlers with Southern drumline ambitions.

"You are absolutely nuts," he whispered against my cheek, the morning scruff rubbing softly and sending pinpricks of sensation up my arm. I inhaled his scent, clean soap, pine and earth. Whether from working outside, or just his body, the man always smelled vaguely like hay and dirt on a hot day after a rainstorm.

"Yet still you love me, so that makes you more nuts." I bit his ear and stepped away to chug a third cup of coffee. "What are you birthing today? Anything good the world needs? Like an antichrist?"

He quirked an eyebrow at me and I smiled.

"You're wearing your amniotic fluid shoes... aka shoes that come off easily so you can exchange them for boots," he stared at his Chucks while I talked, and I wondered if he was aware of his own nuances or if I'd just drawn attention to an unconscious decision making mechanism in his brain.

I had a bad habit of telling people observations and memories of past times they'd shared with me. While they might play it off, their faces registered my memories as "creepy" and "inappropriate".

To which I might argue if it was inappropriate and creepy, why did they share it with me.

I forgot the names of every president after Jefferson and which street connected where. I could be introduced to someone a thousand times and refer to them "hey you" because their name was gone, but I knew the woman I'd shared a table with at Suzie's Diner four years ago liked to add a lot of pepper to her tomato soup and she worried the world was slowly sinking further into space. Thankfully, the stuff I said out loud didn't come close to the threshold of weirdness I kept in, but I was starting to note the Earth's relative position to be certain it wasn't dropping from the sun's orbit.

That or I was on a watch list for my work with telescopes and rulers.

Like an intergalactic watchlist.

"Sheep," he continued to puzzle over his shoes, so I poked him in the ribs as a diversion. "Ow!"

"What? Don't be a baby," I booped his nose and offered another one to Winnie. She whimpered at the poke, but accepted the boop with a head butt for more affection. The dog was as big an attention ho as her grandma, and my mom took public displays of affection to a whole new level.

An illegal level.

An illegal naked level with spectators.

"See, it hurts!" He poked me in the ribs as though attempting to prove his point, but he missed and nudged one of my breasts with his index finger. It slid along the curve of my bra and around the side. Deciding he'd rather pay than seek revenge, he splayed his fingers out along my ribs and slowly moved his hand up.

"What are you doing today?" His words were directed at my chest.

"Hey! I have eyes and they're up here!" Larry dragged his gaze up from where his hand was groping my boob and I offered him an eye roll but answered the question.

"Probably sitting in my office downstairs and contemplating turning this town into a reality show," I shrugged, knowing full well that in the oversized crap show that was Sweet Pea, Ohio, I would probably be the show's star. I would personally argue that aside from the disaster videos on YouTube, I was completely uninteresting in my daily life.

They might then argue that the number of videos available to view disagrees.

I might see fit to point out that a lot of them are remixes of the same incidents.

Probably the network would argue that with the content available on YouTube, there had to be more that the cameras missed and they wanted it.

They would of course be right and I would need to leave my house in an instrument case like Taylor Swift. Except I didn't own or play any instruments, so I'd probably have to be moved in a dog crate. Since I only lived with Winnie, her walking next to a person holding a dog crate looking like their arms might fall off would be a dead giveaway and not worth the neck pain.

Larry squeezed my boob to bring me back to the present.

My "apartment" sat on a quarter of the library's lot. Whoever had built the library over-estimated the number of people in this hick town who would actually read and ultimately walled off part of it to sell as combined office space and living quarters. Beneath the apartment was a small office with a storefront window emblazoned "Sharp Investigations" in gold leaf lettering. The plate-glass window sat beside a heavy wooden door that needed only a talking doorknob to be included in the cast of Alice in Wonderland.

When I'd arrived home from the Army, Mrs. Margot, a local senior citizen, had needed help with a town mystery that left four people dead and a lot of chickens homeless. It had been the first time I shot someone, my fourteenth or fifteenth property damage explosion, and my first real investigation into small town crime. Once my eyebrows grew back, she offered me the office and the living quarters in exchange for investigative services to the town.

Services I may or may not have been qualified for, but the alternative was my parent's basement. I'd lived there for a few months and the house had more horrors than being asked to look into events that may result in death and dismemberment... of other people.

My childhood home had been converted into a shrine of sexual curiosity and experimentation. My old bedroom was an E. L. James inspired grown-up playroom. My brother's was a library of books, tools and research. After that, I'd elected to stop opening doors for safety reasons.

I swallowed the gag that threatened to forfeit my coffee and stomach acid to the floor.

"What time do you start at your actual job?" he asked, referencing my work as an animal technician at the local dairy.

"I'm off today. Something about mediocre white men not wanting to be in a room with me..." I tilted my head and Winnie copied the movement. "I'm guessing that means there's a shareholder meeting and I'm banned after the incident where I made the CFO look like a moron for not knowing the open encumbrance on his pending purchase orders for the fiscal year."

"Do you even know what that means?" He asked and I shrugged.

"Open lines of credit. You learn a lot about how budgets work when the Army shows you an itemized bill for what your disasters cost them in an effort to convince you to stop causing them or forfeit your contract. Did you know emergency fire services are really expensive? Hazmat teams make like forty dollars an hour and they can't leave until the explosive stuff is removed."

"I'm guessing it's a bit more than that, but I have to go bring new life into the world and I feel like you're going to feign ignorance so no one knows how smart you are. My house tonight?" He dropped a kiss on my lips, and I returned it greedily.

"Yeah. I'll bake something," I waved him out and turned to Winnie. "You ready for this, girl?"

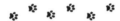

Sweet Pea, Ohio wasn't anything special. The small town sat ten light poles and two cow pastures from Yellow Springs and offered minimal services to the residents. With charming tourist appeal, residents managed to open thriving shops that sold everything from novelty antiques to artisanal baked goods. Though I'd grown up here, every new batch of tourists brought with it a reminder that people were idiots, because the only thing charming about living here was Isabel Charming's headstone in the cemetery that filled up two decades ago.

Instead, we had a rural community of farmers and their offspring sentenced to thirteen years hard time at the single facility school district. Most people born here attended school with the same people, then went to work with them and died without meeting anyone new.

But sure, taking a selfie with a cow and watching movies from the 1990s in our old-school Hollywood theatre could be fun... Especially if you also enjoyed the smell of cow dung, ever-present flies, and mean school children who would smash chocolate pudding on the seat of your pants.

Main Street gave way to four distinct residential neighborhoods that bled into the farms beyond. Many drivers paid for a scenic tour through all four districts and out into the unknown, where the farms funneled into large stretches of absolutely nothing. This was the real reality of living here.

Repetition on a slow march to absolutely nowhere.

And yet, here you are, living here again, my brain supplied. It was an unhelpful thought so I offered a replacement.

Hiding out, staying under the radar until my villain arc begins and I can harness the limitless energy of dogs for world domination. Satisfied, I held onto that thought as I braced myself to open the office for the day.

It was just a temporary stopover on my quest for world domination.

Except then I'd be responsible for the world.

Shudder. I need a new dream.

The moment I slid back the deadbolt in the wooden door, Mo blew in like Dorothy to Oz sans ToTo. A real shame because the dog was always the best character in movies. Bonus was that with ToTo's size, Winnie could enjoy an interactive squeak toy.

"I need sage!"

"Sage advice? Bake your dough before you leave the bakery," I said, plucking a glob of what smelled like rosemary garlic bread out of her hair. The baker was wearing jeans and a T-shirt with an apron in a deep forest green. Based on the location of bread dough, she had been cooking like the Cookie Monster eats.

Dough everywhere and no evidence that any actual bread was made.

"No! Smudging sage! Ever since that bone-"

"Tree root," I interrupted her.

"Evidence of death entered my house, I can sense a presence. An unearthly presence and I want it gone! I could have sworn this morning a stampede of deer was measuring my property!"

"Deer aren't unearthly, they are part of nature."

"Fine, unnatural presence. Talking deer are not natural!"

"How is a bundle of dead plant material called sage somehow not more evidence of death than a tree root? It's the same thing with a different density." I heard a kid ride by on a skateboard through the heavy drapes of the window. The wheels stopped and I heard something that might have been a face against my window... or butt cheeks.

Rotten Kirby kids.

"Are you not listening? My house is haunted by talking deer who measure and you're arguing over whether or not a tree root and smudging sage are the same thing?"

Her frantic arm waving brought my attention back to the real danger- my friend. She was being threatened by deer and femur shaped tree roots. I was being threatened by my friend with flailing arms and unbaked dough over the aforementioned deer and femur resembling tree roots.

Two more globs of dough fell out of her hair as she spoke. Winnie slunk forward and I death glared at her to the dog bed in the corner. I tossed a handful of dog treats from my cargo pocket onto her bed, scooped up the wayward dough and tossed it into the trash.

"They are the same thing, and you are absolutely insane. But I'll play along, what would a deer use to measure the property?" I asked, plucking more dough from her hair and body before it could fall and poison my dog with its garlicky goodness.

"I don't know! But I had a headache and I needed to pee before proofing the bread and something was trampling through the vines behind my house. When I looked, whole sections had been squished and I could have sworn they were arguing about whether it was feet or square feet when they read the listing," I ducked as she punctuated her sentence with an arm thrown skyward. Hungover Mo had a few too many enthusiastic gestures at her disposal that I personally was unprepared to go to the hospital over.

I might be clumsy, but Mo mid-morning was a lethal weapon.

Mo mid-morning and hungover was a toddler with nuclear launch codes and a brightly colored keypad.

"The deer were arguing over units of measurement?" I placed her arm back on her hip, checking once more for any wayward dough before declaring her clean enough for my office. "Wouldn't they use hooves or square hooves?"

I meandered to the heavy curtain protecting and obscuring the front window, drawing the cord down. I risked my peace to let in the hideous light of the daystar. In a slow rhythmic beat, it crept toward the corner in small, measured tugs that I found relaxing.

"You think deer have their own units of measurement?" Mo asked, coming to stand beside the window, hands on hips.

"I think if you don't have feet, how would you know what they are? Time and spatial relevance are all human constructs to give meaning to an otherwise indifferent universe." My eyes trailed off with my words when I spotted a harried woman with dark brown hair in two braids under an orange bandana. Her outfit was nearly identical to the woman in last night's movie, jean short shorts and a tank top that was mercifully still in one piece but barely contained her considerable assets.

She also didn't have any blood or sweat on her, which considering the outdoor temps was actually more terrifying than being chased by a disembodied knife.

"Human constructs are necessarily imposed on the rest of the living. We didn't make it to the top of the food chain by not forcing the rest of the world... Are you listening? What are you looking at?" Her bracelets clattered as she waved her hand in front of my face.

"Yes, but Mo, your house is basically the woods. Even I get lost finding the front door when I visit. Why would deer *not* live there?"

"But-" I cut her off when two people walking the opposite direction paused to gawk at the woman. The couple were two of the town's more notorious residents, my parents excluded, and still she represented some sort of novelty to them. In a town where everyone knew everyone else, a novelty was rare.

A novelty that didn't get the third degree from the senior citizens was dangerous.

"Who is that?" I wondered, even as I pictured her in the place of last night's slasher flick victim. Her body was the right shape, outfit a near carbon copy except for the realistic flush gracing her cheeks. As she got closer, I could see a slight sheen of sweat and declared her human after all. Her eyes crinkled in the corners, raising her age to at least mid-thirties. She also looked to have a fondness for food that kept her from having a flat stomach but enough metabolic grace to stuff a full-size Reese's cup into her mouth and not burst free from her clothes.

Which she proved by pulling out and eating a full-sized Reese's cup.

"I'm not sure..." Mo thought, watching the woman pull a thick folder of paperwork from a large brown handbag I hadn't noticed. Her Reese's had come from her pocket, the wrapper now neatly deposited in the trash bin nearby. "Holy cow, and I thought my purse was too big."

"Your purse *is* too big, that is a satchel. One keeps business documents in a satchel, you keep bricks in your purse cleverly disguised as cookbooks you 'just picked up' even though the same books have been in there for three weeks minimum. Don't even get me started on the slippery substance I found on your wallet all those weeks ago. Phil implied he'd sold it to you ages ago and you specifically asked if it was shelf stable in varying heats!" We watched the woman come even with my front door and stare at the address, then the name on the window and back down at her paper.

Her eyes repeated the movement and Mo held her breath beside me. I scanned her face, waiting for an explanation or a tell.

"What?" I asked and she jumped back, smacking me in the face with a bracelet clad arm.

"Don't do that!" She clutched her chest as I applied pressure to the spot on my cheek that was throbbing. My hand came away without blood, so I tried to shrug it off while giving my friend a wide berth. "You can't just shout at people out of nowhere!"

The brunette opened the door and took a cautious step forward. She smelled like sunshine, sand, and hard work. Manicured fingers caked in dirt clutched the paper, even as she lifted her chin to study us confidently.

Her eye crinkles were accompanied by laugh lines around her mouth and I upped her age to forty.

"It wasn't out of nowhere, I was standing right next to you," I offered the woman a cursory smile as I backed further from the exuberant Mo. Her limbs were once again flailing, and the newcomer elected to stay put near the door.

"Exactly! Right next to me! Why were you yelling?" Mo gave the woman a thousand-watt smile and she relaxed.

Poor woman probably took wooden nickels and bought ice in the arctic, too.

Anyone who thought my best friend was safe and comforting probably also thought wolves would make adorable pets... which included me, so I mentally checked my own bias. Even dangerous things were adorable *some* of the time.

Hell, even decaf smelled like coffee if you didn't know better.

"Can I help you?" I offered without taking my eyes completely off the red head. Her feet hadn't moved, but it was like watching a circular saw mounted into a table: it could still dismember you if you got too close even if it was technically a table saw which was supposedly safe.

"I..." she looked at the paper in her hand, then to me and the dog in the corner. "I think there must be a typo on my deed. Where is the Charlatan Realty Office?"

"The... what?" I asked, walking over and gently taking the paper from her hand. "Charlatan? Like a con person?"

It was a thicker paper, featuring block letterhead at the top declaring Charlatan Realty, J. T. F. Charlatan, Realtor, and my office's address beneath it. The body congratulated one Penny Plootz on her purchase of the house located at... "Mo?"

She came over when I spoke her name and looked down at the paper with me.

"What? Looks like a typo, but I don't know a J. Charlatan." Her eyes skimmed the paper another minute before shrugging it off. "Did you check with city hall? They have a list of town businesses and where they are registered."

"Yes, and this isn't registered to anyone. I thought maybe it was a newer business and Mr. Charlatan hadn't filed the documents with them yet."

"This business isn't empty. Cyn's been operating out of here for six months and..."

I poked her in the ribs as I finished reading the paper.

Outside the window, another skateboarder passed. This one wearing all black and looking a little too old for the sport. He paused in front of the business, checked a paper in his pocket and I held my breath while Penny and Mo continued to argue.

He dropped to his knees behind a trash can. A police cruiser rounded the corner and just as it came level with the window, Skateboard Man popped up, pelting the car with eggs. The cruiser stopped, started to reverse, and the man took off, leaving the skateboard and three eggs behind.

The cruiser came level with my window and Daniel tilted his glasses down to glare at me, but I held up my hands innocently.

"Why is Daniel threatening you?" Mo asked and Penny gaped at the officer in the window, watching him talk into his radio, flip the lights and take off with egg dripping down his car.

"Someone egged him."

"Egged?" I nodded at her and then looked at the paper in my hand, dazed and curious. My eyes scanned the paper again.

"Right, Mo, did you sell your house?"

"What? No," she looked at me as though I sprouted a second head. "Seriously, did you get punched in the head again by a dildo? I would never sell my house."

"Then why does this paper say Penny here owns it?"

Chapter Three:
Catfished

T hough I'd never purchased so much as a travel trailer, I was fairly certain your realtor didn't send you a letter of congratulations. Certainly not one with this many typos or hints of condescension. When Mo confirmed that she had not sold her house, and Penny had begun to wail, we elected to look into it further with the assistance of technology but without the aid of earplugs.

A poor choice really, since I had shooting range hearing protection right up the stairs.

More bizarre than the letter was the listing from which Ms. Plootz purchased the property.

Well, the listing and someone whose legal name was Penny Plootz.

Somehow, she'd made it to adulthood without being bullied into an attic dwelling shrew that flung change at rude children. Yet purchasing a home in her forties had resulted in being swindled out of... however much a house cost.

Probably a lot.

Pulling up a stored listing on her tablet, she used it as visual proof that we were in fact crazy. Obviously no one puts ads for fake things on the Internet. The listing proved that she had purchased the house, was a savvy businesswoman, and we could simply eat our words, because she had bought a house, sight unseen, in an all-cash offer for less than the assumed market value because she was just that good. Only people who are good with money could afford a house, she insisted.

A house that wasn't for sale, Mo corrected.

Wasn't for sale, and for all intents and purposes, not even real I added.

Then the crying went to a pitch Winnie found uncomfortable and we decided to keep the truth to ourselves.

The address was Mo's, but nothing else in the photos matched. After twenty minutes of swiping, not a single image matched any aspect of Mo's property. The house pictured belonged in a New England blue blood neighborhood, with a wrought iron fence and a coat-tail sporting man holding a tray of champagne whenever anyone walked in the front door and offering a cheerful "very good" to any and all requests. The closest we had to anything like that here was Amber's house and it wasn't even technically in Sweet Pea.

"I don't understand," she said for the fortieth time, and I considered whether or not offering her Winnie's tug rope to chew on would be rude or helpful. Denial was the first stage of grief, and my experience with everything that came after was that it was equally annoying. Despite that knowledge, I still wanted her to move on to whatever came next.

It would be a different annoyance and a sign of forward progress.

"I'm not some rube. I'm in investment banking. There is no one better at spotting a false lead in stock than I am."

"Like that fake tip about citrus fruits you've brought up a half-dozen times?" I yawned and she stabbed a manicured finger in my direction.

"Exactly! Nothing gets by me! I'm a research wizard, a numbers goddess, and I never jump headfirst without dipping my toes in the water!"

My stomach clenched for the woman, but I deflected with humor.

"Except apparently the fact that you purchased a fake house at a real address that wasn't for sale... Go back!" I grabbed Mo's wrist just as she swiped right to the next picture. Eyes wide she swiped to the image of a master bath with a jacuzzi tub and one of those toilets that cleanses you with spraying water. The bathroom itself would hardly look reasonable in any Sweet Pea home, but that wasn't what made it worthy of a longer look.

Penny crowded around her iPad so that both women were pressed against my forearms. At Mo's five and a half feet and the other woman's slightly shorter stature, their faces were practically fogging the screen in front of me.

Fogging the screen and wrapping me in a sweaty flesh blanket I did not enjoy.

"Back up," I ordered both of them, trying to channel my drill instructor from Basic Training and ending somewhere close to Dipper Pines in puberty. My voice squeaked and Winnie cocked her head to the side as though examining me for chew toy possibilities.

The human women remained pressed against me.

"I'm serious," and they leaned back a fraction of an inch. I still had two women's breasts pressed against me and I marveled that either of them walked around without holding her spine and dissolving sweaters with body heat. "As impressive as both of your chests are, stop touching me or I'll lick both of you."

Penny jolted backward, new to the game. Mo crowded closer. She knew it was an empty threat as I seriously frowned on putting uncooked meat in my mouth. Proving her point without forfeiting my space, I let out a long low whistle to execute Plan B.

Winnie pounced on Mo, giving her a facial with her tongue that sent the baker sprawling to the floor, crushed under ninety pounds of working dog. There was a short battle during which one of them screamed and one of them barked and Winnie got the upper hand. Penny, for her part, elected to avoid Mo's fate by taking the seat in front of my desk while I leaned against the smooth wooden work top.

"Tell her to get off!" my human best friend called out, or at least I think that's what she said. It sounded more like *toilet ear giraffe* and I decided if I developed any talent, that might have to be my band name.

It totally worked for Ska music.

"Are you going to respect my personal space bubble?" I spoke while zooming in and out on the image of a stylish bathroom with pedestal features. In the corner, there was a smudge, or the hint of a smudge. Something that was possibly supposed to be cropped and wasn't... but it was there and I just needed a closer look.

"Are you going to tell us what you're fixated on?" She'd managed to push my furry partner off her face and now had the ninety-pound furry paperweight in her lap. The dog had succumbed to enthusiastic ear scrunches and the promising scent of baked goods that followed the woman around. If I didn't love them both, I would be supremely miffed that my guard dog had grown up to be such a pushover.

"There's something here... a shadow maybe?" I kept trying to force the image frame to widen, revealing an imperfection that was just out of sight. Every time it was nearly big enough, the image would snap back to thumbnail size.

"That's not weird, I mean... all rooms have shadows," Penny sounded defeated, a sudden departure from denial.

I looked up from the screen to see her face in her palms, two fingers massaging each temple. Her assured cadence somehow broken and diminished to damsel in despair, and part of me broke to see it. I had anticipated anger and bargaining, but not this small, sad show of defeat at her predicament.

Sadness was the only stage of grief that was worse than not moving through them at all.

"It's not the shadow so much as the direction it's coming from." I faced the iPad toward her and zoomed in on the spot. "The room has windows on the wall in front of the camera, looking out at blue skies."

Penny refused to glance for more than a moment and I watched her eyes start to mist. Terrified she might start crying, I plowed on.

"But the shadow is coming from the side of the frame, an area that couldn't have windows, because the tiled wall goes all the way up. It's also going directly to the side, like the light wasn't high up... but all bathroom windows are placed up near the ceiling." I pulled the iPad back toward me and scrolled through the other images again. "The same in the living room image. The windows are level with the shoulder, but the sunlight is coming straight down. Almost like..."

A thought stuttered in my head... it hardly seemed possible. Yet the shadow in the center with the halo of light and the angle of the image... was there another possibility?

"Almost like what?" Mo said from the floor. She now had my furry BFF sprawled on her back, leg kicking punctuated by a rhythmic thumping of her tail.

"Almost like the photographer was taking the picture from above the living room... where it didn't have a roof?" It sounded absurd, there weren't giants walking around taking the roofs off of houses and photographing their guts. I shook off the thought and tuned out Mo's theory of events, acknowledging that words like aliens, Santa Claus, and drones were being used interchangeably.

Perhaps Mo was discussing the plot of a Science Fiction novel and I didn't need to have her committed. In the event that wasn't the case, I was re-purposing the military's nonsense policy of don't ask, don't tell for friendship's sake.

"Is that a black sun?" The words left my mouth before I could grasp the dark black smear outside the window of what was being billed as a second-floor master bedroom. There was a balcony and just beyond it, a circular rising crest of darkness.

"What?" The two women jumped to their feet. Both moved to crowd in again and once more, there were way too many boobs on me. Since I grew only two, the rest needed to vamoose.

"Six inches, ladies," I warned, and they took a single step back while I fiddled with contrast and resolution in a screen grab. Whatever was outside the window was clearly a dusty black circle, small lines indicating some sort of writing engraved in it. "R22..."

I muttered and rotated the tablet left and then right.

"Why does something with R22 written on a dark black circle look like something I've seen before?" My eyes went to the two women. They both were in concentration mode, shouting out answers like audience members at a game show.

"Spaceship?" Mo offered.

"Solar eclipse?" Penny was clearly more realistic, though visions of day walking vampires sent a chill through my spine.

"Armageddon!"

"The second coming of the lord?"

"McRib season!"

I rolled my eyes and signaled for quiet.

"With all of that as a starting point, we have a house with no roof and possibly an incorrect number of walls. It's somewhere that large black round things could conceivably float outside second floor windows with..." A group of children walked past, one clutching a shoebox to her chest as a pair of Daniel Kirby's kids jostled her and threatened to rip the box from her hands. Her eyes watered, face red, and something in my mind snapped.

Women were not helpless.

Women should not be taken advantage of.

Women were not weak.

My feet carried me to the door in a blind rage and I grabbed both boys by the handles on the tops of their backpacks. With a handle firmly in each hand, I lifted the squirming miscreants off the ground until their feet pedaled the air like a cartoon roadrunner.

"Look here you little heathens," I snarled, watching their little faces go red, tiny fists thrashing into the air. Considering what in my arsenal might be remotely terrifying, I called for the first thing that came to mind.

"Oh, Winnie!"

The dog ran out and the boys went pale.

"You are going to learn to leave other kids and other people alone, or you're going to learn what it's like to go flying without a parachute," I lied, recognizing that most people flew without a parachute, unless they were parajumpers, then the whole point of their flight was to jump... eventually. The boys wiggled their arms, fell out of the backpacks and took off up the road as a police car whoop whooped around the corner.

"Ugh," I grumbled, looking at the little girl with dark brown hair and milk chocolate skin. "Is... your box OK?"

She tilted her head and showed me the front.

"It's a diorama," she offered an eye roll at my naivete, and I stifled a laugh. Normally, know-it-all kids were annoying, but something about her confidence and the protective grip on the project in her arms made her correction adorable.

Also, diorama is just a hilarious word.

"So it is," I looked at her display of a spiny-backed dinosaur extending his neck up toward a plastic tree, a hole cut in the top so the tree could rise above the red box previously used for light-up Unicorn Sneakers. "What is that?"

"Spinosaurus," she shrugged and eyed the police car pulling to the curb. "My teacher asked me to bring it back so she could use it as an example for next year's kids. Can I go? That man is..."

Her eyes shifted, and I was willing to bet all the coffee in my house that her mom had trained her not to speak bad of adults. Since the door of the police car swung open and Daniel Kirby stepped out, I offered her a nod.

"Stupider than a sack of doodie?" I didn't bother to lower my voice.

"You're under arrest for harassing my kids and throwing eggs at my car!" His voice carried a southern drawl that was as fake as the sock he most likely stuffed down the front of his uniform trousers. Though it looked impressive on the outside, on the inside it was useful only for making nightmares come to life.

Tiny human nightmares.

It was also an inappropriate use of socks.

"Save yourself," I whispered, and the little girl giggled as she skipped off. "Your kids lost these while being miserable little delinquents. Also, I didn't throw any eggs, Skateboard Man did."

I handed him the book bags. His arms struggled slightly under the weight and I smirked at his loss of muscle tone. The humor sobered when he raised a warning finger.

"They lost them... in your hands when you attacked them!" He didn't have any real conviction behind his accusation.

"I didn't attack them, I warned them to leave an innocent, homework-doing girl alone. I know you don't support academics, but someone in this town needs to get an education!" I jutted my chin out at him. "Otherwise an enigmatic leader will come to town and everyone will drink poison to avoid the apocalypse and then no one will milk the cows and their udders will burst. Savage chickens will overthrow city hall..."

"My kids are excellent students and I told them not to drink Kool-Aid from strangers." His face betrayed his words. Whether the lie was not drinking a stranger's beverages or their academic prowess, he didn't elaborate. Instead, I assumed both and moved on. "But I've told them to stop hassling Kamilla."

"Why are they trying to ruin her homework? Apparently it's already been graded and everything." My question was nearly lost as a bus trundled by, taking a turn on two tires. The vehicle swerved and careened into a potted plant as it came at us. The driver was obscured by something white, fluffy, and attacking his face.

"What the..."

"Do you see..."

The bus jolted toward Daniel's car and he jumped out of the way.

Out of the way and onto the skateboard the egger had left behind. It shot out from under him, sending him to the ground on the leftover eggs. Turning suddenly, the bus missed the car, crushing the skateboard just as the driver came into focus ...

"Is that a chicken?" Daniel asked, but I was staring at the tires.

"Diorama... bus tires..."

"Tires? You were looking at the tires?"

The bus took another turn on two wheels, brakes squealing before the sound of crushing metal filled the morning. I turned away from Daniel, assuming the bus was his problem. Making tracks back into my office, I grabbed the iPad and pulled up the images again. The officer followed Winnie and me back inside.

"Shouldn't you be dealing with the bus?"

He looked around blankly.

"What bus?" A fire truck flew by outside, but he was suddenly blind as well as deaf.

"Whatever," I started scrolling on the iPad and he pressed his chest against my shoulder. Unlike Penny and Mo, his chest was firm, warm, and made my skin crawl.

"Seriously? What the hell, people? Stop touching me!" I flipped the tablet around and forced them to face me like pupils in a school room. Daniel stood leaning against the straight back of Mo's chair while Penny looked to be carefully avoiding the sock sitting uncomfortably at her eye level.

Winnie handled the problem by shoving her face into Daniel's backside to eat the raw egg.

"Ah! Get it off!" he yelled, but we all ignored him. He flapped his arms and danced while Winnie worked to lick the seat of his pants clean.

"This isn't a real house," I started, and Penny rolled her eyes.

"We already knew that..."

"No, I mean it's not even a real house sized house. It's a model... well, I guess more like a toy?" All the images confirmed it as I made another pass.

"A toy? That isn't a toy house!" Penny was on to anger, and I released a breath.

"You know those scale models architects use to show how things will be built?" Everyone more or less nodded. "Someone sold you a house based on pictures of a diorama they took at a bus stop."

Chapter Four: The Collector

"Well, that was easier than a hooker on a date with a millionaire," I muttered, looking down at the four-foot-high model house sitting beside the bus bench. This was only our second bus stop, and while I had anticipated evidence of a fake house, I had no real hope of seeing the fake house.

But it was here and exactly as small as I imagined.

It reminded me of a child's playhouse... if the child was very small. Or maybe a doll house for really big dolls. The model was open at the back to allow interior shots, the front a beautiful façade of a two-story sitcom home. There was a bright red door beside a bay window and a dog face pressed against the window that turned out to be a sticker.

Briefly, I wondered if Penny would let me buy the sticker for my own future house.

"I bought a doll house?"

"Technically, I think it's a little big for dolls, but they would fit in there better than you do," I offered unhelpfully. My eyes watched Penny, her face a mask of the seven stages of grief in rapid succession on loop.

"I bought a damn doll house?!?"

I opened my mouth to make light again, but Mo shot a warning look and I changed tactics.

"You... don't houses have to undergo an inspection to receive funding for the escrow mortgage deal?" Daniel, Penny, and Mo all stared at me like I'd just become a flat earther. "What? I've never bought a house. The only thing I've bought is repairs on other people's homes, businesses, and event spaces when Winnie destroyed them. Those all required a damage inspection and assessment for insurance deals for which I paid the difference."

Proving my point, the dog put two paws on the roof. She was prepared to topple it, but a loud *pooft* escaped her butt. The rank smell filled the area, and she whipped her head around to sniff.

"Yeah, that was your butt, missy. Place!" I gave the command and she moved to stand beside and slightly to the rear of me, flopping in indignation. "What part of that did I get wrong?"

"Escrow is the waiting period between when a housing offer is accepted and the final funding of the loan or seller if paid for directly," Penny was in professor mode, and I pretended the words she was speaking made sense. There was no way buying a house was that complicated, they were messing with me. "A mortgage is the loan you repay when you purchase a house with money borrowed from a bank. The bank can refuse to provide the money if they don't think the asset is worth the amount being requested. So, they conduct a series of inspections to verify the value of the asset and agree that it's worth the financial risk to fund the loan."

"Is there a simple version of all this?" I questioned and got an eye roll from Penny and a pleading look of agreement from Daniel.

My stomach churned at the knowledge that I needed something brought down to Daniel level for me to understand. If my dream of world domination was unrealistic, being as clueless about something as Daniel was unimaginable.

"That *was* the simple version!" Penny looked appalled that I was somehow leading this group. A fact that baffled me as well as I hadn't agreed to be in charge, I just wanted to find a fake house. Now I'd found it, and had fully intended to let Penny walk away with an important life lesson about buying things sight-unseen in a deal too good to be true, and maybe the number to a good attorney to get her money back.

Three sets of expectant eyes demanded I respond.

"The only word I really understood was asset. Is buying a house like a spy training program where banks give you money to make them a new generation of housing inspectors? Is it a four-year contract like the Army or are you enlisted for life like the Black Widow Assassins? Is there a cool outfit? Do you think they need to be oversexualized or is buying a house not the same as overthrowing male led regimes?"

Several blinks and I realized that was not the response they wanted. It also looked unlikely they'd let me walk away and get on with my day. I had somehow become the leader of this ragtag team and I contemplated all the places I could lead them... to the coffee shop seemed like a good idea. Off a bridge seemed even better, but only if the coffee shop was closed and Daniel was in the front.

"Should we maybe avoid the assassins and head to Mo's? I'm running a little low on caffeine and she also has cookies... plus if the assassins follow us, there are knives there."

Three astonished faces stared at me and I chewed my cheek to keep more nonsense from spilling out. Apparently, buying a house was not the same as entering into a pact with madmen bent on world domination, but there were assets, inspections, and funding... sounded like the makings of a secret society death squad to me but if all homeowners were in on it, no one staring at me would admit the truth.

They'd all drunk the Kool-Aid so to speak and were waiting for the promised aliens to set them free.

Except they'd leave behind Penny because she bought a toy house.

"The asset is the house," Mo offered dubiously, and I nodded slowly. "When the bank gives you a loan, they want to be sure you're financially capable of following through on the loan terms and also that they aren't giving you too much money for the value of the purchase. Like they don't want you to owe them ten grand for a house that falls down the next day. Then you won't pay and they will own a pile of rubbish that isn't of any value."

"Still sounds like a conspiracy, but did you see the inspection reports?"

"There wasn't one," Penny sighed. "I watched a drone video of the house, and I was in love, so I paid cash. All transfers were done privately without banks or inspectors, the realtor was a registered settlement agent and seemed trustworthy. I convinced my insurance company to just add it to my policy with the photos alone since I have an impeccable record for claims and quality purchases."

Settlement agent sounded like code for bandits or land grabbers... maybe both. Though I elected to keep that thought to myself after the whole asset/spy network verbal spewage.

No need to ask when there was such a thing as the Internet, where your browser history was judged only by the NSA and whoever marketed me coffee beans.

I searched purchasing a house with cash on my phone as a group of kids too young for school arrived at the housing model with dolls and action figures. A game began where Iron Man married Barbie and they had formed an alliance with the Army men to defend their home from Cinderella and a Cabbage Patch kid. Sides were chosen, Captain America died, and it all ended with Winnie chewing on Barbie's head.

"Winnie!" Her ears drooped as the little boy who'd brought the Barbie cackled with laughter. "Out!"

Barbie's slobber coated head fell to the ground with a wet thwap and the little boy picked it up.

"She has face piercings! Now she can be Iron Woman!" The kids whooped before dashing off to the next most entertaining toy abandoned on the side of the road.

A real feat unless they intended to play with a cow.

"There's something here about checking for liens, did you do that?" I studied the to-do list of buying a home with cash and came to the important conclusion that I would probably never *need* a house badly enough to do any of this.

I could just wait for my parents to join a sex commune and inherit theirs.

"Yes, but your Hall of Records is..." she shuddered and I looked at Daniel.

"We have a Hall of Records?"

He waggled his hand in a *kind of* gesture and I looked back at Penny.

"When I asked about the home's address, she laughed at me. When I asked about the realtor, she popped gum in my ear and hung up. So I shifted to the County Registrar and was able to get the details regarding back taxes and sales history for your address," she nodded toward Mo. "They said the realtor wasn't in their records when I asked about J. T. F. Charlatan, and the address on his realtor website, next to the library, was vacant. Charlatan said it was a paperwork oversight, but it would be corrected."

"Vacant? It's not vacant, Mrs. Margot owns it," I puzzled and wondered if maybe someone at the county had been having fun at Penny's expense.

"Oh, it's owned, but there's no business registered at that address," she offered me a meaningful look and I gave a shrug.

"Hardly anyone pays me, so it's not really a business," I switched to Daniel. "Where is our Hall of Records and the County Registrar?"

"All village numbers are answered by dispatch," he said with a wince that reminded me our town's dispatch was a nosey Jenny who liked gossip and nonsense more than anything in the universe. She also happened to be named Jenny, which I assume was the basis for the nickname since most nosey people were Nelly. "We can go see her. She's at the station, but if you're hoping to avoid a million questions before you have an answer, not asking her is safer. You're better off going in with something for her to confirm than starting a line of reasoning."

"Let's skip her and head to the county. I am not in the mood for Jenny, gossip, or questions." I shuddered at the memory of her vocal range and continuous outpouring of speech. Jenny adored the sound of her own voice more than she cared what it was being used for. Somehow, not as many people were as turned off by that fact as I was, though it might have more to do with her access to juicy gossip than the willingness of others to spend time in her company. Neither of which was worth looking into since both meant being near Jenny and people who enjoyed her brand of entertainment.

As we watched, a VW Beetle driven by a man and a woman in all black pulled up to the bus stop. Behind them followed a pea green pick-up. Two men got out, picked up the house and tossed it into the bed of the truck, splintering one of the walls with a large crack.

"My house!" Penny wailed, the two men turning to give us a quick glance before jumping back into the truck. As they started to drive away, a chicken squawked and charged the car.

The truck braked, sending the house flying forward.

It shattered into a million pieces while Penny's sobbing kicked up a notch.

"Who is the County Registrar?" I asked, hoping to distract everyone as the truck and bug sped away.

"Jenny's mom," he shrugged and gestured us all back to the car park where his cruiser sat beside my Jeep and Penny's Mini Cooper.

"Her mom?" I stammered, but no one heard me as they loaded into the vehicles. "Is it too late to talk to Jenny?"

The chicken squawked its opinion, pecking at the ground.

"Shut up, bird," I growled at it.

Jenny's mom, Maria Dallas, was not my favorite person.

Not my favorite in the same way I wasn't hers. She held petty grudges normal people would have let go and I refused to be the bigger person in anything but stature.

Unlike her daughter, she was perfectly poised, professional, and fashion forward. The last of which was how I ran afoul of her in third grade and I'd yet to redeem myself in her eyes.

Eyes that were now looking at me sternly from above a slightly off-center nose with a bump in the middle. My eyes couldn't leave the spot, another reminder as to why I was banned from playing sports. Evidence of my inadequacies lasted forever.

"Hi, Mrs. Dallas," Mo offered warmly, and I moved aside to allow the town's beloved baker to speak for me. Everyone loved Mo, she was warm, welcoming, and usually held coffee and pastries. "You are looking flawless today. Is that new?"

Mo gestured at the woman's cardigan, a soft pink that appeared seamless and smooth on its owner. Maria's eyes darted in my direction and back to Mo with a tense smile.

"Hello, Mary. It is, thank you. It's Neiman Marcus. Saved up for months but it's just gorgeous," her face spread into a real smile and I considered hiding behind Daniel to keep it there. Her hands stroked the fabric lovingly before her hands halted and a sharp glare attacked me.

Sweaters were a subject best avoided in my presence.

"It's lovely, little warm though?"

"Not in here, dear. Is that what it's like outside?" She glanced toward the outside world, but without windows there wasn't anything to look at. "Warm and sunny was the forecast, but I haven't seen it."

Warm and sunny, just like that day in elementary school.

Maria had been wearing a cream-colored sweater, heading to kiss Jenny goodbye on her way out after dropping off birthday cupcakes for the class. The woman had a skin condition, one that she always kept covered on campus, not that any of us were aware of it until I kicked the soccer ball to Jenny just as her mom arrived on the pitch and... it slammed into her face.

Her nose broke, blood streamed down her face and into her mouth.

"My sweater!" She spat blood as she fought to save the off-white fabric from the torrent of red running down her face. As soon as the sun touched her skin, she howled in agony. The woman was forced to choose between getting blood on her sweater and being in pain. A choice that was made for her when I ran over to help and skidded in mud which sprayed upward, my mud coated body grabbing anything to keep me from falling and ending up face first in the puddle... with the woman's fancy sweater.

"It doesn't matter, she needs to register," Maria broke through my memory and I peeked out from behind Daniel. "If you are doing business within the county and it's advertised as such, you are required to get an EIN, file the paperwork for a fictitious business name, and pay your taxes."

"Penny?" I whispered hopefully, and Mo shook her head with an ominous point in my direction.

"You need to..." but before Mo could finish, a commotion from the parking lot had all eyes turned toward the door. In the split second before the sound was identified, I imagined Winnie leaping from the Jeep, chasing down a man with some sort of food. Hard to say if he taunted her or she just couldn't resist, but the man would have charged toward the nearest shelter: the County Recorder's office.

All of which was confirmed when the door slammed open and a large man with an overly ketchup-y hot dog came in, Winnie on his heels.

He barreled in, Winnie hot on his heels. The hot dog man became level with our group when Winnie launched into a flying leap, hitting the man square between his shoulder blades. The hot dog went flying to land... dead center on Maria's chest, ketchup coating most of the sweater's front.

"Whose. Dog. Is. That?" Her ragged, angry breath sent tendrils of dread running down my back. All eyes shifted to me and hers soon followed. It was another Army flashback, soldiers parting so the guilty party stood alone amid the chaos and ruin.

Maybe you didn't leave a man behind, but you could certainly hang him out to dry.

"You have seventy-two hours to get into compliance, Ms. Sharp, or I will levy an eight-thousand-dollar tax on you weekly until you are either shut down or placed in jail."

Declaration complete, she whirled on a heel only to catch a puddle of spilled ketchup, sending her pump sliding from beneath her. Maria flailed her arms, I moved forward to assist, but nothing could stop gravity. She landed flat on her back in ketchup when Winnie shoved her face into Maria's and tried to clean all of the ketchup from her chest.

"Forty-eight hours, Sharp," she snarled, and I thought I might faint.

"But... you just said..." I started and she held up a finger.

"If you do not leave immediately, it will be twenty-four. The government moves slowly, Ms. Sharp. But they rarely care when I speed up the process of getting them their money." Her index finger started to look like the point of a dagger - sharp, deadly, and covered in the blood of her enemies.

Is that why women wear red nail polish?

"Now, Ms. Sharp. Leave now," she spun on her heel and stalked off leaving us standing there in horror and fear.

"But... I don't know anything about taxes," I whispered.

Chapter Five:
Death and Taxes

I n sixth grade, I had a teacher who phrased statements in a way that made them sound optional. Like "you should read chapters three and four and complete the worksheets on the corresponding pages". This led to classmates regularly asking if "we have to" and she always said, "The only thing you have to do is pay taxes and die."

At the time, none of us thought this was funny.

Or knew what taxes were besides the ten cents per dollar we had to account for to buy candy.

Now, I'm certain it *isn't* funny, I still don't know what taxes are and she was just outright mean. My brain could handle budgets and spreadsheets. It was how I managed repayments to establishments such as the church community room for destruction caused by Winnie, but when tasked with navigating the government website and processes I was useless. Whoever wrote tax law did so with tax attorneys and their bottom line in mind.

The phrasing required professional interpretation that they could bill by the hour.

Like confusing word prostitutes pimping out their brains.

"What is this crap?" I demanded of Mo, but she'd stopped listening to me four websites and six exclamations ago. If she were an emoji, she'd be the middle finger with a fire engine red fingernail. "Did you do all this?"

She turned the page in her cooking magazine and refused to answer.

"This can't be legal! I'm technically still government property, can't they intercede? Or at the very least, repossess me from federal custody when I get arrested? I mean seriously, it would be easier to open a brothel! Can I just charge Larry for sex? They can't tax sex... can they?"

Mo and I had returned to my office and I begged her to help. Within fifteen seconds, I was overwhelmed and refusing to follow instructions. After five minutes, she threw in the towel and announced it was hopeless and I was on my own. As a business owner with experience in education, you would think she was perfectly capable of showing me how to complete the required forms and documents. It was her civic and patriotic duty to make all of this less stupid.

At least that's what I told her before she threw a paperback at my head and went back to reading the magazine. Where she found a cooking magazine in the endless chasm she carted around under the guise of a purse is beyond me, but it was suddenly in her hand. In her hand and infinitely more interesting than the suffering of her childhood friend.

While the woman is a business owner, and trained in education, no professional experience could help her navigate explaining business tax and licensing requirements to me. Not because I was dumb, dense, or un-caffeinated, but I had developed an executive dysfunction to the whole thing. The woman was an above-board merchant who could easily have helped me if I was anything resembling a rational adult and not a toddler in the cereal aisle.

"This is stupid! I don't need to do this! She can't hurt me!" I stomped to my coffee cart, Winnie following closely to eat the ham sandwich crumbs that trailed from my lap. "I should call the governor! Or the President. I served in the military; I don't need an EIN! They already have more information about me than my own mother! Speaking of my mother, do you think she'd give the sexual relaxation spiel and tools to Maria to buy me more time? Can you bribe people with orgasms?"

Mo turned another page and declined to comment.

My feet stomped back to my desk, hands cradling a mug of coffee. It was my dire emergency coffee mug: bright red with big letters "HELP! Someone killed this coffee!" After carefully setting down my reason for continued living un-incarcerated, prison probably had crappy coffee, I flopped in the chair and clicked a link that said IRS and mentioned tax IDs.

"Two-hundred and fifty dollars!" I shouted at the computer. "Mo, you paid $250 for an Employer Identification Number?"

Face twisted in concern, she climbed up from her chair and walked over to look at the screen.

"No, they're free... where *are* you?" She inspected the graphics at the top and took over the mouse. Scrolling, she encountered testimonials and "other services". "This is a scam."

"But the URL said IRS when I clicked on it?" I pleaded and she drew my eye to the top, Tax Services something or other. "What the hell?"

"Anyone can buy a URL and route it to their site. Go back," she stated while clicking the back button herself. "See? They added a dash so it would look legitimate. They are charging people to 'help' with the 'difficult' and 'complicated' government processes."

"So I should pay them?" I begged and she smacked the back of my head. "What? You know I'd pay people to do anything unpleasant for me. If I learned one thing from being in the Army, it's that the ultimate American privilege is sending strangers out to do things that you find unpleasant. Usually fighting wars in inhospitable environments, and dueling to the death, but doing taxes is up there!"

"No! It is neither difficult nor complicated, click here." Again she directed the mouse and we were on the government's most hated agency's website. You could request a tax ID during business hours and four screens later, we were done and I had a number.

It had taken less time than my coffee pot needed to brew a K-Cup.

"They wanted $250 for that?" I demanded and she shrugged. "I could have gotten a half-naked Marine to show me his-"

Mo clamped her hand over my mouth and I swallowed my words. When it came to half-naked Marines, there was always a fair amount of swallowing.

Especially if it was the top half that was naked.

"The world is full of people who prey on the un-informed. Pay enough money, and web browsers will put their ads above the legitimate places to accomplish the same thing. What's next?" She looked at the checklist she'd written out beside the computer.

"Drinking wine and plotting revenge?" I asked hopefully and she sighed.

"No, you lush. I won't come visit you in prison. If you're done whining and throwing tantrums, I might actually be able to help you. Now, get your lazy butt to work and turn this joke into a legitimate business."

"This place isn't a joke-" but I was cut off when a half-dozen clowns walked in. "OK, come on! What the heck? Did you plan this? How do you know this many clowns that aren't Daniel?"

The clowns were almost a comedic stereotype of rodeo clowns. Their fluffed-out wigs sported a rainbow of colors, the baggy pants dirty but previously polka-dotted and bright. What failed to be amusing was their faces.

Angry clowns were definitely not good.

"Look, whatever you're upset about, I can explain! Or pay... whichever this instance calls for," I offered, hoping to mitigate an angry clown homicide.

Two of the clowns responded by honking metal and rubber horns, the harsh sound an indication they would not be easily swayed with words or money. The dirt was contained to their arms and knees, like they'd fallen or been pushed over. Small spots of blood and scabs peeked out of holes in their thin costumes and I had to take a moment to replay the last twenty four hours.

Winnie and I most definitely did not blow up any clown cars or giant tents.

We also hadn't knocked any over or beaten them up.

"What about dry cleaning?" The horns honked more insistently and Winnie howled in unison. The clowns quieted, Winnie quieted, and a new clown entered.

His pants looked oddly lumpy, larger in the legs than all the others and moving. Not just moving with him walking but moving up and down completely against the human constructs of anatomy.

"I'm not qualified to remove living tumors or perform exorcisms," I protested as I jumped out of my chair and retreated. The second something burst free of his body, I was running to Canada and never looking back. America would totally be the first country to get parasitic possession viruses and if I went far enough north it would be too cold for them to survive.

The horns presented an abstract fanfare and the newest clown dropped his pants to Mo's utter mortification. A burst of squawks and feathers poured out of the pants and Winnie let out a startled bark and ran upstairs.

Deciding she was the smartest of us, Mo and I tore off after her while the chickens savagely went after the dog bed in the corner.

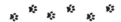

"It was not funny!" I shouted at Larry as I slammed the oven shut. In my hand was a casserole of sorts made of random things Larry had in his freezer. While I was not at Mo's level of culinary skills, I was capable of cooking.

I just usually didn't do it for other people to keep expectations low.

Also, I was pretty sensitive about my cooking and if anyone insulted it, I would dump it on them regardless of temperature. This, I have been informed, counts as assault and is in fact frowned upon... everywhere.

"It took an hour to round up all those damn chickens and then your stupid brother refused to take them!"

The dish smelled like garlic and featured broccoli and chicken in a cream-based sauce over potatoes. I inhaled, long and slow, deciding that I needed to figure out how to get an oven in my apartment.

One could only eat so many Instant Pot tacos and ham sandwiches.

"What is that smell?" Larry asked, summoned to the room with his nose in the air.

"Food," I told him, watching excitedly as he walked toward Winnie, knowing that he'd trip on her and fall on his face as revenge for his laughter.

"It smells... edible." He walked carefully around the dog and I snarled.

"Damnit, you were supposed to trip. Yes, it is edible, I can cook food. So as long as you don't buy inedible food, the odds are good it will serve the requisite purpose of nourishment and mild dietary delight."

Then I stuck my tongue out at him and tried to get Winnie to attack him with silent communication.

Childish, thy name is a woman with fifteen homeless chickens in her Jeep that had her cooking insulted.

"You can take the chickens to my practice," he offered, arms sliding around my waist and lips peppering my neck with kisses. "I have the space and no neighbors. Also probably chicken feed, we'll have to check with Breanne."

"But can I kick your brother's butt for sending the clowns to me in the first place?" My voice came out breathy and his hands started roaming.

"It's your fault the chickens are homeless," he offered, letting me go to grab plates. "While his method sucks, we probably should have done something about the roving poultry gang after Gertrude gave them flying lessons."

I smiled at the memory of Gertrude the mule taking out chickens with swift kicks to the clucks.

"First of all, you can't prove these are the same chickens that were donkey kicked across the dairy. Second, this is not my fault!

You were there when the chicken farm blew up, your cousin brought the explosives. Also, no one can prove those are Roger's chickens. They could be anyone's chickens! But any of Roger's chickens should belong to Mitchell Scott!"

"Except Mitchell has been taken into federal employment/incarceration so you're next in line as owner of the mean biker gang, take no prisoners chickens." He chuckled, serving up the food and handing me a plate and a fork. "Let's be real, the only chickens raised tough enough to make grown men cower belong living with you or in the Russian wilderness where no one can hear the sudden death of unfortunate travelers."

"No! All chickens are mean and biker-like. These chickens aren't any more hostile than all the other chickens in the world." I was talking around a mouthful of food, waving my fork in his direction while Winnie stood by waiting for me to drop or spit food on the ground for her.

"Eat with your mouth closed," he laughed, using an index finger to close my mouth. "Did you get your homework done? I have a treat for dessert if you did."

I swallowed and gave him a face.

"It's too hard," I whined.

"Is it now?" His wiggling eyebrows sent my eyes to the back of my skull. "Where are you stuck?"

"I don't know... I'm still trying to figure out which agencies need to be notified of my status to make tax payments and I have to go back to mad Maria to get the DBA paperwork and send it to a newspaper. But not just any newspaper, a newspaper on a list. And there are people out there who..."

A loud knock filled his house and Winnie took off toward the door, barking loudly with toenails scrabbling.

"Cyn!" Mo called out and I cocked my head. "Cyn, I've texted you twenty times, stop having sex and answer this door immediately!"

She then spoke in rapid fire Spanish, that I only partially understood. *Trabajo... arreglar... estudiar...*

"What's my job to fix?" I asked, yanking the door open while still shoving food in my face. Beside the red-headed baker was a slightly built Latino man, his flannel shirt and jeans well worn. A baseball cap sat delicately between his two callous, work-roughened hands.

"Hi," I said, and he began to wring his hat, eyes darting between me and Mo, before Winnie chose to slam her head into his groin and make introductions awkward.

"Damn-it dog, go to your bed!" I ordered, but the man had recovered and began petting the canine proctologist. She promptly lost all of her bones and came to lay in a fluffy puddle at, and on, his tan work boots.

Mo asked him a question, he nodded and smiled at her.

"*Me gusta tu perro,*" he said to me and I smiled.

"Thank you for lying, she's an asshole." I dropped to my knees to pet her, accepting that his liking her meant he didn't need me to move her. But I wanted to be near her head in case she needed a second look at his man bits... with her whole face. "Que pasa?"

My Spanish sucked, but I thought asking *what's up* was casual enough.

"Can we come in?" Mo asked, and then pushed past me to stand inside. The man stood frozen, looking nervously over my shoulder as though going in would be a fate worse than death. Mo was probably glaring at him for not immediately following, but the man didn't seem the type to just march into someone's home.

"She's pushy... *obstinada*?" I tried, thinking that stubborn might cover her personality better than rude, inconsiderate, and prone to inserting herself in other people's business.

It was also one of the few words I knew in multiple languages after having it applied to me.

Repeatedly.

Across many oceans.

He smiled and nodded before gesturing for permission to come in and I responded with a nod, mentally reciting *stubborn* in all the languages I could remember.

Hartnaeckig.

Burong binh.

Tete de mule.

Of the German, Vietnamese, and French, the last was the most insulting. The French of all people should have been more creative with the insults than mules. They were French, insulting people was as much their language as French itself.

"Lizandro needs your help," she blurted, and he seemed to flinch at her absence of an indoor voice. "*Tiens un papel?*"

I stared between them, not knowing any of those words.

Nervously, he pulled a folded paper from his back pocket and hesitantly handed it to me. Carefully, I separated the quarters and stared at something that looked like a government paper and a letter of some sort with letterhead suggesting "law firm". Except...

"My office isn't a law firm," I said, looking over at Larry. He took the page, studying before he looked between Mo and Lizandro.

A sigh escaped his lips and I waited for someone to clue me in.

"*Has pagado*?" he asked and I looked between the three people in the room, astounded they both knew Spanish and hadn't bothered to teach me. The man nodded, his hat still passing between his hands. "*Cuanto*?"

"*Doscientos cincuenta*," his eyes wide and I knew the number was more than he could afford. "*Ellos iban a ayudar.*"

"*La Migra*?" he asked, and Lizandro nodded fervently. "Crap."

Larry scrubbed his hands over his face, and I looked between everyone for an explanation.

"He paid two-hundred and fifty dollars for help with his immigration papers. He received a letter," he handed me the one that appeared to be from a lawyer. Most of it was in Spanish below the header and I understood none of it besides the threatening use of exclamation points and random numbers mid-sentence. "It states that his visa has expired, and they could help him get permanent residency status."

"Is his visa expired?" I asked, and the man looked down at his shoes. "Never mind, I don't need to know. Do you want your money back?"

Mo asked him something in Spanish and he responded.

"He wants to be a citizen, but when they took his money and disappeared, he can't afford anyone else to help."

His eyes misted over and I let out a long sigh.

"I'll help you, but it's going to cost you." Mo gave me a snarl and I held up a hand before she could yell at me. "*Necesito polla.*"

Lizandro's mouth fell open, his ears bright pink

"Cyn! You can't say that!" she hissed while Larry turned bright red with laughter and Lizandro took a small step back, shaking his head no.

"What? I asked if he needed chickens!"

"No, you implied you wanted his," her voice dropped, "man meat."

My eyes went from Mo to Lizandro, whose hands and hat were now covering his crotch area. His eyes went to Mo and asked her a question, eyes moving from me and back while Larry clutched his gut in silent laughter.

"No! I said *polla*. *Polla* is chicken!"

"*Pollo* is chicken, cooked chicken! *Polla* is penis! You said you needed his penis," Larry stuffed his knuckles in his mouth, doubling over while Lizandro took another step back, alarmed by both of us. He spoke to Mo again and moved his back flush against the door.

"Great! Now he's scared of you! Also, he says he doesn't think his wife will let you work on this if you're going to treat him like a..." he repeated the word and she mulled it around in her mind for a translation.

"Slut?" Larry offered and I punched him in the arm.

"Damn-it, Larry!"

To the terrified man, I offered my gentlest smile... which in hindsight was not the best idea. Showing a terrified man your teeth probably makes you look vicious or into biting. I cleared my throat and tried Winnie's technique for non-threatening.

Laying on the floor, I put my arms and legs in the air and looked up at him.

"Does your wife like chickens? You have to adopt some chickens," I tried again, letting Mo translate and he smiled, but his ears remained a pink tint.

"*Si, un gallina?*" I nodded from the floor with my feet and hands ramrod straight. I had no idea what I was agreeing with but *si* was a promising start to his statement. Mo offered a response and he gave me a side eye before asking again.

"He asked if you're crazy and in need of medical attention," she sighed. "Why are you on the floor?"

"It works for Winnie?"

"You aren't Winnie," Larry countered, and I flopped to my side with a huff. He scooped me up and planted a kiss on my face. Lizandro asked Mo a question about *polla* and she snickered into her hand.

"He'll take your chickens, but you need to get your penis from Larry," her final cackle stayed in the room long after she left.

Chapter Six:
Lesson Learning

D eath would have been more enjoyable.

Floating in a river of mental pain, numbers, and the remnants of what used to be gray matter, I prayed for the end. I was now fourteen hours into my allotted forty-eight and what remained to do was as daunting and murderous as rope climbing... or getting an inappropriate snack back from Winnie without blood loss.

Federal prison had to be better than sorting through the legalese to become a business.

Maybe I could dress up like Lizandro and get deported to Mexico. Hide out from the government there as a significantly taller, agriculturally inept man. Then he could stay here and be a tall blonde ex-soldier with a dog...

Wouldn't work, I couldn't leave Winnie behind or force the man into platform shoes.

There was no choice but death and begging for him to be pardoned as my death wish.

People granted death wishes, right? You get a lifetime of birthday wishes and a single death wish that superseded them all because it could be accomplished by humans.

On the pyre of my death, also known as the desk in my office, sat the instrument of torture I wished to take with me to hell. To hell or wherever the men in Office Space carried that fax machine to meet its demise. My desktop monitor and tower, spinning a rainbow of death where once there was a cursor, had ceased to be helpful over an hour ago and now... now it must pay.

Trial by fire maybe... were computers flammable?

"Damn you technology! Be useful!" I shouted, preparing to throw the mouse across the room. It clicked something and opened a video featuring a woman in a stable. She was wearing nothing but a smile, approaching a horse and the music that accompanied it reminded me of a 1980s porno. She laid down in the hay, the horse mysteriously led closer, manhood on full display as the woman repositioned and...

"Oh my dog!" I set the mouse down and clicked rapidly. Back, back, back until I was looking at the document that held the notes of my hours' worth of research into tax law, immigration law, and the process by which one could naturalize themselves as a sovereign nation on American soil.

The document had a single line: People are jerks.

True, but that wasn't going to help Lizandro get his money or his citizenship, now that the government had been "made aware" of his presence. It had taken a few calls, but whoever had sent the letter had also notified Immigration and Customs. He had a deadline to come into compliance or they would send him back. It was farther out than my deadline, but I'd rather lose my business than let an innocent man be deported for farming without a visa. What sort of government punished hard working immigrants when literally all of them spawned from immigrants?

My brain hopped on the rant train to recover.

Who were they to put up the off-limits sign after they'd pillaged and plundered all of the natural resources? My dark thoughts spiraled to a book about political genocide and trying to start the country again with a clean slate free from arcane notions and prejudice.

Reinforcing the single line on my page: people are jerks.

The man had been running a farm on the outer edges for more years than I'd been alive. He rented the land, started a business, and was a hard-working contributing member to the local economy. On the other hand, rich witch Amber Carter cheated on taxes and tried to frame people for arson without any threat of being kicked out of the country.

Maybe she sent him the letter, stole his money, and then endeavored to get him kicked out so there was one less honorable person to make her look bad. It worked if you didn't require evidence... maybe I could make some evidence...

I was already going to jail for tax evasion anyway, maybe.

"I can't tell if I should offer you more coffee or escort you into a bunker for bomb disposal and clean up your organs after you go," Carla Sharp, my brother's recent wife and new chief of police said as she strode in with confidence. Her pristine uniform and carefully styled hair were the stuff of life goals I couldn't achieve even when the Army required it.

I had probably single handedly kept the hairstyle freezing industry in business during lean times.

"Any luck?" I asked, hoping the sexy auburn-haired bomb shell had managed to glean insight from her former government employer contacts. We'd met when I was investigating a murdered gossip reporter and she was the top suspect. Not normally my deal, but half the town was suspected of killing her and my boss wouldn't let me on the farm until people stopped following me around and demanding help.

He said it scared the livestock. I personally thought he was worried someone would dirty his shiny boots and the plaid shirt destroyed with a flying pudding cup.

Carla had led us on a wild chase, taking my brother with her, to uncover a homicidal ex-baseball player who was stealing money from little old people who subscribed to the paper. She also happened to be my brother's lover, recent fornicator with Amber's dad and, to my utter anti-incestuous dismay, Larry's fling. Thankfully, there was no cross-contamination and she made uncovering the dirty deeds of a local organization her last mission for some alphabet agency no one knew the name of.

Not even her.

The honey trap, female, non-fictional character from TV version of Michael Weston got lucky, though. Carla wasn't trapped in Florida or burned so she still knew people… and didn't have to stay in Florida. If they made a TV show about her, it would be called "Armed and Fabulous" or "Free At Last: Retired and Rocking It".

If they made a show about *me*, it would probably still be called *Burn Notice* for an entirely different reason. Maybe *Burned but Didn't Notice*?

"Kind of," she flopped down in the guest chair, a feat that still managed to be graceful. Despite her luscious hips, her tapered waist kept the utility belt from getting caught on the chair's arms. She fit perfectly on the seat, slouched down in a borderline petulant pose and I had to marvel that she'd married my brother of all people.

Brothers were so gross.

Just look at Larry's.

"The good news, you can stop worrying about Lizandro. He had kids, and he initially had a visa to come here with his wife, so it's a simple adjustment of status which I've taken care of. I haven't had any luck tracing the money, since the con artist required cash and had an exclusive mail-only presence. I'm working with the Postal Inspectors on it, but it's not looking good. All of this is going to cost you a bomb sweep of an estate nearby for a paranoid diplomat." I shrugged and looked at my explosives detection K9.

"She could use the work. He had a visa? He implied there was never anything of the sort."

Carla averted her gaze.

"He must have forgotten. It was a while ago," she'd chosen her words carefully, gaze locked on her perfectly shaped nails. "The documents are definitely there."

"Easy to forget I guess." I went along with it. "And the fake house?"

"As far as Miss Penny," she said the name like the woman was a dominatrix or a kindergarten teacher. Since both must enjoy pain and suffering, the two were not mutually exclusive and both had a lot of latex paint. "She mentioned she was some sort of financial trader. Because of that, her accounts are closely monitored by the corporation she works for, who allow their employees to work anywhere but struggled to picture her in middle America."

"That... sounds illegal and a little judgmental."

"Not if you sign something that says they can monitor your life when they hire you." I nodded at her statement and let out a breath. Some of the tightness in my chest lessened and I acknowledged that I'd earned a sixth cup of coffee, cheese crackers, and the day-old doughnuts Mo had brought by an hour ago. My whole body protested standing with a rhythm any drumline would envy.

"Got it, so they followed her money?"

"They did, and the con artist isn't bright because they left the whole thing in a US based financial institution. It had been created four weeks before the money was moved in and had no transactions before or after. We tried to move it back to her account, but there's a freeze on the funds. Almost like the account owner was trying to hide them from someone else." She worried her bottom lip and I waited to hear what was bothering her while the single-serve coffee machine spit out my reward.

"Normally, in major fraud cases like this, the funds are dispersed into multiple offshore accounts in nominal increments, making it impossible to trace and move back. This person... just left it there. Left it there and trapped it so no one can take it out. Not even the government, which is both terrifying and impressive. Since nine eleven, I didn't believe there was anything the government couldn't touch and take with extreme prejudice."

"Was there a name on the account?" It was a ridiculous question, but she answered anyway.

"Yeah, but not a legitimate one." She scrubbed her hands over her face, leaving a flawless complexion behind. Either she bought really good make-up or she was born that beautiful and didn't need any help. I stuffed several cheese crackers in my mouth and washed it down with a bite of doughnut.

Lucky woman with good genetics. "Everything about it feels off though. It doesn't come with the same sort of malice that Lizandro's threat did."

"So, where do we go from here?" I asked, just as the reminder alarm on my phone blasted *The Song That Never Ends*.

"Work it would seem," she stood and stretched with her statement. "But that's not the whole reason I came in. Your address, this business, is associated with dozens of services providing enterprise websites across the Internet. None have a contact or real presence beyond generic and easily managed content, but if you received a letter and googled the company for back-up, it would look legitimate. Again, except for Penny. I had someone shut them down, they are still running down the IP address, though they aren't very hopeful it will amount to anything."

"What does that mean for me?" I'd frozen with the sprinkle doughnut halfway to my lips. If the websites were shut down, my woes would be over, weren't they?

"It means... you can expect some more visitors." Her tight smile spoke volumes. "Related to that, I talked to Maria over at the County Recorder's Office."

My face brightened, "You got me more time?"

Carla flinched and my gut bottomed out.

"Less time?" It came out as a squeak.

"End of business today to submit your application, get verified, and show proof of payment for listing your fictitious business name in a paper."

"What?! Now I need a fictitious business name? I thought I needed a DBA!"

"You do, it's the same thing." She'd stepped back when I shouted, and I looked down to see a demolished doughnut clasped in my fist. "Was it not any good?"

"My doughnut," I sniffed, looking back up at Carla. "What about DBAs?"

"DBA is a fictitious business name," I stared blankly at her, but she didn't continue.

"How do those letters equal the same thing?" I stammered.

"DBA is doing business as, which means you've made a fictitious business name so that you can operate under an assumed identity, legally." I was willing to bet she memorized that from the internet, but my mouth just opened and closed like a hooked fish. "It's like registering as a superhero."

Now she was just mocking me.

"Then why not call it an... FBN? Why DBA? Why use an acronym that doesn't correspond to the actual name but instead make a new acronym for a nickname?"

Carla shrugged and snitched a doughnut from my box.

"No idea, but you might want to..." her voice trailed off just as the black and tan body of my furry partner landed on my back. She snatched the opened bag of cheese crackers, licked the doughnut residue from my palm, and carried her loot to the dog bed in the corner. "Never mind. Looks like if you want something sweet and brightly colored, you'll have to play dress-up with Larry."

I arrived at the farm with a headache and a bad attitude.

One might argue that the bad attitude was routine, but I would argue that they needed to be punched in the face. Thus, proving their point and ensuring my hand would hurt in addition to my head.

Summer tourism was in full swing at the dairy farm. The red building serving as an ice cream parlor was vomiting a line of customers that snaked into the parking lot. Every human that exited had drips of colorful desserts dripping down vacation couture shirts of Hawaiian prints and dresses that belonged on a beach. These couples were usually followed by a pair or more of smaller humans threatening the careful balance of human existence.

"Cynthia!" Joseph called out and I turned to see him holding a pineapple headband and a hula skirt.

"No way, Joseph," I took a step back toward my Jeep. "I am not playing hula girl. Also, I'm pretty tolerant, but this crosses a line and I am not feeling generous. Push me and I'm going to HR."

"What? No, this is for Winnie." She flattened her ears and whimpered, instantly brightening my mood. "Once you get her settled, I need to speak with you in my office."

An ominous pit opened in my stomach.

"Couldn't you just tell me now? If I'm fired, I don't want to walk to the office and have the anxiety of waiting and wondering beforehand. Tell me and get on with it. No dramatic climax, no building dread and anticipation. Rip off the band aid, man! I'm not your plaything!"

"Holy Christ, Cynthia! You're not fired," he puffed out a breath. "I need your help and it's personal."

The ominous pit filled with slithering snakes, my stomach now home to a slimy sensation that was worse. Personal, in my experience, was sexual.

I had zero interest in learning anything sexual about Joseph. It was bad enough my parent's *personal* business made the news... and had a blog... also a monthly newsletter.

"I uhh..." there was nothing I could point to as a defense. "Okay."

Joseph nodded in his ten-gallon hat and shuffled back to his office. His too-tight blue plaid shirt sitting above crisp jeans and shiny black cowboy boots. The sight would have been laughable if I didn't get the impression he was scared of something.

Something he thought I could fix.

"Let's get you to work, girl," I said, leading her to the ice cream parlor. Jess, a sixteen-year-old with a digital camera, stood ready and waiting. To contribute to the atmosphere, they had Hawaiian themed music playing and the teenager had on a floral shirt and a straw hat. Costume on, Winnie jumped on her hay bale and began her reign as de facto mascot of the ice cream shop.

"Don't give her any ice cream," I warned Jess and she just rolled her eyes.

"No one gives Winnie anything. She's an adorable thief and we are all at her mercy."

A little girl waddled over and pressed her face against the pineapple princess pup. In her hand was an enormous banana that was also smeared down the front of her shirt, face and... then it was gone.

"Told you!" Jess called, as the little girl burst into tears and the mom tutted at us.

In the interest of self-preservation, I ran to Joseph's office and pretended she was someone else's dog. Jess could be in charge of coddling children and calming parents.

Joseph's office wasn't really an office. When he'd become manager of the dairy sometime before I paid attention or existed, he'd converted an old storage shed that was barely bigger than an outhouse, into an office space. The desk was too big, and the only way for him to sit behind it was by crawling over the work surface.

Which is why everyone was invited into the office *after* he'd had time to get in place.

"Come in," he responded to my double knock, and I pried open the door. His ever-present empty box of beer sat in his trash, and the nauseating air freshener that permeated everything somehow made the cow plops outside smell enjoyable.

"Did your office get smaller?" I asked, sitting in the folding chair. It teetered slightly and I braced my hands on his desk.

No way was I falling out of the chair in front of him... again.

He offered a thousand-yard stare that suggested he wasn't listening to me.

"Joseph?" I asked, waving my hand in front of his face.

Still nothing.

"Joseph?" I clapped my hands together an inch from his face and he jumped.

"What!"

"That's what I want to know!"

He adjusted the blotter on his desk, lining up the pen against the edge, angling the post-it notes to sit in one of the date boxes.

"I need you to go down to Mason's and pick up some supplies." He passed me a list and I tilted my head at him.

"Isn't that what Jaimie usually does?" I asked, not mad but also concerned. Jaimie was the best at calming retailers, casual haggling, and looking too tough to mess with.

"Yeah, but he caught some stomach bug. I'd go myself but..."

"But what?" I tilted my head. Joseph seemed like the type of man who'd love to go to the feed and equipment store. Mason's was basically Toys R Us for farmers, cowboys, and farming cowboy enthusiasts.

Also people who liked to shop at yard sales.

"I'm not allowed back in there," he breathed out a sigh. "Mason is claiming I stole a lighter and the change jar at the counter last week and he threatened to pop me one in the nose if I didn't bring it back. When I called him delusional, he banned me from the store and threw a bird roost at my head."

I stuffed my fist in my mouth to stifle the laughter, but it wasn't easy.

"You stole change?" I snickered.

"I didn't steal change. I was home sick the day he said I stole stuff! I can prove it!" His red face looked dangerously close to popping.

"OK," I held up my hands and took the list. "But if he throws anything at my face, you owe me plastic surgery."

Chapter Seven: Attack of the Clones

Mason's was more of an abstract concept than a dedicated farm supply store. Unlike the major known stores in bigger towns, Tractor Supply and anywhere named 'So and So's Hay and Feed', Mason's store was like a Swap Meet that someone moved indoors without bothering to wash it first.

I pulled up to the red building in the dairy truck and stared. If the building had looked like a barn or a firehouse, the color would make sense. Instead, he'd modeled it after some sort of Grecian building with columns and trellises. Instead of looking country chic, it looked like something from a horror movie depicting the barbaric life and bloody death of the Romans.

Probably directed by Mel Gibson.

"They hath painted the walls with the blood of mine enemies," I whispered in my best faux Shakespeare, but Winnie was holding court at the ice cream shop and wouldn't leave to go shopping. "Alas, there is no audience for my play, I truly am Shakespeare. I'll have to die to receive the accolades I so richly deserve."

Again, crickets in the empty truck cab.

"Oh, fine," I grumbled to myself and climbed out to see a man about a list.

Mason's was actually named Mason's Agriculture Collective. He claims to have tried to dub it MAC but the nice people at Apple and the delightful make-up folks took exception. There are rumors of cease and desist orders as well as other terrifying threats of hefty fines, but now that I was familiar with such things, I had a sneaking suspicion the man had made the whole thing up to avoid a semi-truck comparison with his personal figure.

Mr. Mason Mattis was a large man.

At least, large was a good enough descriptor that people felt prepared to meet him. The reality was, nothing could prepare you to meet Mason. Mr. Mattis looked like Andre the Giant had a baby with a sumo wrestler and took up steroids. To add an extra layer of "don't mess with me", he had full sleeves of dark ink tattoos and a ZZ Top beard that he could almost tuck into his brown leather belt with flashy rooster buckle.

The man always wore a brown leather belt and a flashy buckle, but the "Cocky" rooster only made an occasional appearance.

Anthropologists would probably call it a modern day codpiece. Modern day people called it wishful thinking on his part.

Ascending the porch, I took a deep breath and braced myself for the Agriculture Collective. No ordinary store, it was not for the faint of heart or the easily offended. Gathering strength, I pushed open the door and cringed.

It might be June, but the man refused to play anything but Christmas music by country singers.

"*Last Christmas, I gave you my heart*," an early 2000s Taylor Swift sang, and my cheeks went red for her. It would have been a blessing for her Christmas album to have faded into oblivion. Not that I didn't listen to it, but the twang must have sent her cheeks blazing.

"Get your giant ass out of here with that list for Joseph!" Mason boomed from the left and I nearly had a heart attack. "I know you'd never come in here for yourself! I don't sell coffee or dog food."

"Geez, Mason, I could have killed you. Don't sneak up on people," my left palm was pressed to my chest, and I hammed it up to buy some good will. He was absolutely correct on the rest, and not just because he didn't stock the two things I regularly purchased. "You know I was in a war zone. I spent two years in Florida, haven't I suffered enough?"

His response was to pull my arms behind me in a rear wrist lock and start dragging me to the door. My response was to let my body become dead weight and I waited until he adjusted his grip to accommodate the lower center of gravity. He loosened one of my arms and I gave him an elbow to the gut.

He didn't even flinch, but he dropped me on my ass.

"I'm telling your mother," he warned, and I gave him my brightest smile from the floor.

"That's fine, but could you also throw something at my face? Then Joseph has to buy me plastic surgery and there's a little bump..." A plush dog toy pelted me in the face with a squeak. "Hey! When did you start carrying dog toys?"

"Get off your butt and get this over with," he grumbled, lumbering back toward the register. "I may not want the man in my store, but I'll gladly take his money, the thieving, no good..."

His rant trailed off as he leaned beneath the counter and pulled out a giant bag of gummy bears. Stuffing a handful into his mouth, he chewed slowly and considered if the rest of the sentence was worth the hassle of shouting at me.

Deciding against it, he offered me some gummy bears and a tight smile.

"Where's your better half?"

"Posing for pictures in front of the ice cream parlor with children, dressed like a hula girl," I answered, shoving myself up from the floor.

Mason spat masticated gummy bears all over the counter.

"What the hell kinda kinky crap does Joseph have going on up there? The man is a damn doctor!"

I tilted my head.

"Joseph isn't a doctor."

"No, but Larry is and he has the man dressing in drag and taking pictures with children? Is that what this town is coming to? Children considering drag queens entertainment? Also, what the hell with the children? Is Larry..." he searched for a word that went with the horror on his face while I doubled over in laughter.

"Oh geez. First, drag queens are delightful entertainment for all ages." I gasped for air around the words. I grabbed a handful of the offered gummy bears and stuffed them in my mouth. "Second, I thought you meant Winnie. Larry was naked and smiling when I last saw him. Aside from being reasonably certain he isn't naked anymore, I assume he's still smiling. I do damn good work under time constraints."

Some of the concern left Mason's face, but it was replaced with a stern look of disapproval.

"Ladies shouldn't talk about their men and sexual experiences like that in public. Also, that dog fought for this country and you have her playing as a dress-up tourist attraction? Does the Army know what you've done to that dog?" He folded his arms over his chest and my laughter redoubled.

The Army would be relieved she was delighting children and not attacking event leaders in Germany and murdering pretzel statues. That he assumed I had men and not a man boded well for his fate after accusing me of being a lady, but none of that would make me forget that he was a card-carrying member of the chauvinistic prick club.

"So, what's really going on with this whole Joseph thing? You watched him steal a lighter and a change dish?" Changing the topic was a safer bet than challenging his misogyny but I made a mental note to send my mother and her swingers club round to give him lessons on all the things *ladies should be doing in public*.

With or without men.

Mason was asking for a painful lesson in misguided beliefs, and I had a literal army. A real role reversal from when I was part of an army but regularly stood alone.

"No, the slippery bastard." He punched his fist into the palm of his other hand. "I noticed midday the change cup was missing and I went to the footage."

He pulled out his phone and launched an app. The live screen showed me leaning against the counter looking at the phone. With a few swipes and taps, the database of recordings opened and he went to a folder dated three days previously.

"See, watch." He handed me the phone and crossed his arms in smug satisfaction.

Mason was on the video, wrapping something in paper for a man in a bucket hat. Maybe a woman, tops of heads were so universally top of head like. Bucket Hat laughed at something Mason said, and a short tubby man in a plaid shirt and jeans eased into the frame. He appeared to look around casually, shopping until he slid something into the sleeve of his shirt from a display.

Bucket Hat left, Mason turned to answer the phone, and plaid shirt scooped the shared change dish into his hand and slid out of the store while the proprietor was on the phone. It was as smooth as a choreographed dance, but not especially sinister. Even with the shoddy image work, the change dish wasn't exactly folding money.

It was barely chucking money.

"How old are these cameras?" I asked, trying to depixelate and zoom in on the recording. "Because this image quality is shit."

"I don't need good image quality! That is obviously Joseph. No one else shaped like that wearing the same damn outfit every day would be in here!" His voice roared and I took a step back, rubbing my ears.

"You need to calm down. You're being too loud." I hummed the next line of the Taylor Swift song while the man radiated angry heat. Nothing made me happier than telling men to calm down... well besides mocking their toxic masculinity.

"I am calm!" He shouted, smacking his hands on the counter. Someone opened the front door to the shop but when no footsteps followed, I figured the owner had scared them off. "Don't talk to me like I'm some hysterical female. I know what I saw, and after he won a grand from me at poker, that female police chief wouldn't hear any of my story."

That female. *Hysterical* woman.

"First, if you don't stop that macho man garbage, me and my *female* canine are going to come back here and show you exactly how hysterical and fragile we are. Second, that isn't Joseph," I shoved the phone back at him and stomped to a nearby aisle looking for udder ointment.

"If it ain't him, who is it then?" His sneer accompanying the statement was pure malice and condescension. Maybe Winnie poop in his tail pipe would sort this out. There was definitely a reason I ordered her food and toys online.

Even now that he carried dog toys, she'd never be shopping here.

"I don't know. But that person has a pillow stuffed under their shirt to mimic his girth, no one has a square gut," I punctuated my statement by throwing jars into my basket. "He's standing by that display case and his shoulder only reaches two inches above it. Joseph might be limited in stature, but he's easily three inches taller than your suspect."

Mason was now staring at the image, looking for all the tells I'd spotted so easily.

"Finally, that human is wearing sneakers. Joseph doesn't own sneakers, he only wears shiny ill-fitting cowboy boots with..."

My words cut off as I spotted a man palming a hunting knife and sliding it in his pocket.

"What the hell, Jaimie? I thought you were sick."

He strolled toward the display of cast iron wares and I spoke louder.

"Jaimie! What's with the knife?" He turned at the word knife, frowning. "Aren't you sick?"

I moved closer, trying to see his face from under the hat. Jaimie wasn't well-off, and he had a family to feed, but stealing a knife?

His hat tilted and the face was a strange impersonation of Jaimie. The general shape was right but...

"Who are you? Why do you look like Jaimie?" As I moved closer, Mason noticed the knife missing and stormed our direction.

"Damn man and his no-good farm workers, thinking you can steal from me?"

Mr. Mattis charged past me and moved into Jaimie's space. The proprietor was red faced and salivating, but the would-be thief just stood there- impassive. As Mason got closer, Jaimie grew more still, holding his breath as the man pushed through the maze of inventory.

"Give me back my merchandise or I'm calling the cops on all of you!" He came level with the farm-hand lookalike, and just as he reached for the man's collar, the guilty party faked left, bobbed right and sprinted toward the door. I launched forward and caught a foot on his ankle.

We both went down, grappling for purchase to take back our feet. His jeans pocket tore in my hand, sending the knife clattering under a display. Body scrambling in place like Shaggy and Scooby, we got to our feet at the same time and I tried to take him down again.

Eyes never leaving the door, mystery man shoved me aside and dashed into the lot. He had the engine turned over, tires turning up dust before I could catch my breath.

"See? You're trying to prove Joseph is innocent and he arranged to have me looted again! I'm getting that hoity toity police chief back here and you are both going to listen or I'll... I'll..."

All the wind left his sails as he realized nothing had been taken. He reviewed the security cameras while I caught my breath and collected my spilled merchandise. Beneath a display of steak seasoning, I found the knife coated in dust bunnies. A couple quick swipes on my shirt and it was good as new and gently returned to the display from whence it came.

My eye caught a chunk of beige material on the floor. It was roughly where I'd taken the man down, but no one had been injured. Eyeing the nearby shelves, I didn't see any obvious merchandise it would have come from.

Ambling slowly, I lifted the chunk of brownish pink substance and swiped off hair and dust. Though creepy, there was nothing sinister in or about the chunk. It almost looked like...

"A nose?" I asked no one, but felt Mason come up beside me. He stuffed a sausage size finger into the prosthetic and looked to be wiggling it around.

"Did that man playing dress-up try to steal from me?" He cursed to himself, kicking a stack of buckets. "Tried and didn't even wear his own nose?"

I scanned the room again and tried to think like a crook.

"Anything in here worth stealing?" My question sparked an interest that he quickly discounted.

"Nah, but someone wanted to buy the old gal, recently..." he pulled out some drawers and selected a pair of pages on thicker paper than normal, emblazoned with the seal of The State of Ohio. "Here ya' go."

My eyes skimmed from the bottom to the top as I groaned loudly.

"Seriously?" I shouted to the empty space beside me.

"What's wrong?" He asked, studying the paper again and then looking back to me for answers.

"What's wrong is: this is my damn home! Also, don't pay anyone to buy your property. This is a scam." I shoved the cover sheet against his chest after pointing at the return address. "I need a cup of coffee, a cupcake, and some answers."

Seeing none of those things in this building, I slammed down Joseph's money, grabbed the purchased items, and stomped my way outside. As an afterthought, I stuck my head back into the glass doors.

"Call Carla and give her this and that letter."

Mason caught the flying nose and stuffed some more gummy bears into his mouth.

"Then what?"

"Don't take any mail with that return address as serious and call me if anything else comes in," I decided, though, I'd rather swallow sludge than help him.

Sludge or the silicone oral sex training aid my mom tried to send me from Thailand.

"You got it."

Chapter Eight:
Facts and Fingers

"How can you say nothing he did was illegal?" I demanded of Carla. "It was very clearly a planned attack against my partner."

"Because there's no law against that!" She gestured behind me, and I fisted my hands on my hips.

"Give me a list of things that are illegal, he's bound to have done one of them and I will press charges for that!"

My sister-in-law rubbed the spot between her eyes and appeared to consider all of her available options. Hitting me seemed like a contender between rational explanation and ripping off her clothes to live nude in the woods like sasquatch.

At least, that was what I was thinking except I would hit Daniel and not Carla.

We were standing between the barn and the ice cream shop at the dairy. It had been a few hours since I'd returned from Mason's, unloaded the supplies for Joseph, and got down to business. The day had plugged along at a decent clip until her officer, Larry's idiot brother Daniel, had rolled up to get some ice cream.

Holding peanut butter dipped chicken fingers.

Firsthand accounts indicate he carried them toward Winnie on purpose. His version stated he was innocently giving her a wide berth to protect his lunch when he'd tripped and fallen into that path of travel.

No one believed him, but his swift departure when his boss arrived suggested that it wasn't going to amount to anything more than a poor decision stomachache anyway. I mean peanut butter on chicken fingers? To mimic peanut chicken? Was there no culture that man wouldn't bastardize?

"That's not how crime works, you were military police! You above all others know that charging someone with a crime isn't a multiple-choice question with fill in the blank ad libs! If you want to see a book of laws, buy one like normal police recruits! The book is always better than the imaginary movie and you'll be spared the possibility of my hitting you."

"But baiting a police canine is a crime on base! Arrest him for that!" I argued in vain, knowing full well that if Carla could have gotten rid of Daniel, she'd have done it two days after becoming chief of police. "Also, your metaphors are all over the place, you need to spend time with smarter people."

"While antagonizing Winnie is not beneath him, you can't prove that his culinary atrocity was specifically created to tempt her into attacking so that he can... whine. Loudly," she sighed the last word with hands fisted on hips. "Neither of those facts has anything to do with why I'm here and my need for intelligent interaction is hinging mostly on you. Right now, you are not supplying that, and I can feel my gray matter withering. Be a smarter people!"

Daniel had left almost immediately after Winnie's teeth had torn off part of his pants and showed the world he believed commando was work appropriate. A view that had made the Sweet Pea Facebook page and had hundreds of heart reacts. The post sat beside real news articles that had zero reactions and it was hardly a wonder someone had chosen to swindle this town.

"Fine. Yes, I don't believe that was Joseph in the video." She gestured for me to keep going. "I thought I saw Jaimie in the store trying to steal a knife, but he didn't succeed, and prosthetic face foam means it not only wasn't him, it was someone who knew he wasn't going to run into him. Who could even coordinate such a thing besides a doctor?"

"What do you mean?" Carla's sharp eyes zeroed in on my face and I felt as naked as Daniel Kirby's butt after Winnie went for the chicken. He had ink back there and I was both curious as to what it was and horrified at my own intrigue.

But I made a mental note to get the 4-1-1 from Larry.

"It's just a thought, but making yourself look like someone who belongs in a location is risky. Unless you know for a fact they won't be there." I smacked a fly that landed on my arm. "It's like going to a place you used to hang out with your ex, knowing you won't see them because you threw their lifeless corpse overboard in a marina."

"How would they know he wouldn't be there? Also, don't reference *Dexter* like it's a reasonable solution to an average problem, it makes you sound nuts."

It was tough to argue with her logic, so I made a mental note to research normal reactions to break-ups in case Larry betrayed me. Maybe setting all his underwear on fire after shaving his head was a reasonable option. Carrie Underwood went for the truck, but Larry's truck wouldn't notice another scratch.

"Joseph said he was sick. He said the same of Jaimie. Have you talked to the second man? Any evidence of illness or faked incapacitation?"

My eyes drifted to my surroundings. Winnie was off duty, lying on the porch of the ice cream shop with a paw over her face, the hula girl costume packed away for the night. A construction crew had arrived to work on the roadway into the farm last week. They started working after the last tourist left and they were noisily sending dust into the air.

Elsewhere, the farm hands were settling the cattle in for the evening, knowing that even though the sun went down later, they were still leaving at the same time and the livestock would just have to adjust. I caught sight of Joseph staring out of his office window, scratching his exposed belly while chugging a can of beer.

I gave him a disrespectful salute and he responded with a stiff middle finger.

Joseph then made an impatient gesture and tapped his watch to remind me he didn't pay overtime for police cooperation. I dropped to my knees by the collection tank since going home to a cool shower was my number one priority. It was a metal silo where the milk squeezed from the cows was quick-chilled. The temperature gauge remained consistent and the internal temperature of the contents matched the external monitor.

"No," she shifted awkwardly. "He was on the toilet."

"Unwell on the toilet or..." I struggled to find another reason you'd find a man on a toilet that would prevent him from leaving.

Maybe reading Reddit on his phone or playing Sudoku for a moment of quiet.

"Based on the smell, yes. Joseph's wife confirmed the same at his house."

"Were they at the same location the night before they turned up... squishy?" I asked, shoving up to inspect the cow's water and verify the suction was at an appropriate pressure to prevent chafing of the udders.

"They both claim to have attended the two-bit carnival out past the edge of town," she flipped pages in her notebook. "They went on two different nights, but neither could list what they'd eaten besides, and I quote, *everything*."

"Is there a carnival in Sweet Pea? Why haven't I heard about it?" I swatted some flies away from one of the cow's ears and she let out a soft moo of approval.

"I don't know. Your brother and I went with the kids last night. They were really pushing the food, but Sylvie told them it smelled like someone had already eaten it." I snickered at her description of my single-digit niece's attitude. It actually sounded nicer than she behaved normally. "The rides weren't that great, and we left after an hour. Erich had wanted to win a goldfish, but they didn't have any of the traditional midway games. It was like they didn't know what a carnival was supposed to be besides fried everything."

"Are you thinking it was a volume issue versus a quality issue?" I moved onto the next cow. I didn't know Jaimie well, but he looked like a man who should avoid greasy foods.

"Not that I was able to confirm," her eyes darted up and a man was running toward us full speed. Likely by reflex, Carla's hand dropped to the butt of her gun and I offered her a raised brow before she sighed and dropped the hand to her side.

"Habit," she muttered, and I nodded as the early twenties gasped for air in front of us.

"We need..." He wheezed in a breath. "Cyn."

"Because... and who is we that needs Cyn?" I asked, taking a step back when he doubled over and started to gag. "Dude, shoes!"

He sucked in a long steadying breath and gave me a dark look.

"Your shoes are covered in animal poop. Vomit would not be a downgrade," his voice had a saucy edge that warmed me to him. I love a man with an attitude... which probably said more about me than just about any other descriptor of my personal traits.

"So, who is this we and why do you need me?" Carla still looked inclined to shoot him. Apparently, she didn't like the attitude and sass outside of my niece and nephew.

"We were repairing the road into the dairy." He gestured behind him where the CAT machines were stopped and a group of men circled a freshly grated patch of gravel. "And we saw something that didn't look... right. We can't find Joseph, but we were hoping maybe you could..."

I'd already begun walking over, reminded again that if I were a cat, I'd be dead.

Stupid curiosity and thirst for adventure.

"What did you find?" I asked him, striding quickly toward the other crew members who appeared more pale and sweaty the closer I got to them. I turned around, but the sassy messenger had lit a cigarette and was standing beside Carla. She gestured for me, deciding to let me go first and check out the scene.

If Carla were a cat, she'd be a fluffy tyrant who never got her paws dirty.

"What's up guys?" I asked, coming level with them. None of them moved or answered. "Guys!"

Two leapt out of their flesh and I gave an eye roll.

"What's up?"

A few of them gestured toward the road under construction and I inched closer. In the Army, I discovered grown men were basically children always trying to trick you into looking at something gross or disturbing so they can laugh at you. The horror on their faces looked real, but I'd been bamboozled into looking at someone's massive turd a few too many times.

In the grooves where the road had been graded, there were stones and twigs. Nothing looked disturbing or made of poop, so I moved closer and sat back on my heels. The twigs had an odd shape, wider on the end and molded into a bisected mound on the opposite end.

"What am I looking for? I picked up the twig and heard a collective gasp. "What?"

I rolled the twig in my fingers and some of the men went pale.

"You can't just touch that!" One of them hissed and I missed a pass, snapping it in half.

Two men passed out and I looked at the snapped twig in my hand.

It was hollow, jagged... "Is this a bone?"

It was a repeat of my night at Mo's.

Everyone came out, nobody wanted to be the one to make the declaration, but we all knew this was not a tree branch. We all knew that there was nothing to make it a sinister or suspicious discovery.

We all saw the empty BBQ sauce container buried ten feet away.

A chicken bone... maybe another type of bird bone, but it was definitely not human. It had taken three tours through Google to prove that infant femurs were bigger than this, as were their forearms, and none of their bones were hollow. Infant bones were the same density as grown-up bones, though no one seemed willing to trust the internet and yet everyone referenced it as well as fiction and horror movies not based on actual events.

An image of a phalange showed that while the look was similar, they were once again not hollow. Neither those in the toe, nor those in the hand were necessarily the correct length, yet they insisted there were people out there with much bigger hands and feet, thus bigger phalanges. Bigger, and somehow hollow phalanges because large people supported their frame with hollow bones in a logic and physics-defying feat that required scientific study. Their unscientific reasoning was, larger people had insufficient nutrition to fill in their own bones and could only remain upright via metal rigging installed along our bones at birth like Wolverine.

Also, I was a mystical mage with the power to disintegrate my enemies and impale others on my unicorn horn. When I corrected their assumptions with *actual* scientific evidence, I was shot down by fantasy. Using fantasy, I was shot down by religion. When I remarked there was little difference between religion and fiction, they went for the pitchforks.

The only finger they were seeing tonight was my middle finger, raised and displayed to remind them they were on my list for the wasted hours of my life I would never get back. I had been accused of being a bone collector, a relative of Jeffrey Dahmer for snapping it in half. None of my expertise leant itself to bone identification or death investigation of edible creatures, but still my opinion was sought. Sought, coaxed from my lips, and ripped apart as though they knew I would be wrong.

I was envious of the fleshless bones.

At this point, I was ready to show everyone what the bone of a human looked like by ripping someone's skeleton out of their body. Ripping it out, attaching strings and wooden planks, and recreating a scene from an early Disney cartoon about a lying puppet.

"This is stupid!" I finally shoved past everyone and stopped in front of Winnie. Her leash was in Carla's right hand. The woman's left held a double scoop of something chocolatey that smelled vaguely like coffee. I glanced between my two females, took the dog's leash and Carla's ice cream. After several tongue flicks of the frozen treat, I stomped off to the sound of her laughter.

"Guess I'll just get another one then?"

"I need it more than you do," I shouted over my shoulder.

As I scooped a large dollop off the top, the cold sugar set me right again. Right enough to think I should have asked before I jacked her ice cream but not enough to go back and offer to return it. The night stretched before me, an endless stream of possibilities that meant I knew I wasn't headed straight home and to bed.

Curious at my own ambition, I pulled out my phone and called Larry.

"Heard you found a murdered chicken," he said in lieu of an actual greeting. "But they are speculating the bones are sitting on top of a murdered victim to throw people off the scent of a dismemberment motivated serial killer. The local doctor wouldn't come out to confirm because he needed to stop by the church for spiritual protection."

"No, he couldn't come out because he was suturing a stab wound and, I quote, this was 'too dumb for him to waste time on'. I swear this morbid town needs a true crime podcast pumped through hidden speakers like the Hunger Games." I took another bite of ice cream and felt curiosity fight my anger for dominance. "What are you doing tonight?"

Winnie and I arrived at my Jeep and we both jumped in, the engine started with a satisfying rumble. My phone linked to the radio and Larry's voice filled my car.

"Whatever you're doing. I was supposed to go to a card game at Daniel's house but I was uninvited after I told him peanut butter and chicken nuggets were disgusting. He argued that it was better than dog food or Winnie wouldn't have wanted it. I pointed out it *was* dog food, Winnie was right to try and take them," he trailed off and I heard a key tumble in a lock while I smiled into the rearview mirror at my best girl. "He said we deserved each other, I said he deserved an STD, and I was uninvited to hang out with him for the foreseeable future."

"Have I mentioned I love you?" His keys hit the key plate on the other end of the phone and I pictured him kicking off his shoes under the coffee table.

"Yeah, but it's nice to hear it," his voice smiled through the line. "So, what did you want to do tonight?"

"Right... how do you feel about two-bit carnivals?"

Chapter Nine: Deep Fried Flatulence

New Orleans wasn't really on my list of places to visit.

Most of the deep south, with its rampant racism and bribe-based economy, was largely a non-starter for me. As were humidity, alligators, and voodoo practitioners with friends on the other side. For once though, I felt grateful they could not see what has been done with the celebration for which they are most famous.

The Carnival was a roadside attraction that would necessitate a tetanus shot after visiting.

While the concept of a carnival predates even the Carnivale of the south, the liberal use of green and purple made clear their intent to mimic the famed celebration. Once you paid your entrance fee, you were given plastic beads to prove you've paid, a hand stamp of a jester hat, and let loose into the air of nauseating grease and mockery.

This carnival aimed to mimic, insult, and completely decimate by virtue of association.

"Even Fat Tuesday has nothing on this level of greasy gastrointestinal decimation. I think I'm going to be sick," I whispered as a man lumbered past me clutching a deep fried twinkie wrapped in bacon and dipped in cheese sauce. Behind him, booths sizzled with grease and loud carnies barked the contents of their booths. A closer inspection showed they were selling artwork that even a 1970's hippie would find visually offensive.

The food was apparently the main attraction and I'd paid for the opportunity to suffer.

For her part, even Winnie was questioning the edibility of the offerings in the outdoor festival of food. Ears pressed flat against her head, tail tucked behind her, she kept pawing at her nose to get rid of the smell. If I thought it smelled like death, I could only imagine what her superior nose was picking up.

Or how much grease someone could inhale before they needed bypass surgery on their lungs.

"Sorry girl, twenty minutes," I promised, and she let out a small whimper while Larry appeared to be carefully breathing through his mouth.

"Why are we here?" His hard consonants were made soft by his unwillingness to pollute his olfactory senses. I was reminded of the time Winnie had eaten the contents of his trashcan and gotten explosive diarrhea. He cleaned everything by breathing exclusively through his mouth.

Even bleach couldn't eliminate the memory of the smell, and we'd camped out in my apartment for a week until we could forget that particular scent.

"This is where Jaimie and Joseph were before they got sick and then someone impersonated them to commit crimes. We are looking for something suspicious." I spoke around the bile rising in my throat as someone threw what might have been roadkill into a deep fryer. "Something suspicious outside of the obvious gastrointestinal distress of eating anything served here."

We meandered through the stalls of games. There were blinking lights and sirens sounding, but no real prizes worth the money. A game to get softballs in a milk jug yielded mundane prizes like rubber chickens and inflatable golf clubs.

"OK, I've seen inflatable bats and exaggerated hammers, but golf clubs?" I stared at Larry and he had no explanation. "What about that?"

I pointed to an animal hodgepodge that gave taxidermy a bad name. It had faux feathers, a head like a chicken, frog legs and a bill. Not a bill like ducks have, but an actual piece of white plush with squiggly lines and red letters spelling "Past Due".

"Maybe it goes with the golf club? Some sort of birdie reference? Like you're past due on your golf game and they're getting your bird birdied?"

"Ew, you know golf kind of?" I took a step away from him and he dragged me back with a hand wrapped around my waist.

"Don't make me show you my skills with a putter," he whispered against my ear and a flutter traveled the length of my body. In light of alternative options, I wondered how important finding this imposter really was. It's not like anyone had been hurt or that the thief had stolen any real money that impacted livelihood.

No... we could definitely skip this.

At least we could until a man clutching a pretzel cone wrapped in paper and filled with chili topped in breaded onions moved past, timpani of gas following him to the bathroom trailer as I physically choked on the smell. The blue jeans and flannel put him on par for the local course, so to speak, but I didn't readily recognize him. He barely made it through the door before I heard the resounding echo of departing bodily fluids.

"Oh my dog," I fanned my face and Winnie was back to clawing her muzzle. "Why are people eating this? Wouldn't a normal person just stop?"

Larry gave a *who knows* gesture and I had a new thought.

"Do you think he chucked it in the trash can or he's finishing it while disemboweling himself in the toilet?"

"Shut up. Shut up now and look for clues or anything else that means you stop talking and I never have to think about that again."

Our eyes scanned the crowd. Every direction held a food booth with a line of at least three people. The games held little to no appeal to anyone besides the very young, and the handful of rides were less attractions than reminders to check the safety certificate of any and all elevators.

If they were maintained by the people who inspected these rides, everyone's life was in jeopardy.

Fifteen minutes passed and we'd circled the whole carnival twice. Nothing was out of the ordinary aside from the number of people rushing to the bathroom and the persistent lines at the same food establishments sending them there. No one looked to be winning the games, but prizes still changed hands. Screws and bolts rained from the rides, but somehow no one died before our eyes. It was an exercise in *what's the worst that can happen* that never actually played itself out.

"Should we maybe try something to eat?" I looked hesitantly at a line of booths as flames shot from a stovepipe halfway down and a man who was either drunk, a clown, or had red grease paint on his nose applauded. He followed his applause by lighting his own farts and honking a metal horn.

That narrowed it down to either drunk or a clown.

"Nothing here is going in my mouth, yours, or Winnie's," Larry answered, eyes catching on a small group of women egging on a crazy haired member of the group. They chanted, she brandished something and devoured half to their drunken cheers.

When she turned, it was the terrifying woman who ran the town's nursery, Stephanie. In her hand, the other half of a doughnut was basted in funnel cake batter and dripping sugar.

"OK, I kind of want that," I said and Larry shook his head just as Stephanie appeared to sense a disturbance in the force. She froze, looked to burp and then dashed toward the trash can, dumped the treat and hurled her guts out. The ladies behind her laughed and a raven-haired Goth woman collected cash from each of them. "Right... Maybe not."

Most of the customers gave her a wide berth but I noticed the man operating the water gun game watching her closely. His eyes darted to the woman pushing a plastic barrel down the aisle, and she carefully shook her head. By the time I looked back at the man, he had moved on to setting up the next game and the woman with the barrel meandered off toward the other end. A few of the other carnival barkers froze mid game, but others continued on like the pair was invisible.

"What was that?" Larry asked and I shrugged.

"I don't know..." My eyes tracked the two carnies, but they made no new moves toward Stephanie or spared each other another glance. It was like witnessing the beginnings of love at first sight and both parties deciding *never mind* at the same time. "You saw it too though, right?"

He nodded beside me as Stephanie righted herself, chugged water, and moved off toward something safer. Her friends passed her stacks of cash for taking on the challenge and risking her health and well-being. All around us, the carnies seemed to be watching, signaling. They're eyes never strayed far from the eaters of the food but they never got any closer. Whatever the plan, none of it meant anything to me, or Larry if his face was any indication.

"You alright there, kids?" Phil came up beside us with what was either a breaded dildo or some version of an obscene corn dog. Dripping down from the tip was some sort of white condiment or glaze, a crisscross of something red and green dancing down the shaft. It smelled like fried corn and jalapeño with an undercurrent of cardiac arrest.

Visually, it looked obscene and I considered sending my mother a picture.

"How can you eat that?" I asked, secretly envious that despite his food choices and general dominating appearance, the owner of the town's adult novelty shop was still toned with a flawless complexion. He was eating mysterious dough encased meat topped with sperm-like substances and he showed no signs of trauma.

"Got a stomach made of lead," he chuckled, taking a massive bite. "You wanna try?"

He pointed the end toward me and I sniffed cautiously before Larry pulled me back.

"No way, Cyn. Anything that looks like that doesn't belong in your mouth unless it's attached to me." He warned and I studied his face with an eager gaze, before leaning in and taking a cautious bite with excessive eye contact.

Then I may have moaned and licked the sides of the corn dog.

Alarm bells were ringing, but I couldn't stop myself. It was the same instinct that told me to drive a Humvee through a wall and leverage myself from a window to the interior balcony railing of a warehouse for a closer look at caskets, this uncontrollable urge to tempt fate. It moved my teeth through the thick, chewy snack and demanded I just keep eating.

"Oh my dog," I groaned, stealing another bite even as my stomach rolled over. "I need one of those."

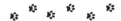

People complain about hangovers. Personally, I've had a few really terrifying mornings after medical procedures and forgetting to eat before drinking, black out gaps in memory combined with bruising or unknown bedfellows that would make any woman hesitate to take "a little something for the pain". It also meant that alcohol, medication, and medical care were viewed through the lens of special consideration one might give buying a car or investing in stock.

I had never once applied those philosophies to food.

No tequila power hour or re-breaking of an improperly set bone came close to the stabbing sensation in my lower abdomen and the bloated gas that refused to escape without taking any and all solid waste with it. It was like being slowly tortured with a knife into my gut. A knife that was being twisted counterclockwise until a scream sat in my throat begging to escape.

A scream I was too womanly to let escape.

"Please kill me," I begged Larry around the agony. We were in the bathroom, where I had been since we'd gotten home just before ten the night before. After that first bite, it was like something alien had taken over my body. One bite led to buying my own corn dog, then I tried the doughnut and the bacon-wrapped twinkie and then it all got a little blurry. The only distinct memory I had was refusing to stop eating until Larry rolled me out like the blueberry girl in Willy Wonka.

"I told you not to eat the pizza stick doughnut," he said, rubbing my back. I had an arm propped on the edge of the toilet, my face pointed into the water of the porcelain bowl. "Or the Corn Dick and the chili cheese cyclone. You were possessed. Winnie and I were powerless until you were too delusional to stop us from forcing you out in a wheelbarrow."

"You did not need a wheelbarrow," I challenged, completely uncertain if that were true. No alcohol passed through my lips, but my body could currently attest to the idea that getting drunk may have been a better choice.

"Winnie was so appalled. She avoided you more than that time you shot off a man's hand, ate four dozen cookies and barfed them all over an unconscious patient," he carried on, his ridicule reminding me why I had been working on concepts such as *moderation* and *mindful eating* with memories of poor choices past. Neither concept had been helpful last night, and in the light of day, were stupid and poorly conceived.

Mindful eating in moderation was a fable pimped out by the diet industry and toothpick yogis' in Lululemon.

The dog for her part was refusing to come near me until I smelled less like carnival induced death. The same as she had when I was covered in vomit and that one time I fell into a vat of spoiled milk fat. Winnie was in the spaceship dog bed beside Larry's bed with her nose under a blanket, looking put out and tortured.

"Hey! I smell your farts. You aren't innocent!" I chastised the dog, but her response was to burrow her nose deeper into the soft material of the bed's lining. "Whatever. You can just pick up your own poop then if we are refusing to acknowledge things that smell. I'll just teach you how to use the plastic bag and grow thumbs…"

Either Larry or Winnie laughed at me.

Probably both.

They sucked.

"I still don't understand how you went from knowing that food was toxic to throwing down fifty dollars eating every last bite of garbage. You knew you would end up here, didn't you?"

I sucked on my inner cheek as I considered his words and their implication.

"It was like being a Pac-Man, once I started, it was impossible to stop." My brain tried to master the memories, but everything was foggy. "I feel both hungover and unreasonably desperate to get more. Is this what drug addiction feels like? Am I a fried food addict? Is there a pimple on my face?"

"I can't say for sure, but maybe? Don't look at your face for like… twenty-four hours." He shook his head as Winnie rolled over. My sweat-soaked hair was scraped from my neck and the cool air felt like heaven. He followed up the gesture with a cool cloth pressed into the space and I nearly orgasmed at the relief.

"I love you," I said in lieu of thank you.

"I'll love you more after you shower and brush your teeth," he responded, pressing his lips to the spot just behind my ear.

Before I could work up a decent insult, an electronic device issued a musical summons. "Be right back."

Larry climbed to his feet, but I didn't have the energy to follow. His soft footsteps disappearing as the clatter of Winnie claws followed him to the land of cell phones and dog food. It would feel like a betrayal, but we passed betrayal eight hours ago when she abandoned me in the bathroom.

"Can I have coffee?" I called, deciding if I was going to die anyway, I needed one last drink to remind me how truly unfortunate death will be. Unless they had coffee on the other side, it was going to be top three on the list of things I'd miss... right beside Winnie and people who yelled at inanimate objects.

I was really going to miss the arbitrary anger.

Larry's voice floated into the room with the sound of percolating coffee, and I tried to decide where he ranked on my death list. I probably didn't love him as much as Winnie, she was just plain cuter. I definitely needed him less than coffee, but he was equally entertaining with the inanimate object attackers.

"What are you doing?" he asked, holding out a pair of antacids and then my phone.

"Trying to decide if I like you more or less than people who shout at stop signs," I answered, crunching on the chalk and taking my phone. "You are presently ranked below Winnie and coffee, but you stand a chance against the third."

The veterinarian bent down to kiss the tip of my nose.

"You never disappoint me." His smile sent my distressed stomach on a sudden trip down Butterfly Lane. Unfortunately for me, Butterfly Lane and Nausea Way were a little too close together to be comfortable labeling the feeling as definitively one or the other.

"Do you have a list? Where do I rank on it?" My question was cut off by a loud angry voice coming from my phone.

"Cynthia! Get your ass down here before I press charges!" I moved the phone out to look at the caller ID before moving it back toward my face. When the person on the other end kept shouting, I elected to keep it away from my face.

I had enough problems without also going deaf.

"Down where? Press charges into what? Is it explosive or are you doing burglary with spark plugs?" Winnie lifted her head at *explosive*, possibly excited to show off her detection skills in exchange for snacks and affection. When there was no confirmatory comment, she flopped back over.

"What? No!"

"Then why bring up charges? If you don't intend to detonate something, you should leave charges out of it. If you put charges in anything, they're more likely to explode than without charges." The cool rag slid down as I spoke, and Larry righted it. In exchange I pinched his butt.

"Not those charges! Legal charges!" The angry man was not done yelling.

"Like Bruce Wayne? Was he a ward of the state? Didn't Alfred call him his young charge?"

"Criminal legal charges, what the hell is wrong with you? Phil just stole six bags of coffee and shoved Jessie into a display of preserves!" The owner of the Coffee Cabin shouted, and I felt my eyebrows disappear into my hairline.

"Why didn't you say that earlier? Phil doesn't drink coffee."

Chapter Ten:
Trivial Pursuit

"Are you sure he went that way?" I asked, hands on hips as I fought the urge to double over. Jene, the short-order Creole cook from the Coffee Cabin nodded. Mel stood behind her, hands on hips. Though he was no longer yelling, his red face and throbbing vein spoke volumes about his proximity to the edge of auditory assault. "It's just empty fields that way."

"If he needed something, why wouldn't he just ask?" Jene spoke the question that boggled my mind as well. Phil was beloved in this town, if he suddenly needed coffee and couldn't pay for it, despite making a mint off my parents and their club, he could have it no questions asked.

Well, except the question of why the heck he suddenly liked coffee.

My stomach made an audible warble, whooshing fluid around with another sharp twist.

"Did you go to the Curious Courtship?" I asked, clearing my throat to hide a fart that followed a burp. "Are you... maybe confusing him with someone else?"

"Yes, and he was there. Baffled and jovial!" Mel was pacing back and forth, my head swimming as I tried to follow him. Stomach fluid shifted and a gurgle burst from my throat followed by a squishy fart. "Jovial! What sort of man gives a bear hug to a business owner he just stole from? Then he had the nerve to laugh at me and drag me to the camera footage..."

The gurgle became a roar and I squeaked.

"Oh dog, bathroom?"

Concerned, Jene and Mel pointed back toward the rear of the Coffee Cabin and I rushed in, clutching my gut and clamping my butt cheeks together. I passed denim and flannel clad men, seated at tables and perusing the shelf items. Despite not selling knives, axes, or lumber, a large number of them were holding bags of coffee and jars of jam with every intention of making a purchase.

A decision that put them squarely in my way.

"Move!" My shout lost under the painful wail of intestinal revolution. "Please!"

Most of the bearded men were taller than me, all were at least twice as broad in the shoulder region, but they parted like the tide when faced with a gut clenching woman making a dash for the bathroom. A few didn't move fast enough and I plowed through them like a linebacker headed for the end zone.

"Tally ho!" A bearded mercenary shouted, grabbing the door and throwing it open for me. His tattooed arms and fanged teeth were more welcoming than the grunt I offered in thanks. I took a moment to wonder why I thought he was a mercenary when another gastrointestinal assault crashed into my abdomen. He closed the door behind me, definitively a man of mercy, and I barely tugged my pants off in time to expel my inner demons.

"Oh my dog," I groaned, the smell combining with whatever I'd consumed to a multi-sense assault. My nose burned, my butt burned, and the backs of my knees were sweating profusely. I had no recollection of bingeing on jalapeno, ghost, or cayenne pepper, but whatever I ate, it was exacting revenge. "Erraahhh!"

Chairs scraped the ground outside in the dining area. Voices murmured, and someone turned on a blender, as though hoping it could drown out my vocal contractions of agony. I convulsed, let out a foghorn fart, and collapsed in on myself as I fell to the floor.

"Never again," I whispered to the filthy tile as I tried to pull my pants back up without standing. "Never, ever, ever…"

"It didn't work." A woman's voice from outside the door came through the gap. "Your information was crap."

"How didn't it work, you looked just like her this morning?" The reply was soft but clear as a bell. They must have been right outside."

"Everyone knows her," the woman hissed in response. "I didn't make it four feet before everyone was staring and whispering. I'm not tall enough, I don't have a dog, and apparently no amount of preparation can make my eyes match. Who the heck actually has purple eyes? Everyone asked if I was new in town, looking for something... I didn't even know the right name to fake!"

My face lifted slightly.

I was tall... I have purple eyes... and I was pretty sure I had a name.

Definitely I had a dog.

Sweat trickled down my back and I struggled to determine if it was from the illness or from the implication that someone wanted to be me... A jolt of pain went through my gut and I had my answer. Anyone willing to be me should have to suffer with the responsibilities of being me, including public recognition and unsolicited conversation.

My ears returned to the conversation to catch the end of her spiel.

"You messed up worse, hitting this place. That man you were impersonating was in his store! The plan only works if they are put out of commission and kept there! I had to throw a cherry bomb into the toilet at a biker bar to buy you time to get away. Who are these people?"

"What? No way! He ate enough to give an elephant diarrhea," the voice challenged. "If he isn't praying to the porcelain gods right now..."

"He isn't! And the man who owns this place tried to take a swing at him until security cameras proved he hadn't left his own store." Her voice took on a shrill quality that stabbed at the already damaged squish in my head. Carefully, and with more effort than it took to recover from pepper spray, I picked myself up off of the floor and flushed the toilet. Then I washed my hands and stumbled through the door just in time to see a large man and a plus-sized blonde high-tailing it out of the store.

"Wait!" I called, but they were already out. I weighed my options: chase them down for answers or go home and hide under a blanket.

Crap.

"These are both bad ideas," I told myself, but curiosity won out over sense.

With that vote of self-confidence, I hurried through the café, the shop, and out the door, watching the two characters come up short at the crosswalk to pass northbound on Main.

"Hey! Wait!" I shouted. The pair glanced in my direction, turned back, whipped their heads back around, and bolted. "Please don't run!"

If they heard me, they declined to listen. With great effort, I moved my feet in the direction they were traveling. My intestines protested, but my feet continued to pick up speed and the running imposters were slowing down. They were taking long shuddering breaths and I knew I wasn't chasing after seasoned athletes.

From the back, I could see that both were wearing all black, form fitting clothing. The man was bald, and the blonde woman had her hair braided in a single plait that ended at her shoulders. Their shoes were also black, and aside from the slight rectangle peeking from the collar of the woman's shirt, they had no distinguishing jewelry or markings.

"Wait!" They glanced back and tried to pick up their pace. "Seriously! Why?"

As I closed in, the pair climbed into an ancient VW Bug and after dumping the clutch and gunning the engine, tore away from the curb. An inch of rubber and a cloud of exhaust lingering in their wake.

"Are the drama kids in trouble?" A young woman was seated on the bench outside the craft store. It was one of seven benches that managed to be near enough to a tree to get shade a few hours of the day. She had a crease between her eyebrows and a paperback in her lap, black hair pulled into a loose ponytail while the shade protected her flesh from the sun.

Probably she wasn't a murderer, so I lumbered that direction.

"Drama kids?" I asked, sitting beside her and pulling up my shirt to mop the sweat from my face. Her giggle forced my memory back to getting dressed this morning. The lack of shouting reminded me that while I *had* remembered a bra today, it was possibly neon pink with cartoon corgis dancing the macarena. Not my most confidence inspiring bra... probably should have been wearing something solid color and underwire for "serious Cyn " days... Except serious Cyn always snuck up on me in the middle of "poor decision-making Cyn" days. Maybe Larry could help me determine which of my bras were the most professional for exposing to the public while wiping sweat off my face... right after he stopped removing them and tossing the garment to destinations unknown where I never found them again.

I pulled my shirt down and tried to look like the grown up I was legally and not think about Larry stealing my bras. Losing my bras was bad, but nothing compared to forced responsible adult behavior.

A challenge most days, but wanting to throw up took the strain to a whole new level.

"Well, I don't know about those kids, but when I was in school, the drama kids wore all black form-fitting clothing like that. Easier to work as a stagehand and pull costumes over for multi-function theatre duties," she tapped a rhythm onto the cover of her book. One, two, one, three, fingers dancing but remaining in the same place.

"Huh," I watched the street, looking for other "performers", and coming up blank. It was possible that a group of performers was casing the town, but there wasn't much to gain from it. My eyes moved from face to face, placing a name or location to each one and coming up short.

If they didn't have a dog or in attendance in my many childhood memory nightmares, I hadn't a clue if they belonged. I barely belonged and I'd yet to live anywhere longer than I'd lived here- world domination plans or no.

"You stim?"

My bench mate pulled my gaze back to her and I followed her line of sight to my hands. It was mirroring the pattern she tapped on the cover of her book.

"I think... I was copying you. Is that what it means to stim?"

My fingers had stopped moving, but her eyes were still fixed on my hand. It twitched to resume the rhythm, but I took a deep breath and stuck my hands in my pocket. Her face lost a bit of expression and I imagined a faux pas had been committed that I didn't understand.

"Did you go to school around here? Or do you?" It was impossible to really pinpoint an age with her hair and clothing choice. Leggings and a plain T-Shirt were a universal choice for people of all ages and there was a cloth cover over her book. It had the dimensions of a mass market paperback, but nothing overt to indicate age or literary preference.

"Went, graduated a few years ago. Doing the college thing, but I'm home on break. Just arrived a few hours ago, but I'm not ready to go home yet." Her fingers resumed their pattern on the cover. "I was in drama. Never knew those people though they're probably not similar enough in age to have attended with me. Their picture would have been up somewhere, though, since the school posts pictures of everything. There are a few new people in town who don't seem to really belong, and none of them have a genuine concern about directionality. Like they are waiting for something while trying to look casual... I'm sorry, what was the question?"

"Are these people who look out of place dressed like theatre people?" I asked, but her answer was cut off by a small man charging toward me wielding a piece of paper.

"You!" His voice was deep, the accent making the word sound more like "view" than you. "What is the meaning of this? You think it is funny?"

He sounded like Dracula, so if the question related to his voice, the answer was most definitely yes.

His blonde hair flopped on his face and I watched my neighbor's fingers speed up without changing the pattern. I wondered again about stimming and if its intensity changed with anxiety. My mental note to look into stimming got an asterisk to also get this woman a metronome to tune because she was better than any computer.

"No... maybe? What are you talking about?" The German man shoved the paper toward my face and I plucked it from his fingers before shoving his hand to the side. "Personal Space."

While he fumed, my eyes flicked over the page.

His name was Eurich and he'd been sent this letter... from my office. It stated that his...

"Wieners contain inedible meat?" My brows drew together as I tried to grab Eurich's attention. The language matched that in Lizandro's letter from my loose interpretation. Threatened exposure, resolution with swift and decisive action. Beneath the line was an offer to rectify the records in exchange for four hundred dollars, paid in cashier's check, and taken to a P.O. Box.

"The P.O. Box is new," I muttered and pulled out my phone to text Larry. I needed to know if there was mention of a P. O. Box on Lizandro's letter. He'd insisted he'd paid cash, but never saw anyone. A P.O. Box would make more sense than a wad of cash taped to the underside of a park bench by the light of a silver moon on the fourth Tuesday of the month as I'd initially imagined.

Also, I needed to stop reading kidnapping thrillers with an eye toward rescuing captives. Probably Mo and I should also give up our addiction to Mark Wahlberg, Liam Neeson, and Keanu

Reeves movies that made us feel invincible. My brain was certain that at any second, an instinct would kick in and I would be able to track bad guys to the edges of the earth and defeat them with a well-placed gut-punch.

My body was certain that if it was a car, it would be dead on the side of the road with a window ticket, broken windows, and spray-painted graffiti.

"You think this is funny!" Small droplets of spit flew from his mouth and I flinched out of the way.

"No. But if I were to think it's funny, why would that be?" I re-read the letter and beside me, the college student tapped at a normal pace looking to read over my shoulder. Her initial anxiety seemed to lessen the farther down the page she got.

Eurich didn't seem to notice the woman sitting there at all, so I passed the paper to her for independent reading.

"Meat? In my wieners? You some kind of sicko? You don't eat my wieners!" I froze.

"Oh my dog! Do you own Pickles? And you didn't warn me before giving me that paper?"

It was a major over-reaction since I'd just been on the floor of a public restroom, but probably nobody had pressed their penis into it... maybe. It seemed unlikely that the employees of Pickles would do such things to office supplies either, but my subconscious wasn't having any of it. The all-male review was largely sanitary and mostly only catered to bachelorette parties and revenge body divorcées. It was loud, glitter-coated, and smelled like briny desperation and sweat.

Either way, I was definitely going to need a shower before work.

"What is *Pickles*? There is no food! I have dog!" He gestured with his hands in the shape of a small box.

"I... also have a dog. But what's your business?"

"Dog! I make and sell dog!"

"Like... that teddy bear making place?"

He gestured to the far end of town square and I saw the boutique pet shop with pure-bred adoptions.

"Oh..." I looked at the business name. "Why would you call it Hot Dogz?"

"Because hot, it is fashion. The dogs have fashion and they are fashion dogs!" His gestures presented his body as though it were wearing formal evening wear and I stared at him blankly. Though he wasn't underdressed for town square, Levi's and a Henley weren't really cream of the fashion crop. Not that my sweat and bathroom floor stained outfit had much room to offer critique, he'd have been better off referencing country chic than high fashion.

"I think he means *haute*," the young woman whispered and I looked back at her.

"Is that the same word with a weird accent?" I said back normally because I hated whispering in public. Not only was it pointless, but anyone close enough to yell at you angrily was probably close enough to hear you whisper.

Also her voice had sent my skin prickling and I hoped to discourage a repeat sound proximity.

"No, it's spelled h-a-u-t-e," she spelled the letters on the book with her finger while speaking them out loud. "It's a fashion term for designer and mainstream, I think... maybe trendy or cutting edge? I'd need to look it up to be sure. Fashion is constantly evolving, and with the recent rise in adoption over birth, dog fashion for the upwardly mobile would be a decent economic strategy. Designer dogs are a great way to encourage mixed breed adoption and limit inbreeding within bloodlines."

My head nodded, but I only vaguely understood the first part of her statement. If something was trendy, then it was mainstream, but wasn't cutting edge new and different? Were those words interchangeable?

Also, it was clothes... for dogs.

No dog looked cool in clothes, not even Winnie.

"So... this letter is trying to get money to help you with a business you don't own?" He nodded at my summary and I shrugged. "Then ignore it and I'll try and make sure you don't get any more."

"You are not understanding, they sent a health inspector!"

"Was there anything for them to inspect?" I asked, head tilting. It was a little odd that a health inspector couldn't figure out there was no food at a pet shop before he or she arrived. With access to public records, they should have known better.

"No, I have dog!" Eurich threw his hands into the air and stomped off, leaving behind the paper my bench mate had placed in my lap.

"Does that... happen to you a lot?" I looked at the young woman and nodded in response to her question. "Then I probably don't want to sit next to you. I don't do well with loud or sudden noises... or just noise in general. My noise canceling headphones died fifteen minutes ago and while I find your company not unpleasant, I think that will change over time if you are frequently visited in such a manner. Could you recommend a location you won't be at, that also has shade and decent people watching where my parents aren't likely to discover I've been home for a while and avoiding them?"

"That seems fair, but you don't have to move," I heaved myself up from the bench. "You were here first, this is your bench. It was nice to meet you though..."

My hand outstretched, I hoped she'd fill in her name.

"Stella," she said, nodding but not accepting my hand. "I don't like to be touched, please don't take offense. The handshake was used to show passersby that you are unarmed, and as you can see both my hands, I assume you are already aware that I lack weapons."

I nodded my understanding and dropped the limb to my side. She did definitely appear to be unarmed... aside from having actual arms.

"Tough town to grow up in. People here have no concept of boundaries."

"It's..." She began, but whatever *it* was got cut off.

Glass shattered behind me, a heavy body smashing into the pavement followed by a barrage of yelling. My eyes flashed to the front of the craft store, where a man in leather stood over a prone cowboy.

"You think you can just waltz back in here?" Jared was shouting at the prone figure of a short pudgy man. "After you slapped my wife's ass and nicked the till? What the hell is wrong with you?"

The round man climbed to his feet as I started walking over, alarmed to see Joseph facing off with our resident ink artist and single member biker gang. Jared was a Grizzly bear clone with less hair on top of his head than poking out of the top of his omnipresent V-neck T-Shirt. When he developed an English turn of phrase was as perplexing as why he was sending my boss through the glass window of the crafting supply store.

"I wasn't..." Joseph stammered, just as I stepped between him and the very angry man. "I swear, I was sick!"

I turned to look back at Joseph before trying to make his case to Jared. A poor choice on my part as Jared wound up and threw his full weight into a punch that landed on the side of my head.

I squealed, very dignified, and everything went dark.

Chapter Eleven: Crafted Catastrophe

"Please don't be dead," I heard from the great beyond, my eyes opening slowly. A gray-black ball of fluff had blocked out the sun. The scent of peppermint and fossil fuels filled my nose and a jagged line of agony flashed through my skull when I tried to bring the fluff into focus. "Cynthia?"

The miraculous scent of dark roast mixed with sugar and baked dough reached my nose, seducing a moan from my lips. It was like waking up in nirvana and I decided I really must be dead and somehow the afterlife came with baked goods and coffee.

"Told you if she wasn't dead, this was how you'd reach her," Mo's sleigh bell laugh followed her declaration and I tried to decide if hitting her would help or hurt my chances of getting the coffee and...

"Cupcakes?" My voice cracked and the dryness in my mouth made the words sound like a Muppet spoke them.

"Muffin. Zucchini, since I heard you had a nutrient deprived night."

A straw touched my lips first and I guzzled the coffee. While it failed to stop the agony coursing through my skull, it did succeed in convincing me that I'd probably live. In the background, a robotic voice announced that live at ten there would be a conference regarding the upcoming measures being passed to crack down on code enforcement and increase tax revenue.

"My head hurts," I said, accepting the muffin but not opening my eyes. My brief stint with vision combined with the noise led me to believe I was no longer outside. I devoured the muffin in two bites and listened to my stomach gurgle in either appreciation or early warning of revolution. "Did I get hit in the head with a baseball bat again?"

"No, I'm so... what does she mean by again?" A rumbly male voice spoke, and a careful lift of a single lid showed the fluffy grayish black puff ball was back. Either it was something attached to a human man, or I was abducted by a planet of poof balls seeking revenge for the key chains we all had in the early 2000s.

As a personal preference, I was hoping for the aliens.

Facial hair on men was scratchy and filled with food particles.

I felt Mo shrug beside me.

"Cyn gets hit a lot. Seems reasonable it was with a baseball bat at some point."

"Seriously?" I muttered and had a second muffin stuck in my mouth. It was unclear if she was protecting her reputation as a gentle ginger, forgotten, or just wasn't interested in reliving childhood embarrassment. It didn't seem possible she'd forget when she was the one swinging the bat that I walked behind. It was an impromptu game of backyard baseball I was mostly ignoring until she was at the plate and I needed to rescue a caterpillar, assuming incorrectly that people only swung the bat in front of them.

Probably it was her reputation.

A little info in this town had a way of blowing up into a natural disaster.

"How is she still alive?" A new voice came into the conversation, and I had the impression of the little old lady from Looney Tunes who tolerated Tweety as a roommate.

No way was that psychotic bird a pet.

"I'm hard to kill," I shoved myself up and immediately regretted it when the floor and the ceiling traded places. "Where am I?"

"Calico Craft Supplies and Brews," Tweety Bird lady answered.

"Calico..." I decided that my ears and brain were not communicating. No way did this boring little town have a bar that also sold crafting supplies. If they did...

I peeled an eye open and was relieved to see the light only hurt a normal amount and the assembled spectators were all well into their twilight years. Around me were neat stacks of yarn, sketch pads, and vinyl. Beneath my hand was a gritty neon pink glitter and the floor smelled of... beer?

Careful not to go too quickly, I sat up again and took a chance opening my other eye.

Beyond the shelves of yarn, glitter, and paint was a wide lacquered bar. In front of the perpetually damp looking surface were green nylon stools mounted into the floor on metal pedestals. A collection of battered and scarred wooden tables held a small group of men in leather vests mingling with soccer dads who probably had one tattoo on their bicep and thought they were cutting edge.

In the corner, a flatscreen the size of a throw blanket took up half of a wall. On screen, a woman in a sharp and crisp pink pantsuit was speaking at a podium, the sound low enough to only catch snippets as the bar area returned to normal volume. At their feet were nylon bags spewing colorful...

"Yarn?" I blinked. Then baffled, I blinked again, but I was not hallucinating. Every man held metal rods, knitting needles and crochet hooks, watching the large screen while watching the oversized screen and drinking beer. "What am I looking at?"

"Yarnbros," the puffball spoke, and I decided it was probably Jared and his impressive beard. "They meet Wednesday afternoons."

"Afternoon? What time is it? I have to go to work..." I shoved away hands offering to help, determined to reclaim my feet on my own. I succeeded briefly before I stumbled face first in the leather vested Jared.

"I'm not sure you should be moving around so much." He adjusted something on the side of my face and I patted my cheek. There was something squishy and cold that was stuck to the impact point of his fist. I raised a questioning brow at the man.

"It's a pain cake, a sticky ice pack. Thought it would help with swelling and it wouldn't fall off if you needed to puke," his explanation explained some things, but I peeled it off my cheek and stared at the circular gel bead-filled pouch.

"Huh... Can I?" He nodded at my incomplete question and I stuck it back to my face. "Can... someone fill me in? What time is it?"

"It's eleven," I recognized Joseph's voice but his shape was somewhere behind me. "But don't worry about the farm. This is much more important."

"Don't..." I turned to stare at the man. "What? I'm an animal technician. How am I going to technician the animals if I'm in a craft bar? Also, why were you thrown through the window of a craft bar?"

"He used to be a member of the Yarnbros until he came in and stole all the money in the register, assaulted my wife, and threw an empty beer bottle at the wall."

Jared concluded his explanation by pointing to a slightly discolored and chipped section of wall near the television.

"It wasn't me! I was framed! Tell him Cyn! I don't want to leave the Yarnbros," Joseph pleaded.

The Earth shifted as I forced my body to face my boss. His face had a few scrapes from going through the window. Most of his body had been protected by flannel and denim, though some of the clothing had become torn, he was largely unaffected by his experience being a projectile.

Lucky bastard.

That was definitely the last time I took a punch for him, accidental or otherwise.

"You... knit?" I asked, studying the canvas tote at his feet. "In public? While drinking with strangers?"

"Yes, and I would like to continue doing so. They aren't strangers though, they're the Yarnbros. Your only job today is going around to all the establishments in town and figuring out how many that damn imposter hit while I was crippled with diarrhea. Then give them my sincere apology and an offer for a free scoop of their choice at the dairy!"

"Don't you think the owners of the dairy would rather I be getting paid for actually treating their livestock and its outputs? Are you really going to buy that many people ice cream? Do I get ice cream for getting punched on your behalf?" I braced an arm around Mo, and she let out an exasperated sigh as she held me up with great effort. The poor little woman was not made to carry me. "Also, didn't you promise the public a shark photo op? No way am I sending Winnie to the farm without me. None of you understand the need to keep dairy products out of her mouth."

As though speaking her name summoned the beast in question, a weighty skull slammed into my crotch.

"Hi girl," I ruffled her ears and saw Mo do the same beside me. "Did Larry banish you?"

"No, Larry is here to escort you to the land of pain medicine and endless ice packs." The man himself removed my weight from Mo and traced his fingers along the edge of my jaw. Carefully, he tilted my face and inspected my pupils. While he lacked medical training to treat humans, he'd witnessed enough of my injuries that it was hard to argue when he assessed me and grunted an all-clear.

"I'm not sure why I'm always surprised when you become injured midday after leaving the house for seemingly ordinary reasons, but could you go one day without marking up your pretty face?" He gently removed the sticky ice pack and kissed the bruise forming on my temple.

It took a minute for my brain to catch up to what the "ordinary reason" had been.

"Phil stealing coffee isn't an ordinary reason," I grumbled and saw Mo wrinkle her brow.

"Phil stole coffee? He doesn't drink coffee. He said if he ever needed to wake up he'd just bump a line of cocaine like he did in the eighties." Jared nodded his agreement to her declaration and I tried to adjust to the idea that the large man had been addicted to white powder substances. Maybe I'd been hit harder than I thought, and this was the twilight zone.

Or an episode of Euphoria.

Or signs declaring this the red-light district.

My eyes scanned for cameras or prostitutes, but only came up with townspeople whose names I'd elected not to remember.

"Don't think about it too hard, doll face. Everyone did coke in the eighties," one of the Yarnbros spoke up, and all the leather clad senior citizens in the room nodded their agreement. Beside them, the clean-shaven polo shirts inched their chairs away, sharing a glance that threatened to break up the group.

Apparently being a pompous jerk was less socially unacceptable than doing drugs.

The more you know, I thought as I rested heavily against Larry until the spinning stopped.

"Can we go home now?" I asked Larry's neck.

"Larry, take her around town and clear my name!" Joseph flapped his arms like an angry bird to get our attention, my eyes opening to catch the tail end of his impromptu performance. "The farm will be fine without you, too."

"He doesn't work at the farm," I loaded more of my ample weight onto his sturdy frame and he wrapped himself more firmly around me. "Also, I need money. You can't kick me out of work and take my pay to save your reputation. I'm not your drug mule or your image consultant, thank dog."

The yuppy dads flinched at the reference to drug mules.

Apparently, I was tarnishing the reputation of this fine establishment full of booze, yarn, and broken windows.

"I already said you'll be paid. And I'll give you a month of free ice cream," he snapped. "Larry, the fowl is feeding nicely, there are no emergency care requests. Routine checks can also wait, but your business account will still be compensated if you drag her around and clear my name!"

"The owners can't possibly like you paying us to do your bidding," my face was buried in Larry's chest again so it was difficult to determine if he heard me or not. "We aren't cheap."

"Too easy," Larry chuckled, so I sucker punched him in the gut. A barely audible gasp was joined by a very masculine chuckle that grated against my ears.

Stupid men.

"What owners? I own the dairy," I snapped my head to look at Joseph and the world shifted. Despite my attack, Larry pulled my back to his front while I tried to bring the world into order.

"What? No. Those old people..." I said, referencing the picture of the older couple that sat framed in the ice cream shop. "Who are sometimes at the Winnie photo spot?"

The dog wagged her tail at the mention of her name.

"It's marketing," he looked annoyed and a bit pink tinged in the region around his ears. "A little old couple owning the dairy sold better to a community-based farm image than... well me. My wife and I aren't adorable old people, we are barely country. I'm a stockbroker from Detroit who cashed in and bought out. I bought the dairy two decades ago and pay the old owners to make appearances now and again."

"Are you kidding me? Why is your office an outhouse? Did you actually take your oversized desk from your old job as a parting gift? Isn't that beneath your New York sensibilities?"

"Detroit and it's not an outhouse! There was no need to waste money on an office, not when there's a whole farm to run and I never needed to call people into the space until *you* were hired. It would have been stupid, so I gave myself the bare minimum," the pink crept higher and the Yarnbros went quiet behind him.

"Is that why you yell at the cows in the middle of the night? To remind you of when you lived in the Big Apple?" I asked, but the newscaster's voice was now audible, and I silenced Joseph before he could reply again that he hadn't lived in New York.

"Adding to the town's abysmal legal practices, an unregistered private eye has been operating in downtown. Now, the retired Army MP is sending people letters demanding money to bring their businesses into compliance while failing to have her own business documentation in order. Of those being ordered into compliance, none is more disturbing than the accusations leveled against an adult shop operating without a liquor license. Whether her spotting the crime or the act itself is more appalling remains to be seen. Amber Carter, local shoe store owner and town darling, is here to offer additional insight into this shocking scam that has rocked the community."

Behind the gray suited man was the Sharp Investigations Office, a half-dozen people clutching picket signs out front. Picket signs, pitchforks and a wooden torch?

No, that was probably a baby with red hair.

Way scarier.

"She has always been jealous of my success and now..." I tuned out Amber's accusations to see Carla stomp into the craft bar. She was in her full uniform, shiny badge and shoes matching the tight bun in her hair. Instead of looking delighted at the idea of being able to craft macrame while enjoying a craft beer, she had "Specialist Cynthia Sharp you are in trouble" face.

Army flashback... shudder.

Under different circumstances I may have saluted her or asked if anyone defecated in her morning crunchies. Under these circumstances, it seemed more hospitable to offer her a beer than risk mangling a turn of phrase.

My mouth opened and daggers fired from her eyes to pin me on the spot.

"You need to come with me. Now!" she ordered. "The town council needs a word."

Chapter Twelve: Council Counseling

The town council rarely assembled for anything besides poker night and wienie roasts.

Despite having grown up here, I'd never met the town council as a group though I'd likely met all the members. For me, they were a shadow organization that existed in the rocky caverns of the Dark Crystal. Dark, hooded Skeksis figured with decaying hands and boney fingers that raised shakily in accusation before devouring Gelflings.

Jim Henson was a very strange man and he probably should have laid off the dope.

In reality, the town council congregated in the gazebo at the center of town. Surrounded by the garden splendor, the sun shining and not a cloud in the sky, it was the most sinister sight of people sitting at a picnic table I had ever seen.

Mostly because they all seemed to be enjoying the sun.

Like some sort of photosynthesizing species or residents of the planet Krypton.

Similar to most town councils, it was an odd-numbered group. If my memory served, there were seven members of the council and the seventh only voted in the event of a tie. All members were appointed based on their position within the community as decided by members of the town voting dynamic. Instead of voting for people, the town voted for occupations and titles, learning who the incumbent was only after they'd been chosen to serve. It was marketed to the membership at large as a campaign to prevent the same bias that occurred in high school elections.

Instead of voting for a person like a popularity contest, you voted for qualifications and positions.

It failed miserably since everyone knew everyone except for me. I knew only their dogs and hadn't voted in a single local election since I was eighteen and the town refused to let me put "the man who hitchhikes in hotpants" as a candidate.

They also refused "woman who acts as Wonder Woman" and "whoever voices the Swedish Chef". The designated vote counters accused me of such crimes as "not taking this seriously" and "making a mockery of a constitutional right". All of those amounted to me resigning myself to sit idly by and watch the catastrophe.

Usually with popcorn and a notepad to document everything for my potential future in stand-up comedy.

Until today, when I was summoned to the table and observed the town council members in the sun-loving flesh. One, two...

Six, someone was missing. It would be impossible to hold a vote unless they already decided.

A small sigh of relief slipped through my lips. No one in this town could make a unanimous decision... could they? My sinking gut searched for tar, feathers, or sticky-fingered toddlers.

Maybe they bought a guillotine. That would be cleaner... except for the blood, but I'd be dead so clean up was someone else's problem.

"Cynthia," Mrs. Margot said, face turned upward like a sunflower. "Please, have a seat."

The entire table was bathed in sunlight, despite being inside a gazebo. A scan showed the sun was on a leisurely descent, hours from approaching the spear on top of the church, yet it managed the perfect angle to increase my suffering. My mouth opened to object, but Carla gave me a firm shove toward the table before slouching against the rail near the solitary exit.

Message sent, there would be no leaving.

"Yes ma'am," I said, and slouched against a railing in the single patch of shade offered by a well-placed post. Unfortunately, I wasn't post-sized, so I had to choose what was most important to keep out of the sun. My face ultimately won, deciding bruised and sunburned weren't an attractive combination. Eyes shielded, I stared up at the council.

Seated around the table were Suzie, the owner and waitress of Suzanna's Diner. Her shift dress in teal and pink, as crisp and flawless as her cat-eye lining skills. Her hair was magenta this week and piled on her head in a bouncy ponytail with a scarf. Mrs. Zuber, my Kindergarten teacher and the town's most notorious lush, was taking secret hits from her flask when she thought no one was looking. Beside her, a hippie out of time, the K-12 school admin, Mr. Meden. As usual, he stunk of the devil's lettuce, wore socks under his sandals with cargo shorts and a tie-dyed shirt.

Though he'd graced the outfit with a bright yellow tie, he was as out of his element as a tsunami in the Midwest. Landlocked states didn't have tidal waves, and town councils shouldn't have old, gay hippies. He was, however, the most visually entertaining member, and I offered a smile even as I squinted at the amount of light he reflected.

The remaining members were new to me. A more mis-matched group couldn't have been assembled if the Avengers had arranged for a multiverse collision... or a toddler was allowed to scoop the Thrifty ice cream without supervision.

"You know Sherry," Mrs. Glen Margot nodded toward Mrs. Zuber and I shuddered. Teachers were not supposed to have first names. Even twenty plus years after grade school, she was not permitted to have a first name. "Suzanna Quentin Williams."

I stifled a laugh that her parents had actually named her Suzie-Q. It explained so much and absolutely nothing because retro was always in fashion and probably a good business strategy.

145

"Mr. Erick Meden, who will stop vaping for the sanctity of this meeting." He took another puff, offered her a thousand-watt grin for catching him, and tucked the e-cig into one of his pockets. "The rest I imagine are new to you. That's Cecily Johnson, she runs the town's business commission."

The thin black woman extended a hand, offering a firm shake under the table and an impressive view of toned biceps under a salmon camisole over white linen pants. It was a look I both envied and knew I could never keep clean. Her hair was braided in thin rows, collected in a ponytail with a perfectly matching salmon scrunchie. She looked at home seated in the town's gazebo, but I couldn't picture her anywhere but strolling a runway with a sash or standing at a podium accepting some sort of prize for solving a worldwide crisis.

"Earl Grey." Her introduction was accompanied with a gesture toward a round man with bright red hair and an affinity for plaid sweater vests that were out of season. Wearing them with nothing underneath was a crime that should be punishable by death. "He was recently elected leader of the local Elks Lodge."

My brows drew together. He was barely forty, if that. Most members of the Elks Lodge were older men, and I was unaware Sweet Pea had a large enough town population to support the organization. While we certainly weren't hurting for membership in any generation, the older folks in this town preferred more... *active* involvement with one another. As though reading my mind, Mrs. Margot offered a tight smile.

"He's presently the organization's only member," her voice strained to get past her clenched teeth.

My teeth grabbed the inside of my cheek to keep from bursting into laughter.

"Ah, Lynn. Thank you for joining us," Mrs. Margot said.

"No, I'm Cyn," I corrected, but her gaze remained firmly behind me. Head on a swivel, I tried to look behind me without vomiting or passing out at the vertigo from my latest concussion. When that failed, I flopped onto the wooden planks with my face toward the entrance waiting to see who would arrive.

"What happened to your face, Cynthia?" Lynn Sharp's voice cut through the open-air gazebo as though it were a steel bunker. Every other member of the council sat up straighter, all eyes on my mother.

All except mine which were clenched shut against the pain in my head and the ringing in my ears.

"Indoor voice," I groaned and a collective gasp left the picnic bench. Apparently, the guillotine was out for my insolence. Children's music and dance concerts were in my future, a slow and loud pain filled death as retribution for speaking to a council member in such a manner.

Never mind that she was my mom.

"Did Jared really punch you in the side of the head?" Her voice was blessedly lower, and the members of the table sucked in air. It was like being on a sitcom with a studio audience and they were all given a script. In my personal version I was given pain medicine and a sensory deprivation chamber to recover.

"Yes, ma'am," Carla filled in for me and cool hands stroked the side of my face. With my mom's hands came the scent of garlic, coffee beans, and peppermint hand cream. She wasn't the cook in our family, my dad held the honor in high esteem, but she made the menu and collected the groceries, acting as sous chef as needed.

"What did you do to get punched in the face this time?" Her gentle voice held an edge of amusement. I wanted to remind my mother that the last time I was "punched in the face" it was with a ten-pound double ended silicone dildo which she was holding. Wanted to but didn't, because I wasn't in the mood for a lecture.

The last time I complained about her personal pleasure parties invading my childhood home, she'd sent Larry a lengthy dissertation on female anatomy and the best places for him to stimulate relaxation and relief. It came complete with semi-nude photos of me she'd taken while I was sleeping in a drug-induced coma with a broken arm last November. As far as I was aware, the photos were taken for "entirely different purposes", but the explanation was far worse than the pictures themselves and I elected to punch myself in the head in an effort to forget.

Still hadn't, but perhaps today's concussion could help with that as well.

"Tried to keep Joseph from getting punched in the face."

"Why was Joseph getting punched in the face?" Her tone took on an edge of concern and my mouth fell open in mock horror.

"How dare you assume that I would do something to deserve getting hit, and he is completely innocent of reasons for hitting! I'll have you know that he shouts at produce and livestock at night. He also owns the dairy, worked as a stock broker in Detroit, and hires cute old people to pose as the owners."

"It's a solid business strategy in this demographic. People associate older couples with stability and genuine intentions," Cecily remarked, taking out her phone and typing into an app. "I have been trying to make that case to a few other business owners who have found they need to spend longer convincing people to give them business. Maybe I can recruit Joseph to help lay out the strategy in fiscal R. O. I. and practical execution."

"Business, business, business... numbers," I muttered, knowing that return on investment applied to marketing campaigns and business upgrades, but hiring in-person actors to fake being in charge still felt like lying to me.

"Actually, Sharp Investigations could use a brand model to serve as the face while you do the work. Statistics show people are more likely to hire a male private investigator than a female one. Do you know anyone who can pull off an Eddie Valiant look?"

"Eddie Valiant? The dude from the Roger Rabbit movie? He was an alcoholic with revenge issues and a wandering eye. Who would want to hire him? I was actually the police... kind of." I shoved my arms crossed at my chest, petulance and defiance radiating off of me.

When all seven of the council members plus Carla burst out laughing, I considered the going rate for eight-person murder... quadruple double homicide? Octocide? Domestic terrorism since they were technically government officials?

I think it was life in prison no matter how many of them I took out, so I might as well get my money's worth.

"Oh, Cynthia, most days you refer to yourself as kind of a detective, and now you are somehow more qualified than a fictional retired detective with psychological trauma to investigate?" My mom was going first for that statement. "Yes, you have some skills, but you often deny them. Was challenging you to hire a front man all it takes to get you to show some confidence in your own abilities?"

"First of all, rude. I don't lack confidence, since, as you may have noticed, I am a complete badass. What I lack is motivation to look into trivial nonsense. Second, most of the skills I have are Winnie's and if anyone should be the face of Sharp Investigations, it's her. Mostly because her face is freaking adorable!" My tirade left me a little breathless, but I powered on for women everywhere. "The skills I do have are weapon and demolition related and I have patches and ribbons that prove I can do both better than ninety percent of the men in the military."

"Demolition? Is this a reference to the incident in Afghanistan or the incident in Germany?" Earl Grey spoke for the first time and I was appalled that his voice was silky smooth. A man who looked as he did should have a nasally whine that got him punched in the face.

The sunburn forming on his pale shoulders would have to satisfy me.

"Or the chicken farmer's trailer, the news office and the back house off the highway outside of town?" Cecily added, seeming to review a dossier on me that she kept in her phone.

"Or the state of Florida?" My mom chimed in.

"All of them," I snapped and deflated against the pole. "Why are we gathered here?"

"The news has a story," Mrs. Margot began. "One that makes you out to be a two-bit con artist and a disgrace to America. You and Carla have helped one gentleman who came to you, but there appear to be dozens of these letters in the area and we need you to clear them up."

"Clear them up?" I asked, as though identity theft were chicken pox instead of acne. "How do I clear up someone or several someone's frauding people with my address? I can verify that the letter wasn't sent by me and help them navigate setting right any legitimate accusations, but..."

"But what, Cynthia? They need your help. While you may not know this, you are held in high esteem in both this community and by this council. There is no one more qualified to get to the bottom of this than you and Carla, but she has her hands full with random acts of violence such as you experienced today."

I looked at Chief Sharp, my sister-in-law and the only person in this gazebo who looked less thrilled to be here than I did.

"I'm having trouble figuring out how they pick their targets." She shrugged, and I tilted my head for her to continue. "Who to impersonate, where to go as that person to not appear out of place... it feels random and poorly researched."

"That's theatre for you," I said without much sympathy. "They either over-research the parts and pull a Shia LaBeouf, or they under-research and are winging it like Chris Pratt on Parks and Rec."

"What do you mean theatre?" Her eyes narrowed and I recounted what I heard while I was sick and the conversation I had with Stella.

"You think they are poisoning people at the carnival? That it wasn't just mine, Joseph's, and Jaimie's poor life choices that put us there?"

"With what? Laxatives?" She suggested. "Laced with sugar so you are so addicted you can't stop eating?"

I gave a half-hearted nod.

"That or America needs to learn portion control and they are just taking advantage of a self-made situation. I can personally attest to the addictive nature of battered, fried, and powdered sugared everything. Don't get me started on cheese, but then what was the man referencing as dosing Phil with? I feel like it can't just be a matter of self-control."

Carla looked between Mrs. Margot, my mom, and Cecily.

"May I be excused?" She spoke like a child at the dinner table.

"Yes, but please keep us posted." Mrs. Margot appeared to be the council voice.

"What about me?" I asked, trying to start my ascent to standing.

"You will remain seated until we are through with your instructions." She narrowed her eyes and I slid back down. "Now, to start off with, how much coffee do you currently have in your office?"

Chapter Thirteen: Customer Service

"This can't be happening," I muttered into the closet where my coffee beans were stored.

Or where they had been stored until seven council members served it to forty plus disgruntled business owners and workers. My address had been used to threaten businesses from florists to legal aid establishments. I felt sick just living there but now... now it was almost completely drunk dry of my coffee stores.

It was both emotionally and physically painful to be a part of this.

"Stop whining, Cynthia. We will buy you more coffee," my mom scolded me from somewhere beside my left elbow. The woman was short, round, and had a blonde bob that was razor sharp at the edges and streaked through with gray and silver. She was also now holding my last four bags of carrot cake coffee and carrying them toward the impromptu coffee bar created with borrowed drip machines and Mo's industrial bean grinder. She was serving my coffee to the masses, chatting with the news people, the blonde reporter mysteriously absent, and generally making me sound like a good person. The entire office area was filled with strangers, drinking my coffee. None of them could manage a moment of silence or a reasonable speaking volume. Everything I had sought to avoid was now bearing down on me from all sides and my mother wouldn't let me leave.

It was on course to be one of the worst days of my life.

It was also a stiff middle finger to any perceptions I may have had about being an adult.

The woman and her conglomerate of suffering had offered coffee and a listening ear to those who had been wronged by the fictitious businesses associated with my address, ones they could assure the townspeople I had nothing to do with. It was a kind gesture, one that I would have undertaken on a smaller scale, but instead I'd lost my sanctuary to the masses and my mother ruled over my office with a welcoming and gracious spirit that ensured no one would leave quickly.

Or possibly ever.

She was that good.

A quick loop of the room revealed that all the council members as well as Larry, Daniel, and Carla were taking notes and statements. Carla had returned soon after her departure, stating that she'd put some feelers out, but it would take more time than she'd thought.

The letters received were being copied and arranged for formal review later in the day. Despite the volume and general hostile air, everything was under control and being handled. Everyone had a job and the system in place satisfied all perceptions of having this disaster under control.

Everything except my bathroom, which had garnered an impressive line and was developing a smell. Given the volume of coffee I had witnessed these gluttons consume, I was going to need toilet paper and a plunger before the end of the day if I had any intention of going pee again.

Or you could just cut your losses and run, my brain supplied helpfully. Winnie was practically radiating joy with all the attention and I knew she wasn't cut out for the nomad life and I needed more coffee access than drive-thrus and gas stations offered.

"Cyn." My name was whispered from somewhere near the rear of the office. On my circuit, I had found the quietest spot to hide was in the back corner. There was nothing in the space and it existed out of my mother's line of sight, but people were desperate to get heard and stayed near the action.

My hiding spot was perfect.

"Cyn!" I swept the room with my eyes and moved slowly toward the door opposite me. Winnie had already migrated that direction for some peace and her wagging tail sticking through the door frame was a good indicator no murderers were waiting on the other side.

Still, Winnie would sell me out to a murderer for a side of beef so the margin of error was higher than one would expect.

"Yes?" I didn't whisper since the volume level in my office rivaled a rock concert. When a gun didn't poke out and assassinate me, I moved a few steps closer. "Are you here to kill me?"

A face appeared in the slightly ajar door, and I smiled at Stella looking out at me. "Hey."

"Hey... could you... leave for a minute? Or thirty-four?" She corrected, appearing to do some sort of mental math and coming to an exact calculation of the time I would need. Winnie's head was pressed against her leg, a hand cradling her cheek and stroking her ear. "Maybe I mean sixty-four. It may take either just over a half hour or a full hour but ideally not more than that."

"I'm told that I'm not a prisoner here." I looked around and saw the council members all deep in conversation with varying victims of fraud. "Do you usually estimate time in thirty-minute increments with even numerals in the one's place?"

She shrugged, "I find it comforting."

"The numbers or the process of estimation?" Still no one was looking our way. A strong indicator we could back out slowly and escape with none the wiser. I took another step, eyes on the lookout for my mom, the most likely person to thwart my disappearance.

Stella's face contorted in thought.

"I'm not sure, can I get back to you?"

"Sure. Keep Winnie close, she'd rat us out for a Cheez-It," I instructed and moved out of the doorway, wondering if she took every question seriously or she'd really never considered it before.

Quietly as possible, I pried open the fire door and burst into the alley. I swept both directions, but the coast appeared to be clear. It was like stepping out of a wind tunnel into a soundproof room and my ears buzzed at the sudden quiet. "What's up?"

The young woman was petting perfect circles on the tip of Winnie's ears in a steady rhythm. Just watching her, I felt my heart rate lower to match the movement. She moved with a measured precision that was both rigid and fluid, a modern dance choreographed by her own mind.

"I... I wanted to show you something. Well... tell and show? It doesn't make sense if I can't show you, but without words it's rather an obtuse data set." Her voice was steady, but the circles she was drawing picked up speed. "The best place would have been your office, or maybe the library, but neither is a very good option for obvious reasons."

"Sure... can we walk there?"

"Yes, but..." she switched from rubbing circles to tapping. Winnie blinked at each tap, but appeared happy with the attention. "It might take longer."

"What's the new estimate?" She was practically bursting to answer me and I wasn't disappointed.

"Ninety-six minutes."

I nodded and gestured for her to lead the way, trying to think of something comforting to say. She was barely ten years younger than me, but her height and gentle nature brought out a maternal instinct I reserved for animals and really good books. I wanted to wrap her in bubble wrap and protect her like a precious gem that hadn't been damaged by the world.

The sensation alarmed me, so I took extra care to not appear too invested in the girl.

Also, because I was fairly certain wrapping humans in bubble wrap was how suffocation happened and my willingness to cause her bodily harm was less than zero.

Right where I thought my maternal instincts were.

"I went by the old school and it looks like they've expanded the computer lab..." she shifted nervously, and I felt my head tilt. "It was the easiest place to try and fix it, but the school's computers were locked. I'd have asked but I'm... not technically allowed there. Please don't tell anyone, Mr. Meden just gave me the passwords so we could get online."

"What? How are you not allowed at the school? I burned down the gym and still had to assist Larry in a presentation there last year." My respect for her grew even as I considered how safe it was to be near her. If two walking disasters walked side-by-side, would the chances of catastrophe increase or decrease? Was it a double negative scenario or multiplying into a deficit of survivable probability?

"When I was diagnosed with autism, they tried to move me into courses that operated with a decreased load at a slower pace. It was infuriating because I was ahead in all my classes and already under stimulated. My neurodivergent behavior just explained why I struggled to work in groups and interact cohesively with peers. Instead of fighting the school, my parents were keen to just 'let the system sort it out'." Her tone remained impassive, but her face was scrunched in distaste. "They said to treat it like a vacation and use the opportunity to flourish in other areas now that academic work would be decreased."

"You don't really seem like a sit back and let it happen kind of person," I offered the remark off-hand, but the same had been said of me. "Also being forced to work under your potential instead of pushing to find its limits would make anyone take action."

"I'm not and I did. Instead of relaxing, I broke into all of the teacher's rooms and copied their lesson plans. In a single week, I completed all the planned coursework for sixth through tenth grade," she smiled, and I felt my face join her. "Unfortunately, the school tried to have me expelled for 'unauthorized access to teaching materials'. The teachers all insisted they'd given me the work, that I'd begged for a challenge, and they had simply allowed me to work at my own pace. Instead of expulsion, my punishment was to return to the normal course level. The teachers accepted the work I'd already done and let me read quietly."

"The teachers at the school are pretty chill. I bet they were impressed and also happy that someone in the room knew what a book was."

She nodded and continued her story as we made the half-mile trek to the all-in-one education emporium of sub-standard learning. My grades had been average because they'd let me pass with below average work, and exceptional test scores. Words like "lazy" and "doesn't apply herself" were thrown around, but as long as I passed, there were no real repercussions they could come up with. I was a late in life baby for my parents and they were too tired to convince me to step it up, even with their positions at the nearby university.

"The teachers were understanding, but they also knew that if I wasn't challenged, I'd get bored and become a problem. They helped me register for community college classes and took turns driving me during the day. I have an affinity for numbers and patterns, so they got me into accounting, budgeting, and multivariable calculus."

"That's... honestly, that sounds awful to me, but it looks like you liked it?" She nodded and considered me as we reached the home stretch to the admin building. I'd seen children on their way with diorama's yesterday morning, but today the small apartment complex looked deserted. No cars were stationed in the parking lot, the fence dummy-locked to keep out any casual miscreants.

I checked my watch to see it was after 1700.

"Yes. You... don't like numbers?" We'd come to a stop at the school's main entrance and I blinked at her in confusion.

"Not really. Is that bad?" Winnie offered her support with a quizzical head tilt.

"I thought an affinity for numbers was universal amongst people like me..."

"You think I'm a people like you?" I asked, wondering if I'd ever been welcomed into a group before.

"There's nothing wrong with people like me," she snapped, and I shook my head.

"No, I know that. It's just... no one has ever wanted to associate themselves with me before, much less admit we shared similarities." My throat tightened, and I felt tears sting the back of my eyes. Someone might actually like me besides Mo and Larry... My world was growing and I hadn't even threatened anyone. "In the Army I became a canine handler because dogs were really the only other service members who could tolerate me. The feeling was mutual, but I think they were more motivated to do something about it than I was."

"No one ever tested you?" She asked calmly and I shook my head. "Right, sorry, I got off track. So, I'd completed coursework through tenth grade in sixth grade, took college accounting courses, and was on track to graduate a year early. Unfortunately, I tend to hold grudges. It's not so much a matter of forgiveness as a sense that when people rub me wrong, and I get the impression they aren't..."

She struggled to explain, but I'd had the same sense before.

"That what everyone else sees isn't real?" I offered and she nodded. "Yeah, I get that."

"So, the principal at the time... Cummins?" She looked at me and I shrugged. "He started when I was in second grade, Hoffman was in charge before that. She was pretty good but transferred to a larger school district. Anyway, he always made me uncomfortable. There was just this sense that he was hiding something sinister. So... I broke into his office."

I smiled again. If moral ambiguity toward trespassing was a bonding characteristic, we were borderline about to be conjoined twins.

"I know, it sounds impressive, but school locks are insanely easy to pop open. Breaking in is really just a matter of calculating the weakest point and applying precision pressure." We were moving again, past the elementary classrooms and junior high toward the cafeteria and the school gym. "I pulled all the accounting documents and did an independent audit. He was intentionally mis-representing the number of students receiving specialized services and underfunding the program. Instead, Cummins was paying himself as three different people: the principal, a special education instructor, and an athletics coordinator. I presented my findings to the district and when they were slow to take action, I notified the IRS and the news media. Long story short, he's in federal custody and I was asked not to come back here for being a 'problem'. I wondered if he was splitting his take with someone at the district level given their animosity toward the topic, but I couldn't prove anything and I was banned."

My cheeks hurt from smiling so big and she stopped in front of the door to a building beside the gym.

"Where are we?" I asked, realizing that we'd traversed the whole campus. Trying to take in the surrounding area, it felt new and foreign. Despite having attended this school for the requisite thirteen years, I had no recollection of this building.

"The performing arts theatre," she offered, jiggling the handle and popping it loose. "All the acting, singing, and other classes are held here."

"This school had that? With what money?" I shared a look with Winnie, but she knew even less than I did. "I don't remember that showing up on the course registration form."

"Yeah, I was thrust into these classes by Mr. Meden." She led me past rows of seats, my eyes scanning the wide stage. I'd never seen this stage, much less performed on it. Would I have joined theatre if I'd known it existed?

"When was this built?" I asked in awe, wondering if I'd ever even ended up here by accident. Nothing looked or felt familiar, but I had suffered a significant number of head traumas.

"Same time as the rest of the school. You've never been here?"

"No... And for all the staff and faculty who complained about me, Mr. Meden never suggested I come here. Do you think he was afraid I'd fall off and die or he didn't think I was cut out for the theatre?" I tried to look everywhere at once. The green velvet chairs, the black stage, the three rows of curtains making entrances and exits from both sides of the stage.

"Probably he thought you weren't in need of social lubricant, though based on what I've heard, I don't know how. Maybe he was smoking more weed when you were here? Anyway, he said autistic people are constantly masking to appear like everyone else. Makes us great actors since arranging our face in a facsimile of emotion is part of daily life."

"What you've heard? People still talk about me? Is it the bullying, the giraffe, athletic ineptitude, or the minor stampede I caused in the agriculture arena because I thought the cows were in danger? Or the gym I facilitated in the renovation of?"

Stella snorted in laughter and paused, considering.

"Honestly, how did you make it to nearly thirty?"

"I'm hard to kill," I shrugged, feeling like Captain America and knowing full well I was Wile E. Coyote. My life was a joke, but one that kept going. "So what are we looking for?"

She stopped halfway through the theatre.

"Right... I..." her eyes scanned the theatre. "We were supposed to go to the computer lab. But... I can bring the computer in here? I need to show you something."

"Need to show me?" I asked, head tilting. "The data set that is useless without words to accompany it?"

She didn't seem to understand I was repeating her own words back to her.

"Yeah... I... made a mistake and I was hoping you could help?" She chewed her cheek and I felt a knot tighten in my gut. "Probably we should just go to the computer lab. I just find the theatre comforting?"

Stella's face went blank with a combination of concern and uncertainty. It was possibly the first time she'd looked into her relationship with the building. I personally found no building on this campus comforting, desirable or enjoyable, but I was glad someone benefited from their time here.

"I'll wait here, go do your thing." I waved her off, reassuring her that I would wait by plopping into a green velvet folding seat. "The alternative is watching strangers drink my coffee and seeing my mom sneak Winnie cheese."

With a quick nod, she darted through the theatre house and I heard a metal door slam. Beside me, Winnie's ears twitched, and then she flopped over in resignation. The air conditioning in the theatre was on, a surprising use of electricity for a school that claimed to need money regularly.

Or maybe they were still making me pay them back for damages caused by me... tough to tell.

I leaned back and closed my eyes, taking in the cool darkness and wondering at a past that held theatre and performances instead of reading and failed sports team tryouts. There was no way to know without a time machine, but the outcome would have likely been the same.

"This isn't working," a voice drifted from stage left and Winnie's ear lifted in questions.

"You can't..." A door shut and the rest of the sentence dimmed into a murmur of voices.

"Stay here, girl," I ordered Winnie, watching as she laid her snout on her crossed front paws and let out a long sigh. "Didn't take much convincing, you lazy bum."

My grumble was met with a resolute sneeze and I rolled my eyes.

"Woman's best friend, my left butt cheek."

I moved toward the stage and found a hallway, hidden in shadows. There was a single door that led to stage left and the door opened into a hallway.

"This is the first small town where we've had this problem," someone spoke from the vicinity of one of the three doors that lead off the hallway. The first was labeled laundry, the second was props, and the third make-up.

Cautiously, I chose to push open door number three.

"Well, what did you want us to do? She wasn't listed on the town website! We should pack up and go." A female voice filled the room filled with lighted mirrors and one continuous counter. Toward the end of the row, on the far side, several mirrors created an ominous sphere of light.

"If we go, we have to start over! The carnival is doing decent business, they'll start to suspect us if we suggest leaving! Especially with cuts he's made." A male voice grumbled into the semi-darkness and I found myself moving closer against all the instincts that screamed to run away. "Everything is nearly ready to move forward. He's already..."

"Shut up!" A female voice spoke in a hiss and I froze. I forced myself to take two steps back, coming up short as a large, warm wall landed along the back of my body.

"You," he grumbled, and I glanced up to see the bald-headed man who was operating the water gun game staring down at me.

"So... the mouse wandered into the cat house," a shorter blonde woman slunk around the corner and ran a sharp manicured claw down my cheek. "You really have purple eyes."

Two over-sized arms pinned mine against more torso. I stomped my foot on the instep of the larger man's shoes, managing only to elicit a chuckle.

"So glad you could join us," the woman continued, gliding closer. "It saves me some effort."

A crackle stole the breath from my lungs, and I saw a small spark in the region of my ass before everything went fuzzy and I fell to the ground thinking it was a terrible day to be tazed.

The warmth in my pants confirmed it.

Chapter Fourteen: Another Day

No one thinks pooping their pants is a good idea.

In my experience, no one wanted to admit that such a thing was possible once a person was fully potty trained but not yet at the age of incontinence. Yet, as a fully-grown adult who'd just been run through with an electrical charge while in the throes of gastrointestinal catastrophe, pooping my pants was the least of my problems.

In fact, it was a little surprising it took the electrical charge for this to happen given how I'd felt this morning. Despite the illness, getting off the floor of Larry's bathroom had been the best decision I'd made today, everything after turning into an unholy disaster, and I was fairly certain the day wasn't over.

There was definitely nothing worse than a day that just wouldn't end.

At least, there wouldn't be if the steady rumble of an engine combined with the scent of diesel hadn't raided my senses. A quick check of my eyelids showed they were open, but no light came in.

Which meant I'd been abducted.

While being taken by strangers was on my list of things to avoid, being taken with underwear full of poop was worse.

Mostly because if I was about to die, these are the underwear they'd have to remove to bury me. My plan had always been cremation but it seemed unlikely I'd remembered to write that down anywhere. If it wasn't in writing, someone would insist people needed to see me dead to prove it possible.

"Winnie?" I asked the warm air around me. I could feel a textured metal platform, a diamond pattern that reminded me of the metal lockers mounted to truck beds. Despite the heat radiating from all directions, it was dark. Outside smelled like asphalt, dirt and... poop.

Possibly the last one was me.

The rumbling slowed and then stopped. An air brake hissed, the truck lurching forward before throwing me backward into the side of my containment unit. I pressed my hands in front of and behind me, kicking out my feet to confirm that I was, in fact, in a metal box.

They're going to bake me in the summer sun, I thought and panicked. Dying in poop-stained pants from being baked in a metal coffin was my fourth least desirable way to die. Fourth or fifth... It definitely made the top ten, below being burned alive and having my head placed in a negative pressure chamber until all the air was sucked out and my head squashed flat like every Barbie I had ever owned.

Voices interrupted my death musings and I tried to focus.

One, two, three, four, five... maybe six different voices. There was some sort of debate on what to do about the problem. Whatever "The Problem" was, it had ruined their plans but was not easily eliminated. Something about thieves not murderers and this was all supposed to be a bit of fun. Nothing they'd taken was worth committing murder over. Knew too much, smelled like crap...

Crap? I'm The Problem?? My brain stuttered on the thought that even locked in a box, taken away from my dog, I'm still a problem.

As though this had all been my idea.

As though I'd woken up this morning and thought: *To hell with my stomach pain. I'm going to go out and get punched in the face, lectured by my mother, and abducted in a giant metal box.*

Anger overtook confusion, and I slammed parts of my body against my solid metal cage. The sound was deafening, my limbs protesting the physical trauma, but I refused to stop. Every atom of my being vibrated with a fury that this was once again my fault, my problem. My feet stomped on the bottom, I threw my shoulders against the floor and when the lid opened, I came up swinging with a right hook.

My fist connected with something that cracked beneath a squishy layer and a warm liquid splashed on my arm. I followed my right hook with a left jab and missed.

"Crap!" A man yelled, and I aimed for that voice, connecting with a malleable body part that grunted in pain. My eyes adjusted to the sun, pushing to stand up with a disgusting squelch as I rose from the metal locker into the bed of a pick-up.

A hideous pea green pick-up truck that should be burned with my pants.

We were somewhere remote. The horizon had brown hills that locals might call mountains. Yellow grass baked in the sun, and there were more trees in Simba's home than the landscape before me. My gaze shifted from the surroundings to the people, noting that the three from the make-up classroom had been joined by a few others in matching black form fitting outfits.

Some of whose outfits were less than form sized and left gaps of skin baking in the harsh light.

There were two women and four men. The ladies were short, this morning's blonde runner among them. Even in heels she'd be lucky to reach my shoulder, the idea of her even trying to be me was entertainment on par with Joseph losing tear away pants to a steer pulling barbed wire. Beside her stood a Filipino man who rivaled her in the vertically challenged department. Stick a couch pillow under his shirt and it would be the imposter Joseph from the video.

"Grab her, idiots!" The second female was a multinational beauty. Based on the lumbering of the man who'd pretended to be Jaimie, she was clearly the leader. He moved at the same time as the man closest in size to Phil lurched up from where he'd landed after being punched.

Their heads collided with a nauseating crack, clutching their individual impact points with simultaneous swears. Both looked unsteady as they nursed their wounds, fake Phil much closer to the edge than not-Jamie. Seizing on the opportunity, I shoved not-Jamie into fake Phil, sending them over the side of the pick-up truck.

Where they landed on the blonde woman and Filipino man. I started toward the end of the truck, watching the tangle of limbs kick up a tornado of roadside dust. The largest man seeming to get shoved to the bottom of the heap, the blond woman on top with a look of despair.

"Enough!" The second woman shouted, and I whipped my head around at the sound of a shotgun ratchet. The universal sound of pain and suffering.

Time paused and everyone appeared to have been hit with a freeze ray. The pile of fallen bodies stopped squirming to get free and the sixth man held the shotgun, squarely on guard beside the woman.

"I swear, I'd have been better off grifting than being saddled with you lot. I'm going to have a long talk with my brother..." her face had a red tinge and a vein throbbed in her head. "Now, Sam and Garth, remove Ms. Sharp from the truck. Hailey, get back in the car with Curtis."

The blonde and short man moved to an ancient white Honda and got into the back seat. Not-Jamie and Fake Phil, aka Sam and Garth, heaved themselves from the ground. Instead of using the tire as a step stool like most Americans, the larger men opened the tailgate and heaved themselves up.

Where they both stopped and eyed me suspiciously.

"What? You've never pooped your pants when electrocuted while having a stomach bug before?" I smiled when they shifted and made a gross face. "Do you want to? I'd be happy to share that life experience with you."

"You do it, G," not Jamie spoke, shoving Fake Phil, now presumably Garth, forward. "You're the one who dosed her."

"It's your taser!" he countered, pushing Sam forward. "You do it."

The woman in charge let out a long-suffering sigh.

"Ms. Sharp, exit the truck. Don't try anything or I'll shoot you." She gestured the two men out of my way but I elected to climb over the side and keep the truck between me and the gun woman. "Thank you, maybe I should have hired you instead of frying your neurons. Live and learn."

The two men exited the truck bed with the grace of baby giraffes at birth. A full-bodied game of rock paper scissors later, Sam had won the position of driver. A disgruntled Garth shoved him, but before either could get in a solid hit, the Honda laid on its horn and the woman cleared her throat.

"This is where we part company. If you survive in this heat..." she shrugged, "keep your mouth shut or I'll be back. This is a warning, Ms. Sharp."

Declaration made, her muscle followed her with his gun at the ready to the Honda. Once she was safely inside with the door closed, he lowered the gun and climbed in. As a single unit, both vehicles started their engines and crunched the dirt on the side of the road as they approached the road, turned onto it, and laid rubber.

"Crap," I muttered, staring at my shoes after their tail lights had disappeared. Darkness was inching its way closer and I needed an idea. Patting down my front pockets, I found a dead cell phone, my wallet, and a losing lottery ticket that I had no recollection of purchasing. My rear pockets had dog fur and some orange crumbs.

A quick tongue flick and I decided they were Cheez-its.

There was nothing to help me contact transportation help or hitch a ride. The smashed fitness tracker on my wrist put the time at seven in the evening. To my left was the sun, to the right was... nothing. My brain tried to picture which end of town the sun was usually on at this time of day and orient myself to the view. Unfortunately, without knowing which side of the street I was on, or having access to a map, I went with instinct. Instinct said to head right, the opposite direction the departing vehicles had gone.

Either one of us was wrong, or they weren't headed back to Sweet Pea.

My throat closed around the frustrated scream threatening to escape. The inside of my mouth was sandpaper, my pants were starting to form a solid unit, and there was no sign that water or showers would be available in the next few minutes.

Even less chance a passerby would pick me up in this condition.

Still, I ambled down the road, and stuck my thumb out when a black sedan approached from the direction I was headed. The driver was obscured by a reflective tint, but the car slowed before making a wide turn and pulling up beside me.

I stared at my own reflection in the Vegas tint and anticipated the muzzle of a black revolver poking out. The window started down, and something moved just on the other side of the glass. Cool air burst out as the window crept lower and something black shoved its way through the opening.

Followed by a brown muzzle, two tan ears, and the enthusiastic eyes of my best friend. Her tail wagging back and forth causing the driver to squeal.

"Winnie, sit before I go blind!"

Stella's face appeared behind her hand pushing the dog's tail back toward her wiggling butt.

"Hey, girl!" I hugged the dog toward my chest. She scented the air and flattened her ears. "Yeah, I know. But you get shot through with ten thousand volts with a stomach thing and see if you end up poop free."

Stella lowered her sunglasses to study my face.

"Trunk," she offered, popping it open. Crossing to the back of her car, I lifted the lid and found two backpacks beside neatly folded sweatpants and a case of water. I took the water first, downing the contents of the plastic bottle before I'd registered even putting it to my lips. With my other hand, I tugged on the zipper of the first backpack to find wet wipes, Chapstick, stain remover pens, and several packets of nuts.

The second backpack held miscellaneous undergarments and a skirt.

"I'm not a survivalist, I just think you should be prepared for an emergency. As far as the other, when you're the weird kid, you get used to needing a change of clothes. In college, I'm sort of the den mom, helping the girls stay safe and covered." Stella said from beside me and I gave her a smile, every part of that I understood.

And every part of me wanted to give her a different life.

"I have a similar backpack. Snacks are usually long eaten before this point in the day."

"Was the pudding thing popular when you went to school?" She asked and I nodded with a pain I tried to mask with dry humor. "And stealing clothes so you had to go naked or wear sweaty crap?"

Another sad nod on my part.

"The cookie smashing failed though, I still got fat." My levity did nothing to brighten her face and I offered a hopeful smile.

"It gets better though... At some point you can adopt a dog. If you get the dog from the military, you also get to play with small and large arms. Sometimes explosives and vehicles that you don't have to pay the insurance premium on if you drive them through a wall or accidentally set them on fire with most of a military base. Then you and the dog can open a PI Office that causes you to end up abducted and abandoned on the side of a road with poopy pants."

Stella shook her head and I decided to believe she was impressed by my military career.

"How did you find me, by the way?"

"Winnie," she said simply and passed me wipes, underwear, a trash bag, and the skirt before leaning against the rear driver side door to grant me some privacy. "She's really smart."

"Yeah, that's why the Army didn't want her... or me, really. We think too much and suck at following directions. I personally just think people should have to explain the big picture and let us find the best way to achieve the goal. Those people think I should just shut up and follow orders and do not appreciate being informed that orders are for drive throughs and the Humvee doesn't fit so they should be flexible."

Stella snickered behind me.

"Did you tell Carla about the abduction? I kind of expected her or one of the idiots," I asked, swiping wipe after wipe over my skin and quickly filling the trash bag. Stella made a sound and I nearly exposed myself in alarm. "What? Was she mad about the leaving thing and decided I sent you to make up a story? Because I feel like she knows enough about me that I wouldn't lie about why I ditched a room full of people. I'd just ditch."

"No... I called the station, but Daniel was the only one there. He was, and I quote 'taking a break from documenting the town's mental illnesses' and there was no such thing as an emergency in this town. When I told him what happened, well I didn't know about the tasing, but I figured you were incapacitated and taken if you hadn't called for Winnie. He asked if I got it on video because he could make a killing on YouTube. Then he said some unflattering things and hung up." Her voice held an anger but no surprise at his behavior.

A sort of peace settled in my gut that some things would never change.

"At least some people are predictable."

"Some people are assholes," she mumbled, and I couldn't have agreed with anything more in my life.

Chapter Fifteen: Disappearance

"Well don't you look nice," my mom commented from where she was sitting behind my desk. I'd been gone for a few hours, yet my office had hardly lost any occupants. "But why would you wear a skirt with those shoes?"

I felt my head tilt, Winnie and Stella mirroring the move beside me.

"Because it's not mine. I needed a change of clothes after getting tazed and dumped on the side of the road outside of town. Didn't you notice I was gone?"

She gave me a quick once over and shrugged. Carla's eyes followed the same path, but she was waylaid by the German man with a pet boutique.

"I just thought you were sulking and being antisocial. Your typical moody self," my mom flicked away my concern like a piece of lint and I wondered what it would take for her to actually be concerned for me. When I'd first got home, she'd nearly attacked a base guard to get to me. Soon after, it was like the novelty of having a child in the area had worn off and she couldn't be bothered with my injuries, disappearances, or catastrophes.

Though to be fair, I'd ended up in the hospital a lot in the past seven months. The hospital, the side of the road, covered in blood (mine and otherwise)... Maybe she just decided it wasn't worth getting worked up over until I was properly dead.

Otherwise it was just another... whatever day of the week this was.

Wednesday maybe?

I considered checking my underwear, but then I remembered I didn't buy day of the week undies. Winnie stuffed her nose up the skirt and I gasped.

I wasn't wearing any underwear at all because Stella's were too small.

"Out!" I hissed and tried to cover my flesh from her cold wet nose. "Get out of there."

"What was that, Cynthia?" My mom called over her shoulder.

"I'm going upstairs." Winnie followed me through the door and up to my apartment, fighting me to get back under the skirt to sniff around. "Seriously? This is why I can only wear cargo pants with you."

She flopped on the floor in front of the couch with a loud exhale. The doggy equivalent of *whatever*. Complete with Valley girl voice and eye roll.

In the interest of self-care, I started a pot of coffee before heading into the bathroom to strip and shower. Despite the discomfort and the embarrassment, the mess and the event hadn't really been that bad. A bunch of amateurs playing at organized crime. They hadn't been overtly threatening, taken anything of consequence, and yet...

I watched the lavender scented shampoo spiral down the drain in foamy white swirls.

A downward spiral seemed likely. But why? They'd known who would be sick, verbally linked to the carnival, but there was something else at play. A bigger picture that hadn't been painted, but was it linked to what was stolen or were the thefts a distraction from something else?

Two short raps on the bathroom door pulled me away from my thoughts and I finished rinsing. The water ran clear, so I was as clean as possible without a lobotomy to rid the memory of having squishy pants.

Stepping out, I wrapped a purple towel around my torso, quickly combed my hair and pulled open the air to a burst of steam. On the other side stood Carla, speaking with Stella and jotting down statements with cool professionalism. The chief's eyes met mine and something sparked, an emotion that spoke volumes about what she thought of our excursion.

"Are you OK?" Her jaw barely moved with the words and I worried for her dentition. Instead of answering, I walked around the counter and pulled down coffee cups. I raised one to each woman and they both offered a nod. I filled all three with coffee and then pulled the Peeps creamer out and offered that as well.

"I'm diabetic, do you have milk?" Stella asked and I re-opened the fridge to offer her milk. She nodded, Carla gestured toward the milk as well and I made the drinks for distribution.

I handed Carla a mug advertising a jungle tour from a theme park. Stella received a cup with a Winnie caricature dressed as a superhero, and mine was plain black, like my current mood. As the ceramic mug heated, paw prints phased in on the cup in a rainbow of colors.

Never mind then, the mug had betrayed me. It was not a rainbow and magic kind of day.

"You want to talk about it?" Carla asked when silence reigned for more than half a cup of coffee.

"We need to go to where the carnival is and check out the make-up room at the theatre," Stella nodded with my declaration and Carla raised a perfect brow at me. "What?"

"Are you kidding me? Just right back to work? Look, I know you're a big bad Army woman, but you can't tell me that getting taken this often doesn't affect you. You can't just ignore what happens to you and hope it goes away. You're not an ostrich."

"If I stop moving, I'll have to think about today and I'm not ready for that. I may not ever be ready. I might drink a bottle of wine and see if I can erase this day." My voice had gone high and, a man might say, hysterical. "Can we maybe put it off? At least for now?"

She chewed her cheek before an almost imperceptible nod.

"Show me where the darts went in," I looked down and saw I was still in my towel. The darts had impaled the outside of my right thigh and when I showed Carla, the angry red swelling had taken on a purple tingle. It was in a fatty part that didn't really hurt but I suspected tomorrow it would be tender.

She let out a long sigh.

"I'll send Daniel out to the carnival with Stella. You and I can check out the school... after we go to the clinic."

"Clinic? For what?" My eyes studied the small puncture site. "This is nothing!"

"It's nothing that could be infected given what I know of your morning and the effects of electricity. I won't make you tell the nice medical people what happened if you let them clean it and give you antibiotics," her voice was cajoling but the implied threat came through. Without having to tell her, she'd known about my pants.

"Tasers are sanitary, though," I grumbled, chugging the rest of my coffee in one long gulp and stomping to my bed area for clothes. I grabbed underwear, cargo pants, a T-shirt with Care Bears giving the finger, and my socks. "It's just red and irritated from the skin being broken."

"Are you certain? What are the chances they re-used taser barbs to save costs if they're stealing petty cash?" Carla called just as I closed the bathroom door. A shudder went through me and I looked closer at the pokes in my skin. They were emitting heat, but nothing excessive, a good sign my body wasn't trying to autoclave an infection.

"You'd tell me if you were infected, right?" I asked the marks and Carla's voice floated into the bathroom.

"Stop talking to your injury and get your clothes on!"

"Stop listening to me in the bathroom!" I shouted back.

She and Stella were moving around the apartment. I heard cabinets open and close, the coffee pot leaving and returning to its plate and lids being attached to cups while I contemplated the wisdom of pants for this visit.

If I were wearing pants, I'd have to drop them. In not pants, I could still cover half my body and only show the injury. The skirt I'd worn home was folded on the toilet tank and it was just the right draping for this purpose.

"Stella! Can I borrow your skirt still?" I asked.

"Yeah, but don't use that one. I have a better one for you," she tapped twice on the door and stuffed a flowing black fabric through a small opening.

While I was easily four sizes bigger than the younger woman, skirts were a bit more forgiving with elastic waists and open entry points for legs. The skirt hit me at knee level and I imagined it reached Stella's ankles. With a quick glance that I looked reasonably well put together, I exited the bathroom and stuffed my feet into my sneakers.

Carla passed me a coffee cup and a cookie before leading us downstairs to our separate missions.

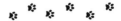

The Urgent Care Center had been relatively quiet. There were only two other patients present, and both had open wounds. I was happy to see them get stitched before someone swabbed my upper thigh and gave me pills. It was barely forty minutes after we departed my apartment that Carla's unmarked police car pulled up beside the Sweet Pea Unified Theatre. In the semi-dark it was indistinguishable from all the other buildings on the campus: a Lego block structure worn by sand, sun, winter storms, and being exposed to children.

"Have you seen any productions here?" I asked Carla and she raised a confused eyebrow in my direction. "Just, for the kids. I could see Sylvie being into theatre."

My smart-mouth niece was only nine, but she had the sense of humor you'd expect from a retired veteran and the attitude of a teenager in the nineties. If I had to guess what the first words out of her mouth were at birth, it would have been "as if".

"Trust me, if she gets into theatre arts, your ass is in the seat next to me," her warning finger forced a calm surrender.

"OK, but it's OK to heckle children's productions, right?"

"Pretty sure Sylvie will be heckling on the stage and what we do from the audience will go unnoticed," she huffed out a breath that cracked the smile on my face into manic levels. "I swear, she was spawned from Satan herself and placed in that kind woman's body to test the patience of man."

"Satan's a woman?" I asked, watching her pull out a key to unlock the side door to the auditorium. It took her the same amount of time to open it with the key that it had taken Stella to pick the thing.

"Of course Satan's a woman. Satan, God, Mother Nature... I think the only masculine representation is Jack Frost because he goes around spraying white crap and trying to kill things. You think a man could have organized a revolt from the kingdom of heaven and then had the wherewithal to establish hell and get a system in place?" Her spiel ended as we arrived at the hallway on house left.

"My mom made you go to church and then sit through her lectures on women's sexual revolution, didn't she?"

Carla shuddered as she popped open the door to the make-up room. No voices had filled the hallway and all the lights were off. I flipped on my phone's flashlight to study the light panel emitting a soft green glow. There was a dimmer switch beside ten individual buttons that dimmed and raised based on how long you held them down. I picked number seven and watched one of the lighted make-up mirrors illuminate gracefully with a dozen bulbs in a rectangle.

"Huh," Carla moved in beside me and jabbed a button in the bottom left, the entire room filled with blinding in seconds.

"What the hell?" I blinked past the spots floating in my vision.

"You were going too slow and it's past my bedtime," she shrugged and I considered plunging the room into darkness as petty revenge but my eyes caught on a half-lit object under the make-up table closest to the props. The cylinder shape was familiar, but out of place in a high school.

"Is that a lighter?" Carla asked, donning a glove to collect the lighter and study its oblong surface. "This looks..."

"Like the lighter Joseph was accused of stealing?" I commented and she nodded. Beside us, the racks of costumes obscured plastic baskets and we shoved aside wool garments to pull out a laundry basket filled with loot.

Inside was the Coffee Cabin coffee, the tip jar from the bar, and a stack of paper cups from Mo's. Carla pulled a notebook from her pocket and compared the contents to various pages, making small check marks and flipping through with speed and precision.

"It's all here," she studied my face as she spoke, looking for answers. "Why go through all the effort of stealing it to cause a scene and then abandoning it in a high school theatre?"

On the make-up counters was evidence of their changing appearances. Foam pieces to change ear and nose shapes, cake make-up in multiple shades, brushes and shading sponges that looked professional to my untrained eye. I wandered up and down the counter, noting contacts and cleaning solutions that mirrored various eye shades.

"They could become anyone with this stuff," I spoke in hushed awe and Carla snorted.

"This is literally amateur high school stuff. They could become anyone who is ambiguous visually to the people in town with cataracts."

Her phone bleated a song about idiots, and she pulled it from her pocket, stabbing the button and speaking without looking.

"What, Daniel?" Her annoyed smirk shifted into confusion and then anger. "That's not possible! Are you sure you went to the right place? You get lost sometimes."

His voice came through the line but his words were lost to me.

"Put Stella on the phone," she barked, and he let out a whining sound that may have been words but was likely the sound of his batteries dying. Someone would have to plug in the living Ken Doll if they needed it to do more.

"Hi, is he in the right place?" She listened to what Stella must have been telling her and swallowed hard. "Take pictures and we'll get out there as soon as we can. You're observant, look for tracks and clues. I trust you more than my employee."

Stella responded and the call ended.

"I'll mark this as a crime scene, but we're going to need to go to another one now." She strode to the door and I followed, watching her lock the room and pull a strip of red tape from a bag I hadn't noticed and place the seal on the door. "Won't stop someone motivated, but at least we'll know if they were here."

I shrugged and tried not to look for signs I had been dragged along this floor... with poop in my pants.

"For now, we're headed out of town."

"Why? What did they find?" I asked and Carla shoved through the crash bar back into the night.

"It's what they didn't find. The Carnival is gone."

Chapter Sixteen: Playbacks and Paybacks

I t was like entering the Twilight Zone.

Last night, the field was filled with cars, artificial turnstiles, and tents. Generator powered light towers had interlaced with lighted rides on metal platforms, midway games and booth after booth of greasy food. There were no tire tracks from previous visitors, no footprints in the hardened dirt of a dis-used field and no holes in the ground from staking and bracing everything.

The only thing that remained was the lingering scent of fried dough and my stomach lurched with the knowledge. Fire trucks were brought out to illuminate the area, Chris searched beside

Barney, the town's second police officer, while Daniel collected statements from families that showed up and expressed certainty the carnival had been here when they drove by hours before.

Somehow, they'd pulled up an entire carnival and erased everything but the olfactory evidence of it in a matter of hours.

"How is this possible?" Carla asked and I worried my lower lip between my teeth.

"Do you think..." I looked for trash, smashed gum, anything that proved we hadn't had a communal town hallucination.

"Think what?" She studied my face, trying to find an answer in my eyes that hadn't fully coagulated in my brain.

"Do you think maybe someone sent all those people to picket my office to distract the town so they could pull up the carnival's roots?" I asked, feeling ridiculous. Lizandro had really been asked to pay a "ransom" for his citizenship. "I mean not all of them... but..."

Carla chewed on her cheek and made a call. She took a few steps away and I stooped to poke at the sand with an index finger that had seen better days. My chipped and split fingernail pushed along the small sediment until a sharp edge cut the nail bed and I hissed out a breath. Bright red blood contrasted with the endless sand and I stuck my finger in my mouth to stem the flow. With my other hand, I shuffled through the sand more gingerly until the folded corner of a worn business card emerged.

It was clearly printed on card stock and cut with a blade, the edges sharp and straight but uneven. The text was faded, the card probably unrelated to the carnival, but I tucked it into my pocket as Carla arrived.

"Your mom is still at your office with Winnie. We are headed there now." She directed me to her car and my face scrunched at the thought.

"It's too late to kick her out and we need to see the papers to see if there are differences that separate the mail fraud from the actors looking to distract and redirect." Her explanation made sense.

"Maybe we can pull up cameras around town? Play them back to see if we can spot the carnival moving out?"

"Couldn't hurt," she shouted next.

"Stella!"

The younger woman appeared beside me, hair swinging behind her in a lopsided ponytail. Despite how long my day had been, this was normal for me. She looked exhilarated, a fact I wanted to attribute to her youth, but I knew the reality.

To anyone else, this mystery was exciting.

"We're getting pizza and reading a whole bunch of boring papers. You wanna come with us or stay and look at dirt?" The question was presented in her most rhetorical voice, but Stella gave it the proper consideration you'd expect of a person purchasing an engagement ring.

"While I find nature fascinating, I'm interested in learning the forensic nuances of the written language." Stella's head took another glance around the area. "I think I've learned all I can from here."

"Great." Carla narrowly avoided the eye roll that matched her tone. "Get in the car."

Indifferent to the mood, Stella bounced to Carla's car and slid into the back seat. Her seatbelt clicked into place and she pulled out her phone. In seconds she was immersed in what appeared to be an eBook while Carla eyed me over the roof of the car.

"Can you explain to me where you go to collect people and how I can unsubscribe you?" She rolled her eyes and climbed in without waiting for an answer.

For the best really, since I was fairly certain Stella had collected me. Most of my friendships were based on their recruitment of me into their lives. Mo had insisted on sharing her crayons in Kindergarten, Larry had insisted on sitting next to me so the bullies would think twice (they did not), and Beth had clung to one of the only other females in Afghanistan that didn't want to claw her eyes out for being hotter than Tyra Banks in her prime.

Nope, all my friends had collected me... Well, except Winnie.

We drove back into town in silence, Stella reading her book and Carla appearing to lose an argument in her head with herself. I made myself useful by ordering several pizzas through the power of my recharged technology, so they were ready by the time Carla pulled up.

"I'll grab the pizza and meet you guys at the office," I said, waving them away as I closed the door. Carla shut off the engine and both women exited the car. "Guys, I got it. I can carry five pizzas. You can head back to the office."

Instead of questioning my volume decisions, Carla turned my body ninety degrees and pointed at my office. The curtains were open, every light was on and the entire sidewalk was illuminated. Inside I could see my mom and the other council members seated in a semi-circle. Between them was some sort of clear bottle and as I watched, two council members leaned in to kiss each other.

"Are they playing Spin the Bottle?" Stella piped up from beside me and I nodded. "Did you know that game was first referenced in the 1920s? It reached peak popularity in the 1970s through the 1980s but has since declined. The first scientific reference to mononucleosis was also cited in the 1920s and its surges in cases aligns similarly with when the game was most popular but it's likely an instance of correlation without causation."

"That makes sense," I said and Carla gave me a look that asked *how*. "Most of the people in that room were born in the 1920s."

Carla snickered and Stella tilted her head.

"I don't think any of them was born before 1946," she corrected, and I decided to move the conversation away from comedic hyperbole. My best material would be wasted on Stella.

"Oh, right," I nodded, the day's events were catching up to me and I was suddenly overwhelmed at the idea of spending more time in the company of others. "So... we can all carry pizza? Quietly maybe?"

Stella beamed and I had to shake my head at the level of enthusiasm.

"You can only carry one and you have to enter the office last," Carla warned her, and I nodded my agreement.

"If she charges, toss the pizza toward one of us and go for the collar." Stella's eyes went wide. "She's fast, but she doesn't turn on a dime. You have a chance with misdirection."

"The council will attack me for pizza?" She asked, doe eyed and innocent.

"Maybe," we answered in unison.

We walked into the parlor and collected the mountain of food. I had prepaid, but we waited patiently for Carla to speak with the man behind the counter. James was in his early twenties, also on break from college and the kind of cute that I reserve for puppies and children who aren't screaming.

Stella, on the other hand, was frozen with her mouth open watching him operate the pizza cutting wheel. If my phone wasn't dead again, I would have taken a picture to stick in the dictionary next to "twitterpated".

Right after someone put twitterpated in the dictionary.

"Hey, Stella!" he called out with a toothy grin.

The woman squeaked and tried to hide behind me.

"James!"

"How's school going? You liking it?" he asked the coward formerly known as a competent human being.

"Fine!" She squeaked again and his smile lost some wattage.

"What she meant was, school would be better if you two hung out more. Could she have your number?" I said and Carla offered him a pen and paper. He hesitated and she peered out to gawk at him. It was like introducing puppies at the dog park, except one was clearly more social than others.

"You can talk to boys," she stage-whispered and his grin came back full force.

"Talk, kiss... you can do all sorts of things with boys when you don't hide behind old ladies." Carla snorted at me and I gave her a thumbs up with my middle finger for the *old lady's* comment. "Do you want to talk to and kiss James?"

Her eyes panicked but she nodded quickly and ducked.

"James, do you want to talk to and kiss Stella?" Carla asked the young man and he cleared his throat.

"Yeah?" Stella peeked back out at his answer and my sister-in-law joined me in saying *awwww*.

"Great, now that that's settled, I have a proposition for you." His face went pink and she cackled. "Not that lover boy, I need you to teach one of my deputies a lesson."

Carla offered him a sizable tip if the man put pineapple on Daniel's next pizza. Under the cheese and soaked in habanero sauce. James agreed with a wicked smile and tried to refuse her money but ultimately accepted when she outlined her plan. Since if James got caught, he could get an earful of Daniel monologue and he deserved pre-payment for that.

"Is there a pizza the council members won't attack me over?" Stella still appeared traumatized and I decided to end the game. We had just forced her to admit to a crush... in front of him.

Thank goodness that had worked out or I would have had to dump melted cheese onto him for hurting her. It only hurts for a few seconds initially, but the burns last for some time and sting whenever you wash your hands.

Not that I knew.

"The council won't attack you. Winnie will attack you for pizza. Maybe also the council, on second thought... if you smell skunk, drop the pizza and run."

"You keep skunks in your office?" Stella's head tilt was almost as cute as Winnie's.

"No... I..." I looked over at Carla. "Is skunk smoke legal here?"

She waggled a hand.

"Skunks are smoking?" Now she was concerned, and I burst into uncontrollable laughter.

"No, she means," Carla paused to hold her thumb and index finger to her lips.

"Playing the kazoo?"

"Seriously, where did you find this kid?" Carla looked over Stella's head at me and I shrugged. The younger woman had mentioned weed earlier, so she wasn't oblivious. Perhaps she'd just never communicated informally. Or while she had knowledge of the substance, she wasn't aware of how it was consumed or what the scent entailed.

"She'll figure it out eventually. Since you mentioned Mono, and it is transmitted via spit, don't join the puff, puff, pass. If they insist... hide under something until they forget about you. Also, if you didn't personally see a cup cleaned, assume it is not and don't drink out of it. The same goes for bars, parties, and anywhere where the male to female ratio feels uncomfortable."

Carla gave a nod of agreement and Stella went slightly paler as we endeavored to impart our decades of wisdom in a fifty-yard walk.

"Also, don't accept water from any of the council members. It is not water. They are all raging alcoholics with livers that have likely shriveled and given up on life, not counting Cyn's mom," Carla added, just as we arrived at the front door. "Are you ready?"

Stella shook her head vehemently.

"Too late," Carla sing-songed as she pulled the door open and I entered first. Winnie came at me and I held the pizzas up in one hand, snagging her with my other and escorting to her bed behind my desk while the rest of the crew came in. Stella stayed completely hidden behind Carla and when she made it to the desk, she dropped to the floor and hid in the space set up for feet. Sensing a game, Winnie joined her.

The entire desk lifted three inches off the ground, Carla and I scooped up the pizza just in time for the entire piece of furniture to tilt and crash to the ground with a crash that could probably be heard in Mo's. My cheap monitor hit the ground, cord pulling free from the USB port and shedding gray plastic pieces of housing.

We relocated the pizza to a semi-kitchenette in the corner that was attached to the wall.

"Everyone grab a slice or several and sober up," I said, laughing as Stella crawled out, ponytail completely disheveled, shirt askew and face wet with slobbery kisses. "If I didn't know it had been Winnie under there, I may have insisted you use protection."

The entire council laughed, and Stella tried to smile but there were too many people looking at her and I suspected she was considering throwing up.

"Sorry, word of warning: don't hide under furniture near Winnie. Especially if you smell like food. We use her to ferret out my nephew when his sister is on a rampage and we need to take him into protective custody." Her smile grew more genuine at my words and the council members meandered toward the food.

"Why does he hide? Is she bigger than him?" She sniffed.

"Nope, he's got a few years on her. My brother mistakenly told him not to fight girls. Unfortunately, Sylvie took that to mean she could just beat him up without repercussions. So, we have to break his fear of fighting back before he gets Mrs. Robinsoned or something equally traumatizing."

"What does that mean? Mrs. Robinsoned?"

Opening my mouth, I shut it again and pretended I hadn't heard her. Some things were best left to Google or ignored altogether. In that moment, I declared lecherous old women in that group.

I turned toward the room and began introductions.

"Let's see... you know Mr. Meden, probably also Mrs. Zuber who will ruin your childhood by giving you small bottles of hooch."

Proving my point, the woman gave her a sealed bottle of Fireball and patted her hand.

"It's great with pizza," she offered sagely, and Stella blinked.

"I'm not twenty-one."

"Neither are we!" Mrs. Margot cackled, and I stared at the normally dowager woman. "Don't look at me like that, Cynthia! I know how to have fun!"

"OK... Moving on, Earl Grey is the portly man passed out in the corner."

Murmurs of lightweight and baby were passed around. His shoulders that were exposed to the sun earlier were a bright pink that would likely blister, peel and freckle before the night was done.

I elected not to point out it was after eleven and reasonable people would be asleep. That the pizza parlor was open was a minor miracle owed to summertime tourism.

"Suzanna, my mom Lynn, Cecily from the business board..." They all waved as they were introduced, and Stella put on her bravest face. When I mentioned my mom, she visibly panicked and I wondered which of the many true and horrifying stories she was thinking of. "Drink that quickly to make this easier and then grab some pizza."

"Did your mom really get an STD from a soda bottle she..." Stella swallowed, her whisper carried, and my mom gave her a look.

"There is nothing wrong with sexual exploration and curiosity young lady. With proper healthcare and safety precautions, all things are safe. Unfortunately, there is a trial-and-error period to all experimentation and I miscalculated cleanliness. You should learn to be open and expressive with your wants and desires."

In lieu of speech, the woman nodded and downed the Fireball in a single swallow.

I didn't have any Fireball, so I stuffed a whole slice of pizza in my mouth.

A knock on the glass window sent our eyes to the front. Penny Plootz stood there with a stack of papers and an expression of determination. I waved her in and she started speaking immediately.

"I had my firm trace the money and it had remained in an account here in town until yesterday where it was all taken out as a cashier's check! They described the woman who took it out as young with long dark hair and... is that pizza?"

"Help yourself, Penny," I gestured to the boxes and Stella stepped forward hesitantly.

"Penny? Penny Plootz?" She asked and the woman startled, not having noticed her before.

"Yes? Who are you?"

"My name is Stella. I uhh...." She pulled a folded paper from her pocket and handed it over. "This is yours. I'm really sorry."

Stella unfolded the paper and I glanced down at a cashier's check made out for...

"Holy guacamole, that's a lot of zeros!" Mrs. Zuber said from Penny's left and I could only nod.

"It was an accident," Stella began. "I was doing a project for school and my partner was commenting on the ridiculousness of the housing market and I wanted to prove that added value was dependent on location and game theory regarding competitive behaviors over finite resources. My partner argued that people would pay for anything if the price is right and there was no real way to commit real estate fraud without complacency."

"What are you saying, Stella?" my mom asked her, and tears shimmered behind Stella's eyes.

"I built a fake house and sold it to Penny."

Chapter Seventeen: Buried Treasure

I t was quiet enough you could hear a church mouse fart.

Since we weren't in church, Winnie filled the job and the stench rivaled mustard gas.

"Mother! You gave her cheese, didn't you?" I turned on her and she shrugged while eating a slice of pizza.

"She wanted it."

"I wanted light up shoes in high school, but you wouldn't get them for me! You could say no!" I countered, and Carla cleared her throat.

"Bigger concerns, ladies. We have bigger concerns. Cyn, Penny, Stella, and I need the room, please, Lynn. Have a good night, council."

"Yes, of course." My mom lingered in front of me, an expression of concern lining her eyes. "Are you OK?"

"Now you ask?" I grumbled and she narrowed her eyes.

"Don't give me that. There were dozens of people around and I wasn't going to make a scene. The nurse from urgent care spoke to a nurse that I'm close to. They mentioned that in addition to the darts, you have a large number of scrapes and bruises. You then disappeared for several more hours without reliable communication."

I nodded.

"I see... we'll discuss this later this week then, Cynthia." Something in my stomach fell onto my toes and I gaped at her. I was somehow going to get lectured for getting attacked.

She kissed my cheek and strode out the door with her purse and a few slices of pizza I hadn't seen her grab. The rest of the office cleared in a matter of moments, the council members taking most of the pizza and their sleeping co-worker with them. When only Carla remained with us, Penny found her words.

"You... sold me the fake house?" Penny looked shaken, the holographic security feature on the paper before her wiggling in her grip. "You're... the criminal mastermind?"

"I'm really sorry!" Stella looked panicked. "No one was supposed to buy the house. It was a social commentary economics experiment. Suddenly my project partner was saying it sold and we're rich and sending congratulatory letters."

"But... you..." Penny's mouth moved but she struggled to find words. It was the complete opposite of the day before and I couldn't figure out if she was tired or her brain exploded. "I'm... shark... trade..."

"The ad was supposed to be up for a week as part of the data collection process for our economic theory course. Once I had the data, I told him to take it down and I began the analysis. But I guess he didn't and then he sold it, but the account used to secure the sale was under a business name that I own through a shell company so after it sold, I think he planned to take the money and run. But he couldn't because I controlled it. When I learned it was there, I froze it until I could look into it further."

"You own a shell company?" I blinked in amazement.

"That's the part you find most pressing?" Carla interjected. "Not that she sold a fake house or that she committed real estate fraud, but that she has a business and a shell company?"

"Hey, I had a hard time getting a tax ID and a fictitious business name. She has a whole..."

"Excuse me?" Penny interrupted and we all turned to her. "Can we focus on the fact that I was conned?"

"Am I going to be arrested?" Stella asked. Penny said yes while Carla and I responded no.

"Excuse me, but I'm pressing charges against her! You have to arrest her!" Penny insisted, hands on hips. "It's the law."

"Yes and no," Carla said, and Penny gasped. "I can arrest someone witnessed committing a crime and you can press charges when a crime is actively being perpetrated against you, but to arrest someone after a crime is committed, I'd need an arrest warrant. And since she returned your property, we would actually need to prove malicious intent in the listing of the property and that she sold the property with the knowledge that she did not possess it."

"That doesn't make any sense!"

"The law rarely makes sense. It's why there are so many rapists and murderers not incarcerated," Carla gave me a dirty look for that addition, but I stood by my statement. "If it wasn't ambiguous, lawyers couldn't stab holes in logic. Don't give me dirty looks, write better laws and hire less sleazy judges."

Penny's anger had morphed into confusion and was now bordering on tears. "I'm homeless."

"I included interest when I paid you back! There should be enough extra there to..." Stella's eyes were also misting, and Carla and I exchanged an alarmed look. Crying people caused me to freeze and panic. Carla was usually worried crying would turn to fighting and then she would have to arrest someone. Her face solidified into business that caused the quivering lips to kick up a notch.

"There's no crying in my office," I declared and they both looked at me horrorstruck. "It's a rule I invented today. Carla, is there sufficient information or evidence to take action this very moment or within the next several?"

She shook her head, so I continued, "Penny, where have you been staying?"

"I rented an Airbnb. It's a back house in the older neighborhood," she sniffed, but her cheeks remained dry.

"So, while you do not have a permanent shelter, you do have shelter for the moment and funds to cover it?" I asked and she confirmed with a nod. "OK, I want you to go there and rest up for the night. Stella?"

The young woman looked at me, red-rimmed eyes owlish.

"Where are you staying?"

"With my parents," her voice quivered, and I gave her a warning point with my index finger to keep those tears in her eyes.

"You're also going to go home. Because it's late, I'm tired, and someone shot metal darts into my ass which they used to electrocute me, then took me hostage. All after I got punched in the head and had public diarrhea." They all blinked. "All in one day!"

"Wasn't it your upper thigh?" Stella asked and I narrowed my eyes at her. As a show of support, she pulled a packet of wet wipes out of her back pocket. "Also I pulled some extras so you could have your own stash."

I accepted them by tossing them into the bag I would now be carrying with me everywhere. It was a flawless plan unless whoever took me left it behind, like they did today with my dog and Stella.

"Either way, I deserve to sleep, and you all need to sleep. In the morning we can reconvene and work through logistics."

"But..." Penny and Stella spoke at once and I held up a hand.

"Upper thigh, not butt."

Only Carla laughed. The other two were statues Michelangelo would kill to paint... or sculpt. Whichever Ninja Turtle he was...

Geez I needed sleep.

Winnie let out yet another fart and they unfroze to fan their faces.

"Yup, stay and suffer folks. Best to flee while you can still smell."

Carla helped me usher them through the door and with a quick two-fingered wave, followed them out. I watched her guide both women toward her car and I deduced she was offering them a ride. Kind of her, considering the impending waterworks.

I glanced around the office. There was one slice of pizza left and I gobbled it in four bites. Winnie yawned in the corner, stretched like a bowing Hippogriff and sat down next to me. I bent down to kiss her head and a small *pooft* escaped.

"You done farting or should I make you sleep outside?" She responded with flat ears and sad eyes.

"Fine, but next time my mom gives you cheese you go home with her." The dog wagged her tail. "Traitor."

She butted her head against my hand and I stroked the soft fur.

"What do you think will happen tomorrow, girl?" I rubbed her ears with the question and her tongue fell out of her mouth. "That's what I was afraid of."

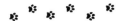

As I suspected, I woke up with a severe aversion to humanity.

There was also an aversion to walking, moving, breathing, and not being made of cheese. Why cheese? No idea, other than it was tasty, melty, and edible on anything ensuring a swift and delicious demise.

My leg was in pain, I had slowly forming cuts and bruises from being dragged into a truck and thrown in a tool chest. The side of my face felt warm and swollen, a fact that was probably true yesterday as well, but I hadn't noticed. Between the attacks and the truth bombs, I needed a day off from being a punching bag and secret repository.

Winnie snuggled in closer.

We definitely had a million reasons to stay in bed. One reason to get out of it was there was a man standing over me. Since it was Larry, it was also a good reason to stay in bed if he joined me. I could muster up a smidgeon of energy for physical activity.

"Uhn," I groaned and he whistled for Winnie. She licked my face for permission, and I agreed. She licked my face again, just to make sure I wasn't going to die on her.

"It's OK. If I'm not dead yet, it's not happening while you potty."

She flung her head around, tags and collar jingling loudly near my head. When I aimed to silence the offending metal, her skull crashed into the bruise on my face. Tears sprung to my eyes unbidden and Larry pressed an ice pack to my face that may have been a bag of peas.

"I'll be back in ten. Don't move."

The sound I emitted was reminiscent of Jurassic Park and he took that as confirmation. Before her jingling collar had receded, I was back asleep.

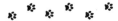

Coffee warmed the ice pack on my face, and I moved my lips like a blind fish. A flexible silicone straw touched my lips. They snapped shut and I sucked and swallowed like a drowning woman looking for air. The slurp of empty air bounced around the cup and I let the straw go with a small sob.

"Cyn, we need to talk," Larry said, and his blurry face came into partial focus when I opened my eye. His light brown hair was mussed, dark circles were under his eyes and there was at least a day's growth of beard on his face. His mouth was held in a grim line, usually light eyes had dulled with worry.

"Uhn."

Stuck for words, I patted the bed beside me and he sat down, hand clasping with mine. Through his wrist, I could feel the rapid rhythm of his pulse.

"Yesterday..." He squeezed my hand and then reached his other hand to my face. With a stroke of his index finger, he pushed my hair away from my face and examined the bruise. "Yesterday, you had a major incident, and no one told me."

I swallowed the sudden dry scratch in my throat.

"Instead of getting a call from you, Carla, ... anyone who actually cares, I had to hear from my brother. My brother bragging about how you got tazed, confirmed by Chris whose friend is the nurse who treated your injury, and still nothing. You didn't even text and tell me you were home alive. We had plans."

My hand reached for his face and he met me halfway. Arms wrapping around his neck to press my head into his chest.

"I was really scared... I know we joke about you getting hurt a lot, but I'm always worried."

A warm drop landed on my cheek, his tears joining mine in their descent. We held each other for a long moment, my heart breaking that I hadn't even thought of him. Once they'd left me on the side of the road, I'd gone into survival mode, and when my mom hadn't seemed concerned, I figured no one would care. He should have been the first person I told, let him check me over with his medical degree.

Animal medical degree, but whatever. He still has a lab coat.

"I'm sorry," I whispered, and he pulled me closer. "My mom made it seem like no big deal so I... let it go."

"I'm not your mom. Also, your mom is a grade A actress because she was freaked out when you got punched in the head," he nuzzled my neck.

"Which time?" I hiccuped and he almost laughed. "Sorry, too soon?"

"If there was any possibility that was an exaggeration, I'd say yes. But not all of them are recent, so it can't be too soon," he kissed the spot gently.

"So, was it the recent one then?"

"It's all of them. You now owe me a night of sleep," he spoke into my hair. "Sleep, dinner, and screaming my name loud enough to wake my neighbors."

"They'll never believe you're murdering me, you big softy."

"Maybe your neighbors will," he spoke just before his lips met mine in a searing kiss that made everything that happened yesterday almost worth it for this moment.

This moment which ended when the fire door at the bottom of my stairs slammed shut and determined footsteps that ascended quickly.

"Cyn, I need you to get dressed," her voice preceded her face and she froze at the sight in front of her. The man in my arms stiffened and though I couldn't see his face the anger rolled off him in waves. Carla was not one to scare easily, but I watched her fight the urge to apologize. "Crap, we didn't tell Larry."

"No, *we* didn't." His jaw tightened, and the words had a layer of frost that Elsa would envy. "She's taking the day off."

"No... she isn't. Something's come up at the carnival site and I need her to come sit with me. We need to read all those papers people dropped off and there's no one to sit at the scene."

"Split the papers and sit with someone else." A vein pulsed in his jaw and her face registered a respect that I hadn't realized she held back. I personally was in too much pain to interject one way or the other. It was a perfect day to let someone else make all my choices for me. "You may be the chief of police, but my girlfriend was attacked, twice, in one day. She is going to rest, and you are going to suck it up and ask someone on your payroll to help."

"Larry, they found something big at the carnival site. Cyn is the second-best trained investigator in this town and I don't know…" her sentence cut off at a chime from her phone. "Daniel is sending me a picture."

"If it's of his dick, send him back one of Cyn's brother's manhood and get out," Larry snapped, grabbing my cup and taking it to the kitchen for a refill. "He'll figure it out eventually."

"Don't bring up my brother's penis!" I shouted, trying to throw something at him and deciding I was too tired and lacking in options.

"It's not…" She tilted her head at him. "I can't tell if you're joking. Has Daniel sent… Never mind, don't answer that. It's not his manly parts, but I do need Cyn to come check it out. Maybe you too."

She went back to looking at her phone, zooming in and out on something.

"What does that look like to you?" She shoved the phone under his nose right as he returned to my bed with coffee. Our eyes studied the image and shared a look.

"It looks like a pile of bones," we both sighed and started getting ready.

Chapter Eighteen: Wordplay

"I always thought of the Grand Canyon as a big ditch. Now that I've seen a big ditch, I owe the National Park an apology."

Carla, Larry, and I stood on the edge of a rectangular hole. If memory served, it was in the location of the Ferris Wheel that had mysteriously vanished. The size and shape were reminiscent of a swimming pool or those water treatment ditches Erin Brockovich was stealing samples from.

Except it was bone dry and dusty lumps sat in the middle.

"Now what?" Larry asked, squinting into the sun. I pulled a baseball hat from my bag and put it on his head. With a quick hand across the top, he adjusted the hat. "Thanks."

We'd both opted for shorts and T-shirts with boots. I'd grabbed the backpack I take to work on impulse, deciding if I was going to have a day like yesterday I would be prepared. Winnie was panting beside me, flopped on her side after attempting to poison all of us on the way over.

"We were going to sit in the car with the AC and read until the techs got here to take pictures, but that's a hazmat zone at the moment," she said with a longing look at her white sedan. All four doors were open, hoping to coax the stale air into clearing the car. "Seriously, how much cheese did your mom give her?"

We all looked down at the dog who'd rolled onto her back and was coating her fur in dust. She sneezed and shot dirt mixed with sand at my ankle, leaving a smear of black.

"Gross," I said ambivalently. She'd definitely put worse stuff on me than dirt boogers. "Are the papers in your car?"

"Yeah, but..." I wandered back to the sedan and popped the trunk. With one hand through the passenger side door, I grabbed the stack of notice letters and folded myself cross legged into the trunk. Winnie leapt up beside me and together we took up the entire cargo space.

"If you fart, you're back to laying on the ground," I warned her. She flattened her ears and wiggled her eyebrows at me. "Fine, but..."

The implied threat sat unexamined since I was out of creative ideas. She licked my hand and snuggled back in while I picked up the thick stack of papers. On top was Penny's congratulatory letter, and I folded that up to tuck on the far side of Winnie. Beneath her letter was Lizandro's and I studied the text, pulling out the numbers within the text. I placed that one beside my left foot.

"Want to hand me some to read?" Larry asked beside me and I shrugged.

"Ask me again in ten minutes," I suggested and read the next one. Though ominous and promising retaliation, there was no mention of money or threat of legal action against the establishment. The next two followed in a similar vein, but the third had mention of a P. O. Box and a cash drop. A neat message printed in the corner with a purple pen said that an agent of justice came by to follow up on the accusation of liquor law violation.

The name at the top was Phil's adult shop, The Curious Courtship. Attached to the page was the item referenced in the text. A small bottle with the image of a tongue "Lick Her Elixir".

"Phil was threatened for lady lube? Why would anyone care?" Larry glanced at the page from where he leaned on the rear quarter panel. "Least of all the Bureau of Alcohol Tobacco and Firearms."

"It's spelled weird in the letter. Phrasing it as though he's selling a liquor called Elixir and not Lick Her Elixir." I handed him the paper and he continued to look at it while I examined the next one. It was Eurich's letter regarding the health inspection. A note on the bottom mentioned the health inspection visit and I compared the numbers of the P. O. Box to Lizandro's letter.

It matched, so I paired them together by my foot.

"I don't think I saw Phil at the office yesterday," Carla had come up behind Larry. I could feel him stiffen at her proximity. They had a past, but it wasn't the traditional 'seen each other naked' level of awkward. This was more hostile than tense. "But the P. O. Boxes match."

"What's going on with you two?" I asked and they shared a look. Larry's irritated, and Carla's confused. So, it was solely a Larry issue, that was interesting but if he had beef I could talk to him about it later.

Preferably naked, post-sex, with coffee and ice cream.

"Forget it. Phil wasn't there? What about his pair of employees?"

"Not that I remember, but one of the council members could have collected it from him personally," she picked up the other letters in my threatened action pile. She studied the addresses and the names of businesses. "Neither of these places are real either."

"The addresses or the business names?" I was reading another letter that had a P.O. Box on it, this one offering to purchase Mason's business.

I hadn't seen Mason either, and the P. O. Box didn't match the other three, but it looked almost identical to the letter he'd pulled out from under the counter that I told him to give to Carla.

Except I'd already found that letter with his greasy fingerprints on it.

"The address is real, but we don't have a porcelain doll store or a rocking chair emporium." I placed the second letter for Mason where the stack Carla held had been. It felt like playing with a loaded deck of cards and you had to sort down the traditional fifty-two to get any real answers. In lieu of dwelling, I quickly flipped through the pile. I removed all pages that had a note of an action taken in regard to the threat and also included a P. O. Box and a request for payment.

I fished out last night's card stock from my pocket and compared the faded lettering to each business. The layout was reminiscent of the actioned threats, but not identical.

Could there be even more?

All the other pages held a threat and no demand for compensation. A recurring theme was the phrase "ordered into compliance". It tickled a memory in my thinking organ, but I couldn't think why. It wasn't an unusual phrase, but "ordered" was a bit military and frankly stretching.

Not only was this America, but it was a small town in America. You couldn't order people here. You could barely order food at a restaurant without adding "if that's OK" at the end. Then apologizing to the server if it was unavailable for picking the thing they didn't have.

My eyes caught on Phil's letter. Adult shop... liquor store... ordered into compliance...

The first breeze of the morning tugged the paper from my hand, and I yelped. Alarmed, Winnie sprung into action, chasing after the paper at full speed. It stopped at the edge of the swimming pool hole, but Winnie could not. With a surprising grace, she swerved and slid sideways into the opening, tail first, to land amid the pile of possible bones.

"Winnie!" I crouched at the edge of the hole, Larry right behind me preparing to slide down to provide emergency medical care. My dog climbed to her feet and wagged her tail, peeing on the nearest bone while happily sniffing the others. "Winnie, no!"

She elected to ignore me and selected one of the pieces. Like a kid with a prize, she loped back up the sheer side wall and flopped down to chew on her pilfered treat.

"I think I'm going to be sick," Daniel muttered from where he appeared beside me, but the object she was chewing distracted me. I got closer, studying the shape and pattern of the internal structure before I sighed and slid into the hole to look at the rest.

"You can't go down there! It's a crime scene!" Daniel hollered, but like most days, I elected to ignore him. At the bottom of the ditch, I moved patches of sand and dust to reveal the pile of bones was a continuous piece of misshapen organic matter, I picked one up and let out another sigh.

"It's just antlers!"

I started up with proof of my findings but misplaced my footing. Off-balance and afraid of dropping the antler, I over-compensated and fell back. My back landed against the ground that was somehow warm and wet, raising red flags as Larry stood above me.

"I landed in Winnie pee, didn't I?" He could only nod as he bit back a laugh.

"I knew I should have stayed in bed."

Once again showered and sporting clean clothes, I let Larry drag me to Suzanne's diner for an early lunch. While I had argued that my apartment had food, he argued that Cheese-Its and Oreos were not food, they were a snack.

He also claimed that coffee didn't count as breakfast, and I nearly broke up with him.

"Sit anywhere you like, kids," Suzanne called out, bright eyed and bushy-tailed, an affront to my pride considering she'd been drunk and kissing my mom last night. "I'll be with you in two shakes of a baby's rattle."

"Baby rattles? Seriously? Have we been reduced to baby rattles as time references?" Instead of answering me, Larry nudged me toward a corner booth where a TV advertising a monster truck rally screamed about *Sunday! Sunday! Sunday!* It was above my head and slightly to the right, my eyes only catching a glimpse of the contents on the screen, but there were no issues hearing the announcer.

I may, however, have issues hearing anything besides freight trains after being in here more than five minutes. Between the TV, the patrons who'd skipped hearing aids and the toddlers upset about the limited crayon colors, starving seemed a better option than staying in here.

"What can I get you kids?" Suzanna asked, pencil in one hand and carbon copy order book in the other.

"Ear plugs," I muttered and Larry poked me in the ribs.

"She'll have eggs scrambled with spinach and cheese with fruit on the side, because she needs nutrients. I will have the same so she doesn't suffer alone. I would like water and she needs more coffee for the safety of society." He finished his order and passed back the menus. Above my head, the breaking news lead in of morse code preceded an announcement.

"Breaking News, the private investigator ordering residents to pay up or ship out has now cost the city its summertime carnival. Stay tuned for more at the top of the hour, with me, Dottie Minerva, on Channel Six News." She spoke clearly and cheerfully, my head whipping around to stare at the on-screen personality. Her hair was still a light brown, but the pink suit was replaced with a billowy sleeveless blouse. The word choice and the inflections mirrored the papers I'd read in the car, and I stood up immediately.

"She sent the fake letters!" I tried to slide out of the booth, but Larry held me in place. "We need to go... something her! She's a..."

While certainly she'd caused an annoying disturbance, nothing in her letters constituted a crime. Creating intrigue to report on it was incredibly rude, but also not a crime. The language of the letters hadn't matched, but the formatting had. Maybe she knew who...

"Get the hell outta here you..." My head whipped again to see Mason, trying to slide his way into the shop. "Misogynistic, geriatric..."

Mason appeared to be oblivious to her words. Suzanne strode over, blocking his path to the register and baked goods on display.

"I told you before, Mason, you aren't welcome here. Not after the last time." Her words caught his attention, but no emotion registered. That's when I noticed his ears. While Mason was distinct in size, his ears poked out in a prominent and borderline comical way.

This man's ears had a seam extending the shell and a plastic apparatus pushing the ears forward.

Quietly, I texted Carla under the table.

Me: *Get to the reporter, I think she wrote the letters. Also, one of the actors is at Suzanne's. We need to talk to him too.*

She sent a thumbs up and an image of the reporter being detained. I stared out the window, looking for the rest of Stella's drama kids, coming up short at the VW bug, white sedan, and a large truck with a trailer. All of them were here.

Me: *Hurry.*

I pressed send just as Suzanna brought the glass pie dish down on the man's head. A crack rang out in the restaurant and the man collapsed into a heap on the floor. The whole room froze, staring at the two-halves of the pie plate Suzanna held and the large man who had a thin line of blood running from his scalp.

Beside his face on the ground was a fake nose and a blob that may have been his chin.

"You literally knocked his face off."

Chapter Nineteen:
Broken News

There are things in life that we, as humans, are not intended to understand.

Why do women's clothing have fake pockets, for example. Who saw a cow nursing her young and said "I'd like a hit off of that", whether or not that man went to whatever that century's version of jail was (because obviously it was a man), and who *really* framed Roger Rabbit? Joining that list now is how a police force of three somehow detained six people in three different vehicles and found pieces of a missing carnival.

"This is weird," I said to no one in particular as I stared at the partitioned off desks in the elementary school buildings. "I always compared school to incarceration and now it really is."

Carla huffed out a breath as we looked in through the rectangle of glass in the second-grade classroom door. The room was frog themed. Students' names were printed on lily pads, declaring the post a "Leaping Leader Board". Another wall held a frog race where the frogs moved forward for every five books a student read, and a Math-phibian board for common solutions to math mistakes.

"Did you pick this room for its resemblance to something you'd find in a serial killer shrine?" I asked, watching the actors shoot furtive glances at the cardboard partitions but remained quiet.

"No. I picked it because Daniel has a thing against frogs and I intended to make him sit in the room with them for hours," she offered a smug smile. We meandered to the neighboring room. The first room had the four male "performers", in the second were the two females and the reporter going by Dottie Minerva.

Instead of frogs, this room was obsessed with Victorian Era charm. Images of men with canes and top hats nodding approvingly at graded papers, a woman with a frock and a croquet mallet talking about getting it into the ten ring.

"Are croquet and darts the same game?" I asked as we watched through the window. While the men had shared glances and clenched jaws, the three women were bored. The two from the carnival crew were attempting to do yoga with their hands cuffed and letting out discontented sighs. The reporter had somehow moved her hands in front of her and was cleaning her fingernails.

"Not that I'm aware of. Maybe I should investigate this school system before letting the step-kids attend," she let out a breath and leaned a shoulder against the wall. "How should we work this?"

"Work what?" I yawned into my iced coffee and sank to sit on the floor with my back against the wall.

"The questionings? I fingerprinted them at the station, but we don't have an interview facility to accommodate this many arrestees. So, we brought them here after processing, with the principal's permission, but we could only have two rooms..." A vein in her temple pulsed. "Honestly, I'd rather not repeat any of the asinine statements that I can only accept as truth."

"I thought the school's principal was arrested for fraud and tax evasion?"

"What?" Carla barked and I shrugged.

"Stella told me that the man after Hoffman was lying about special education needs and paying himself for three positions instead of one and he was sent to federal prison," I summarized, and she relaxed a fraction. "I forgot his name, but you don't look concerned."

"No, I spoke to a Mrs. Meridian who was definitely female and has been as long as she's worked here. She said the other rooms were unavailable due to pest control measures. It looks like the outgoing class of teenagers squirted frosting into every open school window as a prank and now the whole building has ants and small rodents," an eye roll graced her statement. "Do you think the kids would grow up weird if I homeschooled them?"

"They're already weird. But I guess they could get weirder. Are you going in there? Do you need me to call anyone for you?" She looked down at me and raised a brow.

"We are taking them out one at a time for questioning."

"Who is this we? I was just supposed to ID my kidnappers and I have. You have all of them plus a reporter." I slid back up the wall to a standing position. "I'm not a law enforcement officer."

"I deputize you," she countered.

"I didn't agree," I crossed my arms and she raised a perfect eyebrow.

"Look, I have two officers, one in each room. I can't leave interviewees unattended and I need a second set of eyes and ears on these people. If you help me, I will give you two bags of coffee every week until you die and an open tab at Mo's."

"I have an open tab at Mo's, coffee supplied by the town and my GI bill, and no stinkin' badges." I was really going to need more sleep for impressions, because 'stinkin' badges' was more Sylvester the cat level of spit with a whistle like a cartoon gopher.

"Fine. What do you want?" Her eyes were cool and calculating. She knew I had a price, but even I wasn't sure what it was. My opposition wasn't to being deputized; it was to hurting Larry by willingly encouraging participation in dangerous activities.

I had to wait at least a week before I did something stupid again.

"Larry..." I started and she pulled out her phone. She worked the keys and held it in front of her as it rang. In two rings, Larry picked up.

"I need to deputize Cyn, but she won't agree because of you. What do I have to do to get your permission?" She was not in a negotiating mood because when he scoffed, I thought it might actually be possible to kill someone through their own cell phone. "Look, I know I messed up not telling you yesterday, but a bigger mistake would be not allowing her to find answers. She is the best this town has and you need to have some faith in her."

"I do have faith in her. But I also love her and most days it feels like Winnie and I are the only two people trying to keep her out of a shallow grave." I could hear him rubbing his temples over the line. There was a very real possibility that I was ruining this relationship. "Look, she's a grown person. Cyn has more combat training and experience than anyone in your department. She's going to do what she's going to do and I'm not going to hurt her because of it. Just... if anything happens to her, I'm going to make your life a living hell."

Then he hung up.

Carla just stared at her phone.

"You know I don't want you to get hurt, right?" she said, eyes moving from her phone up to me. "I realize I'm demanding of your time and skills, but it's because I respect you and I've seen you work."

"I respect you too. I'm just tired of getting beaten up... and almost blown up... and needing stitches..." I shrugged. "Who should we talk to first?"

"You'll help?"

"Eh, why not? Walking myself home is too much effort and I need to redeem myself by meeting these people with clean pants on."

She smiled.

"Let's start with the men. I anticipate them being useless."

Carla was so accurate in her assessment, that by the time we'd talked to all four only twenty minutes had passed. The pie pan victim had a bandage on his head but was medically cleared for questioning. His inability to form a sentence without cursing... or string together more than four curse words and declaring it a sentence, had us recalling EMS.

He'd also sat down in the child sized chair and broke it, nearly hitting his head again.

His friends said it wasn't a head injury, he was always like that. It was about the only thing they were certain of aside from the names of everyone in the group and how hard it was to erase all traces of a carnival. In addition to Sam, Garth and Hailey, the undisputed leader was Viv, the Filipino man her boyfriend Josh, and the victim of Suzanna's Hulk Smash was Curtis.

None of them were from the area, none of them knew why they were stealing miscellaneous things, but they always left them behind when they moved on from a town. All three times they'd done it, including this one though they made themselves out to be nationally successful criminals.

"What are your thoughts?" Carla asked after we escorted Josh back to the frog room. He had been the most competent and coherent of the group.

"Josh knows more than he's telling. The other three were clearly picked for their inability to distinguish a good idea from a bad idea. Probably also their dedication to arm day," I shrugged and stared at the door he'd exited. "Viv was clearly the leader of this group, but I don't think she's in charge. I think she's just the most bossy and obnoxious, so the others listen to get her to shut up. I'm still supremely concerned about the large quantities of Castor Oil I was exposed to and their delight at making people poop themselves."

"Definitely agree with you on the last, but I think you're extrapolating way farther than reasonable or necessary," Carla responded, and I gave her a *maybe so* face. "You wanna talk to her next then?"

"No... I think it's a waste of time. I want to talk to the reporter."

Carla got up and left the main office.

While she was out, I looked at the pictures on the wall, noting that inside the principal's office was a chronological photo history of leadership past. My principal, Hoffman, then a squat man with pouchy cheeks and the physique of the Stay-puft marshmallow man, and finally a woman who resembled Professor Trelawney.

The timeline gave me an idea and I pulled out my phone before Carla returned.

She got back to the main office four minutes later with Dottie Minerva. The woman half flopped into the office chair we'd wheeled from the administrative office. Her profile on the Channel Six website stated she'd graduated with a degree in broadcast journalism five years before I'd graduated. She supposedly hailed from Strawberry Fields, Kansas, and had been writing news reports since the age of ten.

All of the actors had been hired and handed letters, but none had met Dottie before. They were only advised to make the performance a good one if they wanted to get any airtime. Though more than the six in custody had participated, the rest weren't worth hunting down just yet.

It was not a crime to annoy a Private Investigator and pretend to be an angry business owner.

Sitting in front of her, she was definitely not over thirty. The calm confidence she'd held on-screen had dissipated into a childish petulance that reminded me why I'd never become a teacher.

"What's your name?" I asked and her eyes rolled to me in a manner that made me want holy water.

"Dottie Minerva," her tongue clicked on every hard consonant. "I'm on the news."

"Right, but what's your real name?" I asked, having run a google search on Dottie Minerva's in the field of journalism. The image returns were pretty extensive for a name I'd only heard in cartoons, but none looked anything like the woman in front of me.

I passed the device to Carla.

"Dot-tie," she spoke the syllables slowly as though I was hard of hearing or mentally incapacitated by her beauty.

"Li-ar," I enunciated back at her. "This is Dottie Minerva, graduate of BYU School of Journalism."

Carla handed me back my phone and I turned it around to show the image of a woman in her thirties working as a White House correspondent. She had the dignified professionalism of a woman fighting against men to prove she belonged. Run down, world weary, in most photos she was sporting slacks and a blazer. Her hair pulled back and severe, the real Dottie would cut you before she submitted.

Her only concession to traditional gender stereotypes was a whisper of make-up that probably took hours to look effortless.

"More than one person can have a name, you know."

"Yeah, but I got your resume from Channel Six, and this is who you claimed to be. Down to the ten-year-old field reporting," she shrugged. Carla had switched to working on her phone and was making periodic grunts of acknowledgement. "So... who gave you the ID and what were they asking you for?"

"Nothing. I wanted to be an on-camera reporter. So, I found someone and faked it." She tried to toss her hair over her shoulder and accidentally hit herself in the face with handcuffs. "That's totally assault, I want a lawyer."

"Sure. But what is your name?"

"Lawyer," she spoke the word as though it had four distinct sections. Carla set her phone down and gave her a serpentine smile.

"OK, Bleu," Carla stood, taking her arm. "We'll get you a lawyer."

"What did you say?" She snapped her head toward the police chief.

"Bleu. Your name. Bleu Henders, born on June tenth in 1998 in... now I might say this wrong, but Cornholee, Missouri? You used your own social security number to get the job. I made some calls. We could have helped you if you helped us, but now I got all the answers without you," she smirked as the young woman wilted. I personally would have wilted when my birth certificate said corn-holy.

But hey, some people are more noble than I.

"Fine, I'll tell you whatever you want to know." She flicked an imaginary piece of lint from her shirt. "Whatever, I told my great-aunt it wouldn't work. I can't believe she got blackmailed into sending those letters."

"Your great aunt put you up to this?" Carla asked, eye roll at the ready.

"Yeah, she told me that she needed a reporter to draw attention to an incident, that everyone would be there, I just needed to get a camera on it. She told me what to say. The head guy at the station is out on an *Eat, Pray, Love* quest, so it was pretty easy to just say the network hired me, flash some fake credentials and cleavage, and step in front of the camera."

With a long-suffering sigh, we pretended to take the bait.

"Who's your great-aunt?" I asked, prepared to roll my eyes.

"Maria Dallas. She's the county's Registrar, she can get records from anywhere."

Chapter Twenty:
Water Pistols

"So... your mom just *went* on vacation? Suddenly and without any previous mention of intention?" I asked Jenny, staring at her from across the dispatch desk at Sweet Pea's police complex. She had a wide face, a high ponytail ending in curls, and wore poodle skirts and neck scarves on a daily basis.

Her mom may have been fashion forward, but Jenny was fashion retro and I wondered if they approved of the other... just not enough to ask either of them.

"Yeah, I guess," she took a call and jotted notes on a pad while Carla and I stood awkwardly in the trailer. The floor creaked when we moved and yet standing still was torture while the woman cackled at something being said on the other end of the line.

Sweet Pea's police station wasn't really a station.

The facility had been earmarked for government buildings at the town's founding and then someone dumped horse urine on someone in power. Whoever got pissed, literally and figuratively, decided to build a jail first and stick the miscreant inside. The building was a bunker, partially underground and constructed with concrete and bricks.

Unfortunately, he'd built only the jail and a few decades later actual police services were needed. A series of portable trailers were rented, a fence erected around all except the main entrance trailer, and plans drafted to make the facility permanent.

That was in the nineteen seventies and the city now owned the portable trailers. They were also no longer portable due to structural integrity loss but not actually secure without a foundation beneath them.

"What is this even about?" Jenny demanded, and I realized her call had ended.

"Do you know Bleu?" I asked instead and she lifted a disgusted lip.

"Ugh, yes. Little hoochie stole my crayons and then there was this time Skylar..." I zoned out. None of this was relevant except to prove she probably wasn't working with her mom. A relief since arresting her would mean there would be no one to take phone calls, but also unfortunate since we had no idea where to start looking.

"... then she convinced my mom that the hideous things were amazing and she should start selling on that craft website, Eternity or whatever. But no one bought any and she had debt from materials purchases..."

"Wait!" I interrupted and her eyes went wide. "Your mom had an Etsy business?"

"Obviously. I literally just said that, were you listening to me?"

"No, not really. She started a failed craft business and had debts, then what?" This was the first useful lead Jenny had ever provided. If Maria was in debt, someone could leverage it against her.

"I don't know, this was a couple months ago. My mom got kinda cagey, stuffing papers in a drawer whenever I came over and physically blocking it until I left. Like I'm some sort of Harriet the Spy who would invade anyone's privacy for my own personal entertainment..."

"Which drawers?" Carla interrupted this time, and Jenny shot daggers out of her eyes.

"It was just one drawer. The drawer of the end table at her house. I don't know why she bought it, the claw foot look doesn't work on a white and green..."

"Do you have a key?" I asked and I was fairly certain she would have strangled me if there wasn't a witness sworn to protect and serve. Apparently she'd been needing to vent about this table for a long time and I was stealing her relief.

"Yes, but..." Carla held out her hand and Jenny let out an exasperated breath. She handed over a single silver key and prepared to launch into a speech that was cut off with a phone call. "Whatever."

She dropped the key into Carla's palm and returned to her all-important task of documenting all town gossip and shenanigans. Despite being paid to dispatch calls and assist the town, I was fairly certain that Jenny intended to put the information on Facebook before she actually dispatched the call. We left the trailer housing dispatch and prisoner processing to cross the yard and exit in silence.

Blissful, delightful silence.

"Now what?" I asked, both of us staring at the key.

"I guess I need to go get a warrant from a judge," she considered for a moment and then looked to me. "Do you think she's the perpetrator or just another victim?"

"No idea, but let me know when you have answers," I shrugged and climbed into my Jeep while she angled into her squad card. "I'll be around."

Without any better options, I found myself sitting in the Sharp Investigation's Office with a very large iced coffee reading threatening letters. The ones we felt were legitimate had been taken in by Carla as evidence. The rest of the letters were much more similar than I'd previously realized. They all skirted a line, not quite an accusation but stronger than a warning, that on a second read-through was desperate. Whoever had written these letters was begging the receiver to do the right thing. It read like a coded message, but not one I could decipher.

The door opened and Larry came in with a freshly bathed Winnie.

"You're here," he said, Winnie bounding toward me for affection while checking my clothes for spilled food and snacks. "I thought you'd still be with Carla."

"Nah, she needed to see a judge about a warrant. What's up with you two?" I decided not to wait for sex and ice cream since I had coffee.

He averted his gaze.

"I don't know what you mean," he told Winnie's tail and I growled at him.

"If you lie to me again..."

"OK, I know what you're talking about. It's not really an 'us two' as much as it's a me thing. Since she moved into town... seeing her every day and knowing what I know, it's hard to trust that there isn't an ulterior motive." His hands splayed out on my desk and then folded back in. "It was all fun and games, but every time you get hurt and she pulls you right back into the world, I wonder if she's actually any different than the ruthless government agent we knew at the beginning."

I felt the skin on my neck bristle.

"Do you think she'd hurt Sylvie or Erich?"

"No. Definitely not. I don't think she'd hurt anyone in your family, but I also don't think she would hesitate to push limits and boundaries to get what she wants." His gaze was far off, but he shook his head clear. "Just... be careful. My history with her makes me biased, but I don't think she's as out of the spy life as she claims."

"Careful is my middle name," I spoke around my iced coffee and he let out a sharp bark of laughter.

"Yeah, and Chernobyl was just a minor radiation leak."

"How... How are those two things related?" I wondered as a man entered the office and stared.

"If you got a letter, the police are collecting them to look into."

A bead of sweat appeared at his temple, and he licked his lips. He was wearing carpenter's jeans and a button down of the same material. His mussed hair was thinning, and the work boots he sported were coated in a fine layer of white dust.

"N-no, I didn't get a letter," He shifted from foot to foot and wrung his hands. Small puffs of dust came off his shoes, floated to the ground and settled like a snowy blanket on the industrial patterned rug. "I think I've been swindled."

"Swindled on what?" I asked, eyes on the white dust. If he said cocaine, I was sending him to the Yarnbros for recovery. They knew way more about cocaine than I did and probably weren't related to the chief of police.

"Toilets."

"You... I'm sorry, what?"

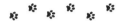

Ten minutes later, I was standing in an apartment complex that was under construction. The concrete floor was in place, wooden frames marking where the walls would appear, and criss crossed wires and pipes filled the space in between.

Shattered in the middle of a small square was a porcelain toilet.

"Huh... are toilets easy to break?" I directed my question to Larry but he could only shrug.

"Not that I know of... at least not until they're installed and subjected to toddler levels of toilet paper." He crouched down to study the fragments. "What did you say this was made of?"

"Porcelain. Toilets are made of porcelain," Contractor Timmy said. When he'd said his name was Timmy and pulled on a hard hat, it had been a real struggle not to offer him a Christmas goose or coal for his fire.

"Smells like plaster," Larry said and Winnie crowded his space to sniff, and promptly sneezed white powder across the room. She flattened her ears and I wondered if it reminded her more of the vet's office where she clearly saw a dog casted or one of my many broken bones.

Plaster was a substance all of us would be familiar with.

"You can't make a toilet with plaster. It would break the second someone sat on it," he scoffed, and Larry joined me in staring at him until the facts clicked. "What? Why are you staring at me?"

Perhaps we were overly optimistic in humanity.

"Where did you get the toilet?" I asked, deciding to move along.

"I have a vendor. The toilet is a TOTO, they are the best money can buy," he spoke pointing to an emblem behind where the seat was mounted.

"OK, what did the manufacturer say? If they cost as much as you're implying, they probably have some sort of exchange... why are you shaking your head at me?"

"I didn't get it from the manufacturer," Timmy looked appalled at my implication. "I'm a contractor, I don't pay retail."

"Wholesale?" Larry asked, leaning against a sink mounted to one of the single hung pieces of drywall. The top edge of the drywall connected to the unit's ceiling and it was already sporting signs of water damage, despite not having rained in this area for at least four weeks.

"Not quite. I know a guy who gets better rates than both wholesalers and the manufacturer but he didn't supply these. His intended shipment fell off a truck."

The sink collapsed under Larry, he fell back and straight through the drywall. There was no insulation and he kept falling until he landed hard on yet another sink that had completely shattered.

"What the hell, man?" Larry asked, rubbing his ass and trying to stand. "Whoever your 'guy' is should be sued, these fixtures are garbage."

Just as he grabbed onto a wooden cross beam, the pressure joint of the water pipe gave, dumping a gallon of water on all of us.

"What... how..." Timmy sputtered, rushing to the edge of the building where I assumed the water main was housed. His foot caught in a puddle, legs sliding out from under him, to slide feet first on his back toward another water pipe.

Timmy bent his legs to brace for impact but miscalculated. Legs spread, he ran crotch first into the pipe, cracking it to shoot water in his face while he screamed in pain at the possibility of needing testicle retrieval surgery. Both he and Larry groaned in pain, Winnie prancing to each man in turn to offer tongue baths of comfort that neither appreciated.

Gingerly, I followed the contractor's path toward the edge of the foundation. On the other side of what had yet to become a wall was a hard plastic housing that flipped open to reveal pipes and a large spigot. A metal rod with a forked foot and a triangle handle leaned beside the box and I shoved it against the metal valve release and turned.

Water thrummed behind me as every pipe shot out more water and began to crack. More water pushed out, widening the openings. Winnie ran back and forth through the waterfall barking while Timmy yelled around a mouthful of water to turn it the other way.

A sharp turn later and the waterworks had stopped. On the ground were two soggy men and a soaked dog danced in the pooling water.

"What the hell, man?" I asked, watching the drywall droop and ooze down itself to join the cracked plaster fixtures. "Who did your plumbing?"

He spat water, face red.

"Some guy in all black offered to do it cheap. He even had his own fixtures, all for less than my usual guy. His stuff is usually recovered from police auctions. This dude, though... I thought it was a little weird his work crew was carnies and a couple clowns, but..." He trailed off at the sight of destruction around him. "So, I did get swindled! You'll help me now, right?"

"Nope," I said, answering the ringing phone. "You pay for cheap work and plumbing, you get cheap work and plumbing. Also, I'm posting online that no one should rent these. No way are they safe or livable."

"Cyn!" My phone was shouting at me... right, I'd answered a call.

"Where are you?" Carla asked through the phone, voice a little louder than I found comfortable.

"Somewhere between Yellow Springs and Dayton where a contractor cut corners and almost drowned." I could hear her pause on the other end. "The whole structure has nearly collapsed; I wouldn't worry about anyone being tricked into living here for a while. Did you get the warrant?"

"Yeah, and you'll never guess what he used as leverage against the good county registrar."

"Sweater fraud? Was she misrepresenting designer brands?" I asked hopefully and I could hear her eyes roll.

"Nope, failure to register and file tax documents for her Etsy business."

My jaw clenched, forcing my teeth to protest.

"That dirty little kettle!"

Chapter Twenty-One: Pot Meet Kettle

D umb luck still counts as luck.

At least, that's what I gleaned from watching Daniel work most days. Despite that, I still couldn't understand the amount of universal cooperation that had him bringing in the very person we needed to talk to. In his words, it was skill.

In my words, it was just dumb luck.

He'd been on his way to the construction site at Carla's urgings and saw a vehicle on the side of the road. It was a gray early 2000s Ford Taurus and the vehicle was completely dark, a technical violation for a vehicle parked on the shoulder after dark. If it was disabled and unoccupied, the vehicle needed to be removed. If it wasn't disabled, it needed to turn on its lights to not get smashed by a deer.

Daniel activated his yellow flashers, pulled up behind it, and shined a spotlight into the car. When something moved, he exited his vehicle to address the safety issues, only to find a woman in a heated frenzy with a carnival worker.

That woman was Maria Dallas, and he collected her and her paramour for questioning. Just as he pulled away, a semi carrying a concrete pipe took a curve too sharp. The tie-downs snapped, and her car was completely crushed on the side of the road... a sight that caused her to lose consciousness, and the Mr. Happy in the man's pants wilted to a Mr. Flaccid.

"Daniel saved someone's life," Carla said, aghast and a bit annoyed. "He found my suspect, detained her, and in doing so saved her life. How? How and why?"

I passed her an iced coffee and we stared at the sobbing woman in the interview trailer. Her disheveled hair matched her red, swollen eyes and splotchy skin. Beside her, the man was perfectly still. He had the panicked look of shock about him that could easily be recreated with recreational sedatives.

"Do you think she'll stop soon?" I asked as another wail cut through the room and I flinched. "Maybe you have a tranquilizer? Or wine?"

Carla shook her head and sucked up half the coffee with a single drink.

"I've got a better idea," she declared, looking at Winnie. The dog had poofed into a cotton ball and smelled... like a wet dog while laying sprawled out beside a small breakroom table. In the closed-up trailer, her smell was stronger than anything that had lingered here before. It felt like wearing a wet fur blanket, but I found the smell comforting. A reminder that I had a best friend.

"Winnie?"

She lifted an ear toward Carla and one eyelid slid open.

"Do you mind?" She gestured toward the interviewees and the dog looked at me.

"Up to you. I'm not going in there."

"I'll give you a treat?"

The bribe had Winnie's attention. Her eyebrows danced on her forehead, eyes shifting between me and my sister-in-law. With a long sigh, she dragged herself off the floor. Ears drooping, she slouched into the interview room and went right for the woman who was mid-sniffle.

Maria screamed.

"Get it out! Get it away from me! Help! Police!" All traces of the waterworks were gone and beside her, the man blinked for a few seconds. His head was bald, though genetically or by choice was indeterminate. The prints we ran on him came back to a Paul, but the identification photo was older than Winnie and I couldn't be certain if it was actually the same person or someone had made less intelligent clones and were a little loosey goosey with the toner.

"It's a dog." He held out his hand to Winnie and she butted her head against his open palm. "The dog is wet. It feels so weird on my hand. The fur is bristly but smooth. Have you ever petted something wet?"

Then he snickered and Maria smacked him on his bald head.

"Hey! We don't hit people." Carla strode in as though she'd just arrived and tossed Winnie a treat. The dog wagged her tail and pranced over to flop next to the chief's chair. I was motioned to the one beside it and we all stared blankly across the scarred and lacquered table. "We need to ask you some questions."

"Can I pet the doggy?" Paul asked and I tilted my head at him. "It's soft... so soft and the textures..."

And with that I knew how he came to find himself hot and heavy in a Ford Taurus.

"When did you drop the E?" He blinked at me and stroked the table. Underneath, he'd kicked off his shoes and was drawing circles with his big toe on the ridged carpet. "Paul?"

"This table feels incredible..." Maria's eyes went wide and I fought back a snicker.

"He's on drugs?" she hissed and Carla watched the older woman carefully for signs of the same.

"Most likely. We haven't checked though and no one was behind the wheel of the car so it's a legal gray area as to if we even can. You want to tell me how you came to be on the side of the road headed toward public indecency while supposedly on vacation?"

She tapped a pen against the palm of her hand. It was such a small movement, but it reminded me of Stella and her tapping. In front of Carla, Maria's leg bounced off nervous energy. Paul... was now rubbing his naked scalp.

"It prickles."

"Hey, Paul? How did you meet Maria?" I asked him, pulling out a velvet textured hair scrunchy and dragging it back and forth in front of him like a cat toy. "Did she give you a letter?"

"Yeah! She came to the carnival and hired all of the performers. Said we'd get more airtime if we were incensed. That we'd be on the news." He took the scrunchie and started stroking it in a disturbing circle. Maria appeared horrified and mildly aroused beside him. "There was a small group of custodians and booth workers who were upset about it and said we would draw unnecessary attention but we were like 'paid gig, heck yeah!' So they were out-voted."

"This small group, did it include Viv and Josh?" Carla asked, pulling out a textured gum wrapper and giving it to the man. If he weren't on drugs, I wonder if this would have worked anyway. He came across as a man who'd collect shiny things and stick them in a shoebox under his bed.

"Yeah! Viv is kinda a witch with a B, but Josh is too lovesick to care. I can't figure out how Hailey and the rest got looped in. Well, besides Curtis. He'll do literally anything. I once convinced him to drink a two-gallon tub of ranch dressing for a dollar. He puked everywhere, it was so sick."

I laughed but he didn't seem to register his own pun. Maria had gone a little green at the edges as he spoke, playing with the scrunchie and the wrapper alternately.

"I almost made love to him," she choked and I tilted my head.

"An encounter in a car with a virtual stranger isn't 'making love'," I hooked air quotes around the words. "It's just fu-"

"Don't be vulgar, Cynthia," she scolded me, even as the flush in her cheeks returned, watching his fingers on the scrunchie. My eyes bounced between the two and I understood how she came to be in the throes of passion with a less than full capacity male. His fingers were somewhat skilled. "Yes, I organized and provided additional actors to stage a scene outside your office. It was to draw attention to the business so you couldn't get away with tax and registration evasion. Too many members of your family are skirting the law."

Her pointed look at Carla cost me my composure.

"Like you skirted the law with your Etsy business, and someone blackmailed you into helping them? That's why you made a bunch of letters and distributed them, falsified your great niece's records and recruited her to steal the identity of a reporter?" Carla squeezed my leg under the table, and I sucked in a breath. "Let's start over and try honesty."

Her hackles rose, and I watched her mouth work like a hooked fish. It was interesting to see the tables turned on someone so full of their own benevolence that they believed themselves untouchable.

"No, you don't get to be offended, Maria. You were literally engaged in public fornication at the time you were discovered on the side of the road. We have the letters, your niece's statement, and Paul here. Eat crow and speak up."

"What Cyn meant to say," Carla interrupted with a pointed look in my direction. I crossed my arms and slouched. Nothing irked me more than showing compassion and finesse to self-indulgent harpies. "Is that we'd like to know when you became aware of the tax stipulations and how you came to be leveraged to this task?"

The woman deflated, but I still wanted to hit her so I sat on my hands.

"I didn't know when I signed up to make my shop that if I didn't let the company handle the tax portion I would be responsible for reporting and submitting payment to both the local and federal legislation. When I got the first letter a few months ago, I dismissed it as spam. When the second letter came, referencing the need for assistance in exchange for their silence, I looked it up," she spoke to her hands clasped on the table.

"It turns out whoever sent the letter was correct. I was a government employee out of compliance with business legislation. When the third letter came with the instruction that I insert a reporter and collect some performers, I contacted my niece. She's big on that app with the dance trends and was thrilled to be on broadcast television. With access to local records, I knew how to get everything I needed to get her the job and set up her success. She actually did surprisingly well considering she's an insufferable twat."

Carla sucked in a breath and I wondered why Bleu hadn't been as candid about her aunt.

Was it possible she was a better person?

"Right..." The chief rubbed her temples and we paused to watch Paul play with the wood paneling on the wall. He had his finger dragging along the seam between two boards when he switched to using his tongue.

"Paul! Enough!" I commanded the same way I did Winnie and he dropped back into his chair.

"Geez, you don't need to bark orders," he grumbled and Carla gave me a curious look that I returned with understanding.

"When did your blackmailer speak to you?" Carla asked and I marveled at the open-ended question that was also incriminating. "Was it in person or over the phone?"

"Phone," she plucked lint from her sweater. "He called because letters took too long. He asked me for an address where no businesses were registered and I pulled Cyn's address. When it came out there was a business there, he told me to fix it so the owner would seem the obvious choice."

"So, he didn't give you the word 'ordered'? You came up with it as a military reference on your own after learning I worked in the building?" I asked and she blinked at me.

"What? No No. I didn't write the letters. A courier delivered them. My solution was to use the same leverage he had against me. Only it backfired when you actually followed through on all of that tedious paperwork and then he said he had a way to link it back to you if I just held up my end of the deal and got the news coverage. I didn't know until Bleu's report that you had been in the Army."

"You were in the Army? That's so weird! Viv's brother was in the Army. I wonder if you met him! It was a little weird that such a short pudgy dude managed to meet the fitness requirements, but he was always watching Army movies and going on and on about the good ol' days, so he must have." He was back to making light reflect off the green gum wrapper. "He became a school dude after he left. Like, around here. How weird is that?"

"What's her brother's name?" Carla asked, pulling up a file on her phone. "Can you confirm Viv's last name?"

"I don't know his name, but I think it was Cummins." He let out a high-pitched giggle. "Maybe that's why Josh was into her. Viv Cummins, getting the juices flowing."

He tried to get a high five from one of the women seated at the table, but we all declined so he slapped his own hand. He made it look like a jumping jack without the jumping or jacking part.

"Do you..." I started, but the trailer window shattered as water rushed in through the shattered glass. The pressure ripped off the wood paneling and flipped the interview table. Grabbing the druggie and Winnie's collar, I followed Carla out. She'd started calling for reinforcements and assistance, but the geyser ceased, and an engine gunned it just as we rounded the building. All we saw was a water cannon truck taking a left turn on two wheels, before the taillights faded into the darkness.

Chapter Twenty-Two: Wash and Repeat

"What the hell was that?" Carla was shouting into her radio, Maria angrily screaming about her ruined designer something or other. My eyes went to Paul, staring at his saucer eyes and wondering if there was some interaction between E and high-pressured water that no one had studied before.

"That was so sick!" He leapt into the air like the end of Breakfast club and whooped. Carla turned on him but came up short at the soggy Maria. She was pulling a full-on Karen, demanding reparations and repayment for the water damaged clothing.

"Will you shut up? That was an attack. We were just attacked. Nobody cares about your clothes, Maria!" Her patience was gone, eyes red and squinting. The normally perfect bun on top of her head was wilting, and with it the scent of hair products dripping down her face. I pulled off my T-shirt and handed it to Carla. Nothing burned like sweaty hairspray in the eyes and her clothing was impossible to remove quickly, least of all when wet.

"Thanks," she muttered, getting the hair products out of her eyes. Jenny poked her head out of her trailer, snapped a few quick pictures, and disappeared back inside like a groundhog.

"You can't tell me to shut up, my tax dollars pay your salary!"

"I can't believe they got her working!" Paul hollered.

"If that had been an armed attack with a gun, you and your clothes would be dead, so can it!"

Daniel and Barney's lights illuminated the police complex in eerie reds and blues. Sirens on full wail with stutter stops echoed into the night. Every inch of rubber on pavement seemed magnified as the night settled in, both police cars rounding the corner, engines straining to catch the long since departed...

"Got who working?" I asked, registering bits of the noise.

"Britina the Water Truck! Man, she's been in repair mode since forever. I heard back when there was a rodeo component, the clowns would use her like a giant seltzer bottle. But then they downsized when the new dude bought the carnival." He clapped his hands and then stopped, mesmerized at the feel of his own flesh and slid his palms back and forth.

"Could we have been shot to death? At the police station? I want to speak to the mayor and my congressman..."

"You would have been fine!" Carla shouted back at the hysterical criminal. Paul continued to play with his hands, speaking irreverently about water trucks and the joys of being a rodeo clown. The noise was too much, and I gestured to my soaking wet canine. While everyone was arguing, we left without my shirt.

A silence swallowed us as we drove back toward town. After the rushing water, yelling and sirens, even the night seemed to be taking a break from making noise. No crickets chirped, the stale night air failed to make even the grass whisper as we transitioned from the emptiness of the farmland to the quiet township.

Main Street was dark. Even the fairy lights had been turned off for the night, casting shadows where normally you could see for miles. When I first got back, I'd run in the middle of the night to avoid questions and wandering eyes, but it had been a while since we'd been out after sundown.

"Have all the lights ever been off before, girl?" I asked Winnie, and she responded with a loud snore as I cruised slowly to an intersection with a four way stop. I searched all directions, nothing looked out of place, but I felt something. The still night held a nervous energy, movement in the darkness just beyond the reaches of my headlights.

My shoes squished on the brake, water seeping between my toes to splash onto an already waterlogged floor mat. The sensation was gross and sent another wave of discomfort through my body as I stared into the darkness and willed it to show me what was hiding. A second passed, my eyes straining to adjust to the low levels of light. Another second passed and a person ran full into the headlights of my Jeep, dressed in all black and wearing gloves.

"Hey!" I called out, shutting off the truck and climbing out, Winnie behind me. The figure had frozen for hardly a moment, but a flash of bright blue eyes met mine and took off into the dark. My dog gave chase, but the whole night was suddenly alive with black clad figures, moving in the impenetrable dark. My hand flew out and connected with a forearm. I gripped tight, dodging a fist flung out toward my head, as I dragged the form toward the headlights of the truck. A second figure charged, coming up short at a well placed foot, sending him sliding into home at the headlights of my car.

Except it was a her, and I recognized her face even as I registered her gaze placed at chest level.

"Carnival workers?" I asked, checking the face of the person in my grasp. He was also staring at my lack of shirt and I nearly shouted about the legitimate nature of bras as shirts... even if it did have sharks on it.

"Let me go!" he shouted and turned into dead weight to counter my grip.

"Not until you tell me what's going on!" I insisted and he shook his head.

"I don't know!" He hissed as more figures danced on the periphery. "They packed up the carnival early, hired us to protest at a random office and now he wants us to be a silent flash mob. He even cut the lights. Now let me go!"

He twisted his arm and this time I released it. Winnie returned with the glove and beanie hat of the blue-eyed worker moving through the night. Long blonde hairs were left inside and I pictured Hailey.

Except she wouldn't be out, would she? We scurried back to the Jeep, grasping for my phone that had been on the front seat while reaching for my keys.

They were both gone.

I checked my wet pockets, the floorboard... There was no light, no phone and no keys. Winnie and I were sitting ducks in a motionless car and against all rational thought, I ran. The figures moving from the dark scattered, throwing themselves out of the way as I high tailed it across town.

We turned once, stopping at the back-alley entrance to my office. I pulled the spare key from Winnie's collar and shoved through the fire door into my office. On my desk was an old landline that Mrs. Margot had required I keep for historical purposes. I picked it up and called the only number I knew by heart.

"Larry! All the lights are out in town!" I was whispering, despite being safely locked into my own building. I reached for light switches, flicking them up and down, but nothing happened.

"It's a planned outage. There was a post on the Sweet Pea page," he answered sleepily. "Where are you? Do you need me to help you get dry? I think some of the dust was cement, my pants stand up on their own now..."

"Larry, there are people moving in the night. They stole my keys and my cellphone. It's all the carnies, but I can't call Carla. I need to tell Carla!" My voice had reached a pitch that Winnie responded to with discomfort.

"OK, so call Carla," he yawned, and the call ended before I could ask for the number. Before I could call back, the phone rang in my hand, and I answered the call.

"Thank you! I need the num-"

"Cynthia Sharp, the second most annoying woman in this town," a male voice filled the line and I had an urge to reach through the line and strangle him. "You ruined my fun, so I'm making a new game. One that comes with the added benefit of revenge and suffering. The rules are simple, I've taken something of yours. The only way to get it back is to move through the shadow forest, deliver the bounty and surrender the light!"

A silence stretched through the line as I fought down a hysterical giggle.

"I'm sorry, what?"

He heaved a sigh at me, a trickle of fear snaking up my back. It wasn't a joke?

"I hate repeating myself, so listen closely. Every cent owed to me will be collected. Find the total, secure it, and follow the clues to delivery. If you don't deliver by sunrise, I take something from you and you'll never get it back," he laughed, and I scrunched my eyes together.

"What did you take? My phone and keys, those are replaceable. If you want me to play..."

A small voice took over for the man on the line, "Cyn?"

"Stella?" I asked, but the man was back.

"Tick tock, Cynthia. Tick tock, we'll be watching."

The line went dead, and a face pressed against the glass before a fist slammed beside it. A small scream slipped through my lips and then we were alone.

Chapter Twenty-Three: Yield to Night

Three terse phone calls later, I stepped out into the darkness. The consensus was that whoever had Stella was definitely nuts, but no one could say for certain why she would be targeted. Of all the people who had collected me over the years, she was the most recent and least well known in my orbit.

He'd mentioned revenge in his first iteration. Did I know him? The name Cummins... Did I know him?

My wet clothes had been replaced with dry, a new shirt firmly in place, my backpack filled with supplies, and Winnie... looked like a drowned rat at bedtime. But she had a look of determination that poked holes in the rising fear that sat in my chest.

If I had her, I could do this. Nothing was impossible with a Winnie dog by my side.

Pinned to the front door of my office was the first clue, a few lines on a three by five card in a loopy handwriting that was equal parts dramatic and childish.

A settlement fines, the sum of each letter ten times.

Pinning to each an alpha value.

Then Fetch.

I stared at the words and considered screaming. He'd chosen to place someone's life in jeopardy and make a Dr. Seuss rhyme to save her? What sort of person...

There was no need to finish the thought. I knew what sort of person, and with a deep exhale, I read the note again and worked through the rhymes.

The man wanted me to use alpha numeric values to calculate the money he felt owed to him, and multiply it by ten. Since most of the letters were in the first half of the alphabet, that would make the majority of numbers less than thirteen. Just the number of letters in "A Settlement Fines" times ten was $1600 and the ability to get that, let alone the total he had indirectly quoted, was absurd.

The paper shook in my hand. Most of the letters lived in the first half of the alphabet, but I couldn't concentrate, couldn't count.

It was too much money.

Add in that it was the middle of the night and the town had no power, and the whole thing would have been hopeless. Within walking distance of my building were four ATMs, and the total drastically exceeded the withdrawal limit of each one individually. I took off at a brisk jog toward the closest, knowing that I could do more with the sum of the clues than I could by just collapsing in tears.

Not that I considered that an option.

Around me, the shadowy figures moved. It was disorienting, and disturbing, but they made no move to stop or redirect me. Winnie kept pace beside me and we ate up the distance, reaching the darkened machine within a few minutes.

Breathless, shaking, and a little lost.

Without power, the automated teller was useless. A laugh bubbled over and pierced the night, hysteria that the criminal mastermind behind this quest clearly misunderstood the meaning of a power outage, and the automated portion of the acronym ATM required power. Shaking and hoping the contents of my backpack would save her, I plucked off the note.

All the world will see the show...

It was incomplete and I quickly assessed I was supposed to visit every cash machine in the area. Focusing on my breath, I pushed myself to run to the next closest ATM while my brain tried to figure out the ending at the beginning. We were against the clock and there was no shortcut, not if I wanted to keep Stella safe. Every footfall reminded me that I wasn't alone in the dark, the figures watching. A sudden flash or blast of sound was meant to disorient me, my brain pulling off the note with the next crash of metal trash cans.

Merely players when the curtains close.

The third ATM was nearly visible from this one, and a new energy joined the night. A thrill of excitement with an edge of terror. Winnie and I could do this, the clues rhymed, but they weren't obtuse. Shows? Players? It niggled at something in my memory, but I pushed on.

We had to make it.

Breathy, I pulled off the third note at the next ATM. A bead of sweat dripped from my brow to smear one of the words.

The stage alone

is just

a plank.

My brain stuttered at the word plank. Was this a pirate reference?

Was this a play on the quote "All the world's a stage, the men and women merely players"? Is this a performance? What did it mean for Stella that he kept insisting the curtains would close? That he referenced a plank of wood, was he intending to try and drown us... again? Was he hoping to throw me off or was it just an elaborate ruse to make sure I visited all the machines?

Our town didn't even have a stage, did it?

I shrugged off the uncertainty and ran to the fourth machine. My brain went into overdrive with mental lists to determine if there were any more in this town. To determine if he could see me and knew there would be no money. He'd taken my car, indirectly, so everything had to be reachable by foot. Without my phone, he would have to make sure the locations were ones I would know.

Unless he didn't think it through.

Unless he wanted revenge more than money.

We got to the fourth ATM, this one lit up by headlights, the low rumble of an engine filling the otherwise silent night.

Until all the actors assemble, there is no show.

To men the women must go.

Misogynistic and creepy, I felt my stomach roll over.

If he touched her...

If all this was a clever way to distract me while he... or worse. My brain couldn't even form the words.

Stay the course or try and find the end earlier? The question was a nonstarter. Aside from money and poor theatre references,

I didn't know enough to skip to the end. The name, theatre, it all niggled, but I couldn't find the thread.

The rumbling engine drew me closer, shadowy figures seeming to direct me toward the light with their movement. Cautiously, I inched forward, raising a palm to shield my eyes as I stepped around to the driver's side door.

It was my Jeep. No worse for the wear, a pool of water on the floorboard exactly as I'd left it. Keys were in the ignition, another clue taped to the center of the steering wheel. My pulse quickened, the words a direct punch to my memory and a reminder of what could go wrong in the dark of night.

You have to pay your dues, but you can't

play where

you live.

Then where would you work?

I played where I work.

Now we'll play chicken farmer,

and work where you played.

Place your bets to see who's left standing.

When everything around you burns.

Winnie leapt into the back seat and licked my cheek. I touched the spot to find warm salty tears mingling with the sweat that dripped down my face. It was too soon to be threatened with fire again, too soon to be threatened at all, but... Stella.

"We can't mess this up Winnie," I whispered, picturing Stella's face sitting on the bench. "Her light can't go out. It's too soon."

My hand jerked the truck into gear and on instinct, I pointed it away from town. There was only one place I had ever played chicken farmer, watching everything go up in flames, and it would seem he expected me to go back.

I was willing to bet on it.

Chapter Twenty-Four: Hollowed Out Memories

D espite the darkness, I could still make out where Roger's trailer had once been. Instead of a four-walled structure, pieces remained like ancient ruins. Jutting into the darkness in shapeless lumps, it cast shadows upon the existing shadows until all there was couldn't be distinguished from the darkness it cast and the darkness around it.

All the life and energy had been sucked completely out of the space.

"It's like he still lives here," I breathed to Winnie.

His house had been surrounded by a wooden fence in the front, and chain link with dark green plastic slats around the rest. In my mind, they had both been knocked down, but in reality, they had stayed upright with only a few gaps where the wood had burned. We got out of the Jeep and peered through one of the larger gaps.

"See if you can find Stella," I whispered, holding out the wet wipes I'd moved to my pocket. She sniffed the pouch, then me and seemed to realize who she was looking for.

On the other side was a treasure trove of half-destroyed automotive and carpentry pieces. The once shabby chicken coop now sagging into the category of chicken slums, a single rooster clawing at the dirt.

"Have you come to place your bets?" I leapt out of my skin. A man in bright white face paint and intentionally drab tuxedo whisked a top hat from his head, bowing before extending it to accept payment. "The only way to win is to pay, kind madam."

"Win what?" I asked, catching sight of Winnie out of the corner of my eye. She was sniffing a grid pattern, back and forth across the yard. Her tail at half-mast, indicating she didn't smell anything yet.

A decent sign she wouldn't smell anything at all, Stella wasn't here.

Lazy as she was, Winnie was too good to not have found her already. It had been a ruse and we were losing time. I glared at the ringmaster.

"What was taken from you? Have you brought the fine for stolen time?" His rhyme scheme made my eye twitch. Every sentence a gut punch to my anxiety, the urge to cause him pain was starting to overpower the need to find Stella and lock her in a tower away from the chaos that surrounded me.

"Yeah," I pulled out a small, zippered pouch and dropped it into his hat. From the ruffled sleeve of his top, he flourished another paper.

"While we count, you must beware. Lying will end the game before you get there." He smirked, a laughing face that stung the corners of my cheeks and without warning, I slammed my fist into his face. White grease paint smeared my knuckles and Winnie raced back at the sound.

"You can't play with people's lives!" My voice carried in the night and I watched the energy drain from his face.

"Lives? What lives?" He started to panic on the ground. "I was told this was an elaborate scavenger hunt. Like the thefts Viv's crew did, just a show and we always leave the goods behind. Here, look!"

He handed me his phone and I looked at the instructions included in an email attachment. The lines were written out, his instruction was to count the bags contents and send confirmation. Once he'd done that, they were to meet back at the carnival site and split the fee.

"Where is the carnival site? I thought they took it down," I didn't bother to return his phone. Winnie head butted his form until something clattered out of his pocket and I took custody of his keys as well.

"They took it down, but they parked it at the school. There's an outdoor arena with plenty of space to park the rigs. He said if all goes well, we'd set up in a new town tomorrow."

"Who is *he*?" I asked, sparing a glance at the note. The school had a stage... I'd completely forgotten. A stage and something else, someone else... Was Stella on-stage at the school?

YOU'VE BOUGHT YOUR TICKET TO SEE THE SHOW.

HURRY NOW, THE CURTAINS CLOSE.

"Fred Cummins," he stammered when I pulled out a gun from the waistband of my pants. I checked that it was loaded and took a single shot at the tires of his pea-green minivan.

My aim was true, as usual, and the air leaked out in a quiet hiss while I dumped his keys back into his hand.

"Who is Fred Cummins?" I asked, tucking the gun back into place and working his cellphone to send a message before dropping that at his feet as well.

"He owns the carnival. Said he used to work here before that little brat got him fired."

The pouchy cheek man stood center stage at the theatre when I walked in, looking like a marshmallow with legs. He was holding a rifle, weight too much for him, balanced on one forearm with his finger massaging the trigger.

Beside him, Stella was taped to a chair, mouth covered and eyes wide.

"Well, well, that was quicker than I expected."

Cold steel brushed my arm before shoving hard into my kidneys and I doubled over in pain while Penny relieved me of my backpack.

"How nice of you to join us," she tossed it onto a theatre seat four rows up. "Won't you join the show?"

The request was accentuated by another gun barrel to the ribs, and I held in a scream.

"What the hell, Penny?" I hissed through clenched teeth.

"Oh, please, no. Call me Kimberly Hester, District Chancellor." Before I could ask a follow-up question, the woman pushed me forward and down the sloping house toward the stage. "My greatest performance to date and you're here for the finale. How delightful."

"I should have known no one named Penny Plootz would actually exist," I muttered as she shoved me to move again. "How did you steal hundreds of thousands of dollars from yourself?"

"Shut up and keep walking, Cynthia."

My brain worked overtime. Stella had ended Cummins's career as a principal, the revenge he'd mentioned was against her. It was where I'd heard the name when Paul brought it up but why would the school district help him lie?

"Hard to believe you're related to Viv," I told the pasty white dough man. "She's... and then there's you."

"Half-sister," he snorted. "The better half, I'd say."

"Not from what I can see, you racist..."

Penny/Kimberly brought the butt of her gun down on my face. The strike sent my head snapping to the side, eyes watering and a pop from the base of my skull.

Everything went fuzzy as she half-dragged me up the steps and into the lights of the stage.

"No talking, Cynthia. I heard enough from and about you these past two decades. I'm not listening to it anymore." She shoved me into a wooden chair and grabbed the gray tape to bind me to it beside Stella. "The pair of you cost me thousands. When the dough boy here failed to secure the funds from little Stella's fake project, I never dreamed she'd just hand me someone else's money. Never dreamed the cops and the company she works at would be so quick to help me without any proof of identity. That Penny Plootz character must be either very rich and several hundred thousand is nothing, or she is very poorly regarded in her community."

I blinked at her in confusion as tape covered my mouth.

"Oh yes, Penny Plootz is real, and it was her money that was used to purchase the home. Freddy here was supposed to con some college kid into setting up a phony listing as part of a group project and sell a fake house to someone with more money than sense. Then he had to add his own agenda... Who brings the crime back to an area they have a connection to? Then bring the carnival here to commit petty fraud and extortion..." She rolled her eyes and studied the gun in her hand. "It was hardly a problem when he went around taking cash from easily duped fools, but he brought it back into my house. I told him to stay the hell out of Sweet Pea... Guess serving time didn't teach him anything and it's up to me."

She fired two shots into his chest, and I heard Stella scream through her tape as the warm red blood splattered us both and his lifeless form fell heavily into her lap. Her legs shoved back until he fell onto the floor with a heavy thud and she screamed again as her hands clawed to get free of the chair.

"Oh, don't act like you wouldn't have done it," she muttered, pulling a slim metal case from her pocket. Flicking open the mirror, she used the back of my shirt to wipe off what little blood had landed on her. "Now that I have the money, I don't need to play school chancellor or hire a traveling circus to distract the town while we extort their citizens. Honestly, those fraud letters were strangely lucrative considering the dough pile that thought of them. I had no idea this was what he'd started when he got out, but I was willing to take over when I was done with him. Now I don't have to work nearly as hard."

My hand inched toward the gun in my waistband, even as I knew it would be impossible to get in a shot without hitting myself. Mentally, I went back to college anatomy. There were non-critical body parts in my abdomen, I just needed to avoid anything that would be hard to sew up... like my spine.

The gun was right behind my love handles and the only way to shoot was through them with my thumb depressing the trigger. It slipped free and I tried to concentrate on lining up the shot, deciding angling out was safer than angling in, but I couldn't miss.

There would only be one shot to get this right.

I took a deep breath, swallowing air and picturing Stella's fingers on Winnie's ears. My heart tried to match the even cadence she tapped in, the quiet place in my mind where aim was true and pain was temporary. One, two...

A movement in the shadow caught my eye. The stage lights were bright, the need for dramatic effect clear, but I could still see something moving along the wall. On the other side of the stage, another movement, this time from the hallway to the make-up rooms. Additional movement at the rear of the house and then it felt as though the entire room were alive and swarming with ants.

I held my breath, refusing to shoot if there was a chance I could hit someone else.

Someone innocent.

The house lights came up, light flooding every inch of the theatre and startling Kimberly. She took a step back and I pushed up to my feet, still attached to the chair, and tackled her into the orchestra pit. A sickening crack echoed around the theatre, the ants coming into focus as the performers in all black from the streets of Sweet Pea. Bringing up the rear with Carla and Daniel was the clown in coat tails from Roger's farm, all three lead by Winnie who'd been placed outside as a beacon.

Daniel checked on the gun woman while Carla released Stella and me from our bindings. With a thick sniff, Stella collapsed into my lap and cried.

"I'm sorry. I'm so sorry," she gasped into my shirt and I held her close. "I should have figured out who my partner was sooner.

271

Should have looked into the School District more... shouldn't have trusted a stranger who wanted to meet at the theatre..."

"Shhh... you shouldn't have done anything but stay safe," I whispered back, and joined her in crying while hundreds of performers watched.

Chapter
Twenty-Five:
Internalization

"**S**eriously, who wanted this?" I asked Stella, the sounds and lights nearly too much in the blinding light of day.

All around, children ran and screamed amid the tents and games. The reconstructed carnival was twice the size it had been, the actors pulling out all the stops with the lofty payment the council presented in gratitude for services rendered and an impressive endowment from Mrs. Zuber to the new owner.

Viv, it turned out, had been feeding the authorities info on her brother, but they weren't too interested until he turned up dead. Now she had a carnival and a drunken financier to make it bigger than ever.

Also replacing my phone as an apology for almost getting me killed.

The town council had deeper pockets than even I was aware, because my coffee stores were fully restocked, and the school's theatre cleaned of blood, gore and corpses. There was also another endowment made to provide the theatre upgrades and replace the window of the craft bar.

Kimberly hadn't made it and no family had come forward to claim her body.

"Me... and you. Now that there's no castor oil in the food, do you want a Cheesenado?" Winnie perked her ears up and let out a soft bark of approval. Apparently, her aversion the night we attended hadn't been to the food, it had been to the toxic levels of laxative she smelled in it.

Smelled and didn't tell me about, the rat.

Stella tossed her a dog cookie from my cargo pocket.

"Definitely do not," I declared, phantom stomach pains shooting through me at the smell. "Maybe not ever. But your date's here. Are you guys going to hold hands and lick tonsils?"

My elbow banged against her in a not-so-subtle gesture that made James laugh as he approached.

"Now kids," I began as Larry walked up behind me and wrapped his arms around my waist. "Be careful with the hand holding, I heard a rumor that that's how Mormons make babies. Remember what I said about kissing and the sharing of fluids and you'll turn into a pumpkin at midnight."

"What did she say about fluids?" Larry asked, a sly smile on his face.

"To do it responsibly," Stella answered and took a cautious look at James. "Twenty nine percent of the adult population has kissed between two and ten people. When have you most recently engaged in a salivary exchange and did you feel any ill effects? My experience is several years old, chaste, and I had no reaction."

I felt Larry flinch, James just smiled wider.

"I haven't in... a year maybe. And no ill effects. What about your experience? Did you enjoy it?" They were sharing a look that made me think we should leave them alone, but my long-dormant and suspected non-existent maternal instinct insisted I chaperone to hide his dead body that would be made by me if he hurt her.

Winnie shoved her head into his crotch and he released an oof of pain that satisfied my need to issue threats. After nearly losing Stella a week ago, I was well aware that she was my people. Winnie had accepted her into her herd of Sheeple and the rest of us had been collected alongside her.

Maybe the real glue of my life's relationships was Winnie.

"I have never exchanged saliva," Stella admitted, ears tinged red even as her voice held only factual intonations. "I'm not sure I will enjoy it, but I'm willing to try. Is that acceptable?"

"Do you want to try?" He asked, gripping her bicep and then sliding his hand down into hers. It was as though the warning had made the contact acceptable.

"Do you find it enjoyable?" Her face was moving toward his and I decided this was my cue to depart.

No one wanted an audience for their first kiss in which saliva would be exchanged.

"Be safe you two!" I called over my shoulder. Before making it four steps, a form slammed into my back and I turned around to hug Stella back.

"You'll be at therapy Friday?" She asked and I nodded confirmation. "And I'll see you tomorrow to start my internship?"

"You don't have to jump in right away. It's technically slave labor since I can't pay you," I said into her hair. "Carla's offer was better than mine and you turned her down."

"I don't need money... I just want to feel safe," she whispered and I nodded my head. "And Carla comes with Daniel and the man who may or may not be related to Dudley Dursley. Do you think his mother believed naming him Barney Fife would keep his size proportions in check?"

"I have no idea, but I'll teach you everything I know," I spoke into her hair and tried to choke back a laugh that threatened to turn into crying. "But for now, you should go learn what James knows and if you need help with that, ask my mom. She's the family expert and has... diagrams."

Stella went pale as the air shifted around me.

"Is she right behind me?" I asked, straightening up. Stella nodded. "Run away while you can."

"Cynthia!" My mom extended her arm and the young woman hugged her. "Stop telling people to run away from me! I am not some sort of predator. She is right about my knowledge though, dears. When you're ready to take that next step, I'm a bottomless resource and I have plenty of materials for practical and experimental intercourse. What is your skill level, son?"

James went pink and Stella looked on the verge of a nervous breakdown.

I mouthed *Told you to run*, just before my mom put an arm around each of them. She escorted them a few steps before pausing to look me over with a satisfied nod.

"What? I'm not bloody!" I protested and saw something dark cross her eyes.

"We still need to talk. Don't think I've forgotten." Her message sent, the two college students were directed toward one of the merchandise booths where a smiling Phil sat.

"Oh man... she's going to need a lot more therapy," I muttered and Larry gave me a gentle kiss.

"Do you think she'll need more or less than you after you finally have that conversation with your mom?" he whispered, lips caressing my ear. "Because I think if I try hard enough, I can get you to scream yourself deaf to miss most of it. You do owe me the privilege of convincing my neighbors I'm a killer."

"How hard we talking?" I asked, and he pressed into me with a nip on my ear. "Oh, that's pretty hard. Probably we don't need anything from Phil's booth."

"Wanna head home and soften it up?" He purred and I smiled.

"Yes, definitely. Can I have coffee?"

"Before, during and after, babe. I'm full-service and have everything you need," his words warmed all my good spots and I briefly forgot we were in public as I groped behind me. Larry laughed and stepped away. "Ah ah, good girls have patience."

Winnie let out a soft bark and I smiled down at her.

"Some things are worth waiting for... just not too long. My attention span isn't that long."

"You know what's long?" Larry gave a very male eye waggle and I looked him over.

"Show me?"

Sneak Peek of Book 6: Growling at the Gentry

Chapter One: Furry Situation

"For the love of dog, STOP!" I shouted, pumping my legs faster.

The olive drab cotton shirt I was wearing was stained with more condiments than even I could name, and the smears over my sweat outlined boobs smelled alarmingly like manure.

Though that could have been my pants... or my shoes.

Possibly the house itself.

Sweat dripped down my face, stinging my eyes but I didn't dare wipe it off or blink. If I blinked, I'd lose the little gremlin. If I wiped my face off, whatever was on my sleeve would end up on my face. Between days at the farm and nights spent babysitting, my entire world was a foul-smelling rollercoaster of physical endurance and psychological warfare.

"I'm serious!" I shouted again, but my niece cackled as she ran through the house. We'd started in the kitchen, cut through the dining room, and she had just thwarted my plan of corralling her in the downstairs bathroom. The little demon was now charging toward the living room and I couldn't fathom what would happen if she got away with her stolen goods.

Clutched in her hand was a bright orange square of cheese, and behind her was Winnie.

Sgt. Winnifred Pupperson, Army canine retired, was a lactose intolerant German shepherd-Malinois mix. Also known as Winnie, her love of cheese was rivaled only by my love of breathing without noxious gas asphyxiation. My niece, Sylvia... was a jerk who liked to steal my fresh air.

For an eight-year-old, she had a well-developed sense of violence and warfare. In the 1990s, they would have blamed video games or rock music by the likes of Marilyn Manson. In the early 2000's, they'd have blamed the parents and the decline of the nuclear family. As the century progressed though, it was more likely the result of either over-exposure to influencers on the Internet or a genetic predisposition to unleash chaos upon the world.

Considering my military career of destruction, it was probably genetics.

Coupled with my parents' penchant for public fornication and bondage, it could have come from either side of our family tree; and while my brother Seth's deceased wife was a saint, none of her personality traits were passed on to Sylvia.

The little clone of her mom served as a reminder that looks are often misleading.

"If you don't stuff that cheese in your mouth and sit down right now..." I started, but my toe caught on an end table. On that table was a hideous lamp shaped like an elephant that began to topple. My hand shot out to grab it and connected with a frog figurine that went flying toward the wall. My hand grasped for the lamp, pulled on the cord and it tangled around my feet, sending all size sixteen, six feet of me crashing to the ground with the ceramic elephant lamp.

A lamp that had been plugged in.

The lightbulb shattered, sparks arcing across the filament and traveled back down into the lamp. I yanked the cord hoping it would kill the spark traveling the insulated wire. My plan failed, the current continued and arced to the outlet with a puff of smoke and the smell of burning hair... before plunging the whole house into darkness.

"Her tongue tickles, Aunt Cyn!" Sylvia shouted, as my former partner made the slobbery sounds of consumption.

Please let her be eating something else.

"I need to get more cheese!"

Of course it was the cheese, I thought, banging my head on the floor. *Could this night possibly get any worse?*

A reminder, really, to never ask that question. It was followed by the sound of my nephew Eric shouting and my niece threatening him with a peanut butter facial.

Winnie's claws clattered in the dark and I blew out a breath.

"You all suck," I muttered.

"Your daughter belongs in a zoo. If I take this money, I could go down for being a paid accomplice to a future serial killer," I said, passing my brother back the small stack of cash he'd paid me for risking life and limb so he and his wife could have a date night. "And I'd call social services over the fact that you gave your child a chainsaw, but I think you deserve to suffer for that poor choice all on your own. Also, I don't have a phone and yours is useless without power."

"What?" He stuffed the money in my pants and pinched my love handles like all jerk brothers are known to do. "I didn't give her a chainsaw."

His teasing would cost him, since I decided to keep it to pay for the extra therapy sessions I'd need after this.

Also, something in my pants smelled like garlic cow farts and I wasn't ready to touch them.

My pants, garlic, or cow farts.

"Well, you gave her something. She threatened Eric with it after stealing his noise canceling headphones when the peanut butter facial re-aligned Winnie to his side of the war. I wrestled the headphones back from her before he fell apart, but I had to promise her free rein to destroy a small village until she was ultimately brought down by Dogzilla's gas. It seemed fitting her own weapon would bring about her downfall, but I have to take that weapon home and I don't think you paid me enough for the amount of cheese she gave Winnie. I'm going to ask that all cheese be removed from your house if I'm ever tricked into coming back. Your lamp and frog are totaled, your house has no power, and I'm fairly certain you need to call one of those companies that cleans up houses where violent crimes have happened because there is crap on the floor I wouldn't touch without a hazmat suit and a respirator."

Seth shrugged while beside him Carla held in a laugh.

"That's kind of how it normally looks... and smells."

"Then I guess there's no point in telling you about the sinkhole or the toilet. Eric needs new batteries in his headphones and a sensory deprivation chamber if you aren't shipping the terror off to Neverland," I added the last with a pang of guilt that I had zero control over his sister. My niece and nephew are unique and special in their own way, but my autistic nephew deserved better than being a second-class citizen to the madness that was Sylvia. For the most part, he played quietly and did his own thing, only asking for stuff to be kept at a low volume and not to be physically crowded.

In an act of unprecedented cruelty, the universe gave their family Sylvia.

With Sylvia around, there was no quiet, personal space, or cleanliness.

Especially since she discovered Daniel Kirby's kids had access to fireworks. One friendship led to another and now Sylvia was headed down the express lane to fugitive incarceration. My mom insists she's a "free spirit" and just needs to "work through it".

I'm fairly certain the only way to save mankind is to send her to a deserted island for reformation training by the world's top psychologists and behavioral experts. Like wherever they put Harley Quinn in *Suicide Squad.*

My mom said I was an exaggerating drama queen.

I told my mom that she'd regret that accusation when Sylvia succeeded in world domination and forced her to dance like a marionette puppet.

My mom threw a silicone dildo at my head and I declared her the official winner of our argument.

"Why do you have glow in the dark magic marker on your face?"

I swiped the back of my hand across my forehead and saw incandescent smears mixed with a chunky green fluid. My eyelids shut as I replayed the night's horrors in my mind. Some were already scheduled for traumatic memory suppression or whatever happened to Bing Bong in *Inside Out.*

I gagged when I remembered what had been on my sleeve that was now on my face.

"Uck, yeah. Eric decided to use my face as a distraction beacon. I'm leaving now... your house is a mess and your kids lost consciousness on the couch. Next time you need a night out, contact a prison warden," I started walking away as Carla gave up and burst out laughing. "If you ever ask me to do this again, I refuse to monitor your children in any place that isn't padded, surrounded by water with me on the other side, and devoid of sharp objects."

"If anyone in our family is there, there's always a Sharp object!" Seth shouted back and I offered him a stiff middle finger at the reminder of our last name. Opening the door, I climbed into my Jeep after Winnie. She leapt in gracelessly, clambered into the back, and flopped on her side, white belly exposed beside the tan and black fur. My entry wasn't much more graceful as I plopped into my seat and dropped my face on the steering wheel.

Two long inhales and exhales, and I felt my shoulders release some tension. At least enough that I could lift my head again. Around me, darkness covered everything in a veil of anonymity and I felt a calming silence settle in. It was the most peace I'd had in four hours and Winnie's light snore indicated she was spent right along with me.

But we'd survived and the horror was over. At least for tonight.

A second-floor window of my brother's house shattered and I heard Sylvia cackling.

"Oh my dog, she's escaped!" I shouted, turning over the engine and squealing the tires out of Seth's driveway. My Jeep zoomed down the street, revealing that my brother's house was the only one plunged into darkness on the block. I drove past house after house illuminated and spewing pajama clad residents onto their lawns to rubberneck a suspected murder in progress.

OK, so it was one neighbor and she was getting her mail, but it was only a matter of time before red and blue lights flooded this neighborhood.

Lost in thought, I came toa sudden stop when I realized I almost ran a stop sign. Pausing, I checked both directions and blinked at a movement in the shadows. It retained an almost alien shape as it moved with the speed of a sloth. Like a predator, my eyes tracked the figure, attempting to discern whether it was real or a trauma induced hallucination that would easily become an obsession if I started down the path, like children looking for the treasure at the end of the rainbow. Each movement swayed along with a stale breeze, a serpentine path over a deserted road by a... something.

Something big.

Something big that just fell over into the shrubs beside a white picket fence.

"Just go home, Cynthia," I whispered to myself as the figure staggered to upright, though potentially still hunched, and stumbled. My finger tapped on the steering wheel before flicking on the blinker. "Why aren't we going home?"

The car made a right turn and Winnie let out a loud snore from the back seat that sent my skin jumping after the total silence. Her claws clicked against each other, running in her sleep that was punctuated by a fart that rivaled air raid sirens in World War2.

"Real smooth, girl. Now we…" The smell hit my nose and I gagged, choking and jerking the car until I slammed the brakes and came to a full stop. I threw my Jeep into park, and jumped out, dry heaving and gagging while my military working dog didn't so much as flutter an eyelid.

In front of my Jeep, the figure had frozen. It was roughly the size of a human adult, but on top of what would traditionally be the head were pointy protrusions that made the spiked arc of a regal crown perched atop. My eyes tried to zero in on the outline and identify the shape as it staggered closer, my heart racing as I braced myself to choose between physical pain and olfactory assault.

"Hey!" A muffled sound came from the approaching monster and I crouched low in anticipation of a tackle. "Help!"

My ears twitched, waiting for the figure to move into the pools of light created by the Jeep's Pelican headlamps. My breath stopped as first a furry black stick stepped in.

Next was a leg.

Then the whole figure toppled forward to reveal…

"Are you… wearing a cat costume?" I asked, relaxing and striding forward. The figure had landed on its face and I gracelessly hauled it to its feet.

While the nose looked a little dented from the fall, the rest of the outfit was a loose-fitting fur suit in black with white patches on the gloves and chest portion. Mesh green eyes let out the scent of alcohol and another plea for help.

"The clip is stuck and I can't get out!" The voice was male, but not very deep. Cautiously, I tilted up the cat head and saw a bicycle helmet clip securely fastened under a jaw with a few bristly hairs. I took a breath and yanked my face back.

"Holy cow, how much have you had to drink? And how did you drink it"

"Straws and a lot. I need to pee and maybe throw up. But I sewed the paws as part of the suit and I can't take them off to operate the buckle," I studied the arms of the cat suit and didn't see any gapping or seams to indicate they can be removed.

"Fine, hold your breath," I ordered the cat while following my own advice. Against all better judgment, I stuck my hands in the cat head and grasped for the plastic buckle I'd seen. It took a minute to press the release, a slippery sheen of sweat coating the clip and the strap around it.

At least I told myself it was sweat after the vomit warning I'd been given.

He did not smell like the vomit was a "maybe".

Once it was released, the cat threw off his head and heaved, vomiting all over my pants and shoes with an alcohol content that could peel paint. At the same time, I saw him clench his thighs together, either because he was peeing or trying desperately not to.

He should have tried harder with the vomit.

A long sigh escaped, but I carefully inhaled through my mouth as I watched the cat hunch on the side of the road. After two more heaves, it staggered upright and swayed back tome.

"Sorry," he mumbled. Acne scarred skin and bright blue eyes rimmed in red blood-shot vessels blinked at me. "I need more help."

He turned his back and showed me a fluffy tail. Furry paws grasped at a seam, peeling Velcro that immediately stuck to his paws.

"Take off my clothes."

"Shouldn't I buy you dinner first?" I asked, taking a step back when he heaved again.

"Please don't mention food." He swiped at his mouth with a paw and I grimaced at the smeared bile on the costume fur's white patch.

"Right.... Turn around and hold your breath."

He followed my instructions and I yanked apart the Velcro to get to the plastic zipper. He exhaled painfully and I realized that drunk and barfing was ill-suited to breath holding. He could only manage for so long and I was taking more time than he had. My fingers shook in horror as I slowly lowered the zipper and tried to move my face as far from him as possible.

"Oh my dog, you're naked!" I screamed and jumped away. With enough of the zipper down, he pulled apart the rest and the costume pooled at the base of his eerily thin frame. Unlike part of my face, his skin didn't quite glow in the dark but he wasn't wearing magic marker. The exposed flesh of his butt cheeks reflected my headlights in a display that would make Bart Simpson proud and reminded me that someone made a song about wearing sunglasses at night.

"Oh thank god," he staggered to the side of the road, taking with him the costume puddled around his ankles. He stopped by a fence post, leaned against it, and let loose a stream of urine so long and loud, it woke Winnie up and she pressed her nose to the glass to watch.

"Right... I'm gonna..." I gestured to my car, still impressed by the steadily growing puddle at his feet. If I didn't work on a farm, this might have been the most urine I'd seen come from a living creature and I felt the urge to hold up a scorecard with the number nine.

"Wait!" He held a finger above his head, even as the puddle threatened to get onto his cat costume. "I need to get back to the party."

"I think you need to go home and go to bed," I countered, slowly backing away. He turned suddenly, giving me a full frontal and a clear view of his swinging junk.

Like a freeway car wreck, I couldn't look away from the wrinkled flesh of his manhood.

"I can't! My pants are at the party."

His voice was coming from his face, but I couldn't bring myself to meet his gaze.

"Do you only own one pair of pants? Can't you forfeit them? Submit a request that they be sold to benefit an organization that... neuters cats?"

"No... My keys are in there. And my wallet... and..." he trailed off when he noticed I was still staring at his one-eyed snake. "A condom?"

My eyes snapped up and I choked on my spit.

"What? No, I have a boyfriend. I'm just terrified that if I look away it will get fluids on me like your mouth did! How did so much urine come out of... that?" My face burned and he shrugged, pulling the costume completely off and bundling it into his cat head.

"Mr. Wiggles has a lot of skills... Your boyfriend must not be very good if you're shopping around and Mr. Wiggles is available," he smirked.

"You named your penis Mr. Wiggles and speak about it in the third person?"

"Yeah. Wanna know what I'd name your tits?" He wiggled his eyebrows and I wanted to choose violence.

Wanted to but didn't.

Not for the moral high ground but for the crucial life goal of never touching him.

"Larry is perfectly suited to fulfill my-"

"Larry? Larry Kirby?" He interrupted and I nodded. His eyes were unfocused, and a small stream of drool was slipping out of his mouth, but he apparently knew there was only one Larry in Sweet Pea.

"I was going to swing by his house and say goodnight before heading home. So I don't need-"

"Perfect, you can drop me off," he swayed and staggered toward the passenger side door. Winnie scented the air and just as he gripped the handle, she let out a whimper. Her body disappeared into the back seat as the naked man placed his uncovered junk on my cloth seats.

At a loss, I went to the driver's side door and yanked it open.

He was rubbing his naked butt on the upholstery trying to get comfortable, really grinding in that naked man scent.

"Where am I dropping you off?" I grumbled, hoping it wasn't far. Between the grime on my outfit and the fluids on his cat costume, my car was going to need sage, bleach, and possibly an autoclave to ever feel clean again.

"Larry's house. That's where Amber's party is."

Made in the USA
Las Vegas, NV
10 December 2024